I0760901

RUTHLESS

BOOK TWO OF COTERIE OF MAGES

THOMAS K. CARPENTER

Ruthless

Book Two of Coterie of Mages

Hardcover Version

by Thomas K. Carpenter

Published by Black Moon Books

Cover design by
G&S Cover Designs

Chapter Heading by HelenaKrivoruchko

Discover other titles by this author on:
www.thomaskcarpenter.com

ISBN-13: 978-1-958498-29-3

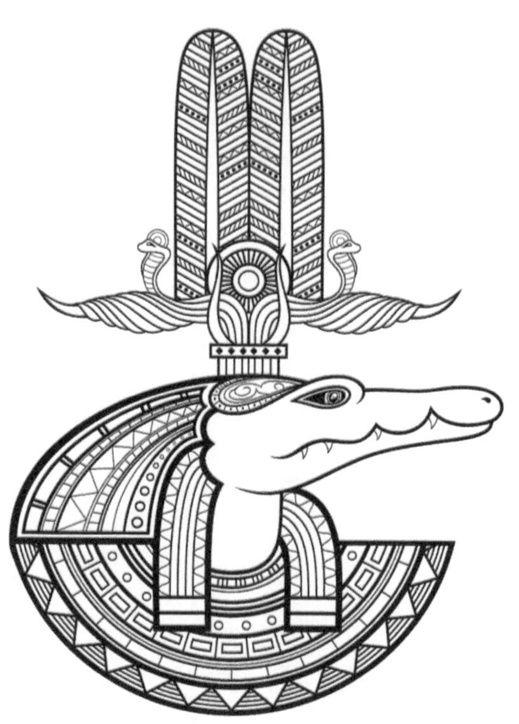

RUTHLESS

The Hundred Halls Universe

<u>Season One</u>

THE HUNDRED HALLS
Trials of Magic
Web of Lies
Alchemy of Souls
Gathering of Shadows
City of Sorcery

THE RELUCTANT ASSASSIN
The Reluctant Assassin
The Sorcerous Spy
The Veiled Diplomat
Agent Unraveled
The Webs That Bind

GAMEMAKERS ONLINE
The Warped Forest
Gladiators of Warsong
Citadel of Broken Dreams
Enter the Daemonpits
Plane of Twilight

ANIMALIANS HALL
Wild Magic
Bane of the Hunter
Mark of the Phoenix
Arcane Mutations
Untamed Destiny

STONE SINGERS HALL
Song of Siren and Blood
House of Snake and Tome
Storm of Dragon and Stone
Sonata of Shadow and Thorn
Well of Demon and Bone

THE ORDER OF MERLIN
The Order of Merlin
Infernal Alliances
Tower of Horn and Blood

The Hundred Halls Universe

Season Two

THE CRYSTAL HALLS
Shadows in Amber
The Emerald Eclipse
The Sapphire Strategem
Chains of Obsidian
The Bloodstone Rebellion

AURA HEALERS HALL
Half-Pint Hex
Full Moon Demon
Blood Witch Curse
Twilight Horn
Deathless King

COTERIE OF MAGES
Monstrous
Ruthless
Vicious
Merciless
Bloodlust

Other Works

ALEXANDRIAN SAGA
Fires of Alexandria
Heirs of Alexandria
Legacy of Alexandria
Warmachines of Alexandria
Empire of Alexandria
Voyage of Alexandria
Goddess of Alexandria

OTHER SERIES
The Dashkova Memoirs
Kingmakers Saga
Gamers
Mirror Shards

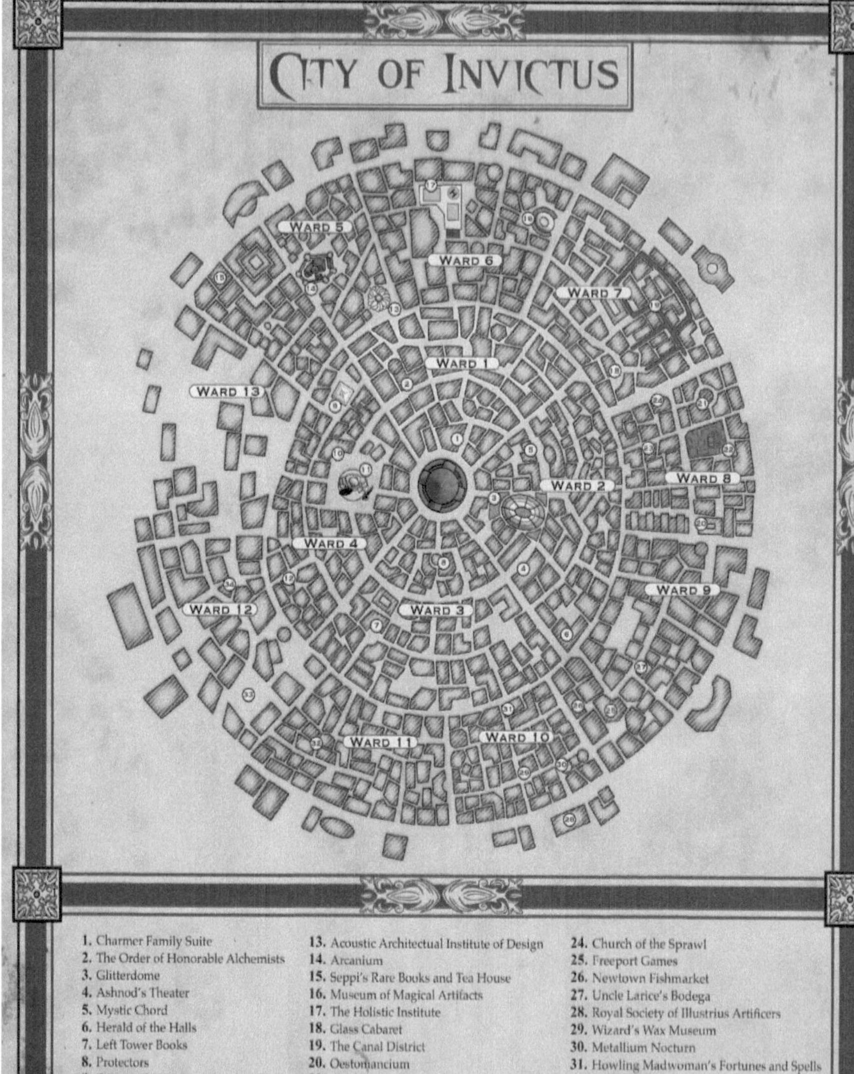

1. Charmer Family Suite
2. The Order of Honorable Alchemists
3. Glitterdome
4. Ashnod's Theater
5. Mystic Chord
6. Herald of the Halls
7. Left Tower Books
8. Protectors
9. Coterie of Mages
10. City Library
11. Statue of Invictus
12. Amber & Smoke
13. Acoustic Architectual Institute of Design
14. Arcanium
15. Seppi's Rare Books and Tea House
16. Museum of Magical Artifacts
17. The Holistic Institute
18. Glass Cabaret
19. The Canal District
20. Oestomancium
21. Animalians
22. Invictus Menagerie and Cryptozoo
23. Goblin's Romp
24. Church of the Sprawl
25. Freeport Games
26. Newtown Fishmarket
27. Uncle Larice's Bodega
28. Royal Society of Illustrius Artificers
29. Wizard's Wax Museum
30. Metallium Nocturn
31. Howling Madwoman's Fortunes and Spells
32. Enoichian District
33. Oba's Autumnal Garden
34. Gamemakers Hall

Obelisk MAP

Third Level
PYRAMID
Second Level
OASIS
First Level
Level Five - Telchine's Star, Kill Rooms, Classrooms
Level Four - Telchine's Circle, Classrooms, Testing Rooms
Level Three - Professor Living Quarters
Level Two - Student Living Quarters
Level One - Dining Hall, Meeting Rooms, Grand Hall

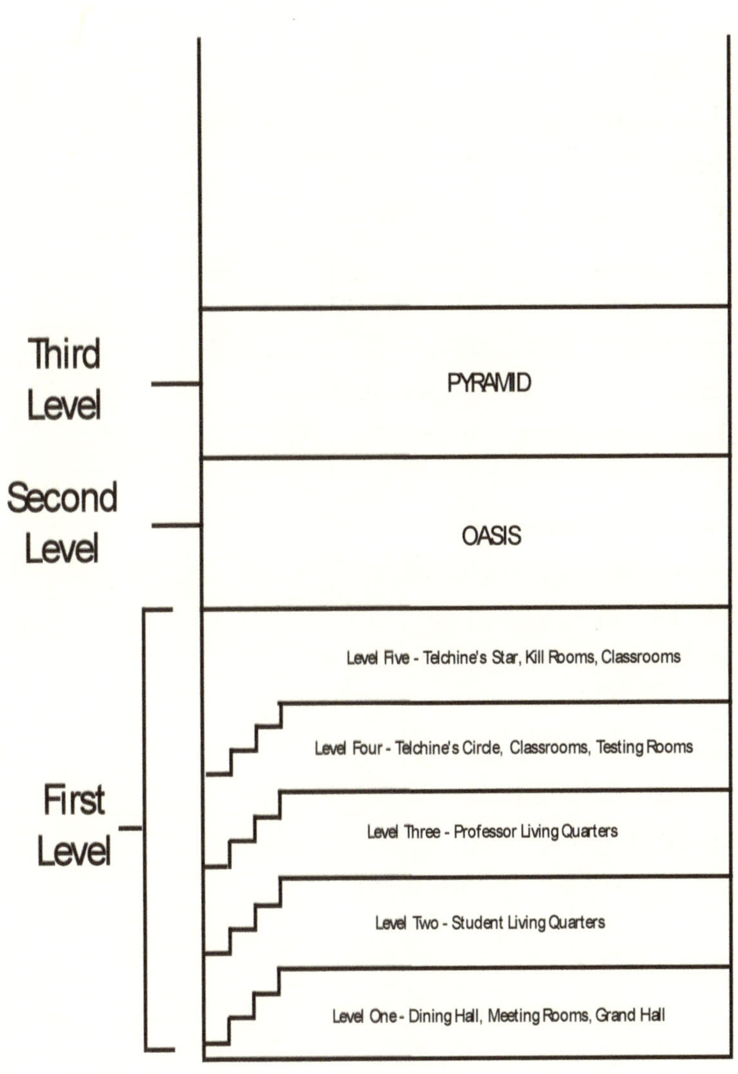

Arcanium loves books
Coterie adores power
Assassins will kill you
Stone Singers has a stone flower

Animalians is a zoo
Alchemists, you'll devour
Tinkers loves gadgets
Protectors makes you cower

Aura Healers wants to fix you
Blue Flame has a tower
Dramatics loves the spectacle
Oculus has grown sour

One Hundred Halls
Each with their own magic
The Patrons protect
Because faez madness is tragic

In the city of sorcery
Invictus is the Head
His students are many
But the foolish end up dead

- A Children's Rhyme

ONE

Screaming children in the nearby park put Ilyana's teeth on edge. They were chasing each other through the jungle equipment while their parents watched from benches, flipping through their phones, barely paying attention. Easy prey. But she didn't have time for such games.

Ilyana strode down the sidewalk in her thigh-high black leather boots. She flicked her finger and the lead child tripped over nothing, smashing their face into the metal slide. The screams changed from joy to horror, and parents came running. Ilyana let her tongue rest on the bottom of her teeth as she enjoyed the metallic scent of blood spilled on a fine Sunday morning.

She stopped at the corner, peering down one of the spoke roads that led to the center of the City of Sorcery. The Spire was like a bright candle, glowing before the world. Fenris had always told her to avoid the city. That there was too much power. Too many people. And too many mages.

It wasn't the place for their family.

But now that she'd seen it, Ilyana disagreed. The powerful never had enough of it, and the more they desired, the more opportunities there were to subvert their interests. She would tell him as much when she found him.

The question was: where was he?

Her father liked to disappear at times. There was a nearly two-decade period when he'd headed into the frozen Siberian wastes and only emerged when he was gaunt and skeletal, but he'd found what he'd been looking for. A lost tome filled with ancient Egyptian secrets. No one had any idea how it'd gotten all the way up there, but it didn't matter, and he never explained what had happened.

Nor had Ilyana ever gotten to learn what was in that book. Maybe when she tracked him down to his new hiding place, she'd ask about it. He'd told her previously that it wasn't the time.

On the other hand, the condition of that backwater farmhouse did not portend good tidings. It wasn't unusual for her father to have destroyed his hiding place once he was done with it, to keep old enemies from tracking him, but it felt so sloppy, so careless and hurried, that she worried what that meant. She would ask him that too when she found him.

Or her half-sister Iona. She'd never laid eyes on the girl, only heard about her through correspondence with her father. The prodigy. That girl would never love him like she did.

The address brought her to an antique store on the corner of a residential district. A handsome young man wearing a tailored three-piece suit was sitting on a wooden chair eating out of a bag of popcorn. The quality of his clothing didn't match the dusty old antiques displayed on the shelves.

She handed over a card when she reached him. The handsome gentleman sniffed the card before letting the corners of his lips curl up.

"New to the city. Could I interest—"

"Spare me the sales pitch. I need information, and not the boring-ass tourist crap you're peddling."

His amusement turned to incredulity as he rested his fingers against his chest.

"What is that delicious accent? It almost sounds Hungarian with more than a touch of French. *Hogy szereted a véred?*"

"*Eclaboussé sur ton cou.*"

"Touchy."

"I'm looking for Fenris."

The handsome gentleman's eyebrows wagged upward.

"*He's* in the city?"

"He is. Has he not inquired about your services?"

"No," said the gentleman with more than a hint of disgust. "And it pains me. Have we lost our way so much that the Great Fenris Storm does not visit upon us? When did he come to the city?"

"Last year sometime."

"We have no record of his attendance at any of our establishments."

Ilyana tried not to let her anger betray her mood, but there were only so many complications she could endure. What had started as a short family visit was turning into an annoying slog.

"What about Iona Storm?"

"Who, pray tell, is that?"

"His daughter. My half-sister."

"Charming."

"I have no idea. I've never met her. But she was living with Fenris until recently."

The gentleman rolled his eyes.

"Let me check our network. Maybe she dined at a different place." He thumbed through his phone for a few minutes before exhaling deeply. "My apologies, there's no sign of an Iona Storm in our records. The only thing I can find is that there was an Iona Storm that joined the Halls."

"What?"

"I couldn't find her name, so I did a simple search. Amazing what technology can do."

"Where is she at? Which Hall?"

"It appears she joined Coterie of Mages. What a surprise, really. Is that why we haven't seen Fenris? Did he pull some strings to get her in? It would be like him. Which means he has some plan in mind. Am I right?"

Ilyana scoured her memories for anything he might have said about Coterie of Mages. Of all the Halls, why that one? She could recall that he'd mentioned it in the past, but it'd been decades. The details were lost to time. Had something changed? Did he send Iona into the Hall to retrieve something for him? It would make sense. They were the most powerful Hall. She'd heard rumors of the artifacts and secrets the Obelisk contained. What she wouldn't give to get a peek inside.

If he'd gotten Iona into Coterie, it meant he'd be lurking nearby. He'd probably sniffed out how insufferable the Cadre had become and decided to avoid them. He had that power and right, after all.

"This isn't your problem. Keep it to yourself."

"I have a duty to my superiors," he said.

Ilyana leaned into his perfect face.

"Would you like me to tell my father about your insolence?"

His jaw dropped.

"I'm only doing my job."

"Your job is to keep your mouth shut."

She placed a long fingernail on his upper lip, pulling it down until they were sealed.

"See. Wasn't that easy?"

He gave a subtle nod and she removed her fingernail.

"Is there anything else you desire?"

Ilyana was preparing to tell him that he had nothing she wanted, but then her stomach rumbled imperceptibly.

"The address of your finest dining establishment."

He pulled out a felt-tip pen and, using the back of her card, wrote in neat penmanship, then held it out between his first two fingers.

"I'll notify them that you're coming."

Ilyana turned on her heel and strode out of the antique store. The hunger was making her a little irritated, but she had one more thing she wanted to do before she sated her needs. A taxi provided transportation. She could have used the Cadre's services, but didn't want them to know where she was going, not that they couldn't figure it out.

The taxi wound through the busy streets. The Trials of Magic were currently in swing, so more families and tourists were clogging up the side-walks than normal. Ilyana wondered what it'd have been like to enter the Trials. Not that she needed them. Fenris had been all the teacher she'd ever needed, but she was curious how well she might have done.

And it was another thing that annoyed her about this half-sister, Iona.

The taxi pulled to a stop outside a wrought iron gate in the fourth ward. The vehicle could pull no closer.

Ilyana joined the other tourists gawking at the smooth black structure in the middle of a wide square. The Spire, which was only a dozen blocks away, was more grandiose, more impressive in its size and majesty, but the Obelisk was something entirely different: a pillar as tall as a skyscraper, made of glossy black obsidian that reflected nothing. Not a single sur-rounding building could be seen in its surface. An enigma. Much like the Coterie of Mages with all their power and secrets.

Ilyana had a good idea that Fenris had sent Iona into the Obelisk to plunder those secrets. Why else would she have joined the Halls?

But it begged the question. Where was Fenris?

She tapped a long fingernail on her bottom lip, ignoring the insipid tourists and their inane conversations as she considered her next steps.

First food, then I must speak to this Iona Storm.

TWO

The sizzle of cooking filled the spacious apartment as Iona studied the spell tome. The finger gestures were causing her hands to cramp, but she was determined to learn the protective ward. The only problem was the smell of meat cooking was distracting and her stomach growled in solidarity.

"Not too cooked, please! Just a little searing on the outside and extra-runny eggs too!"

Zuri acknowledged her request and let her know that it would be served soon, so Iona closed the tome and stretched her hands, working out the knot in one palm.

What a difference a year made. This time last year, she'd just passed the Trials and was preparing to head to Coterie of Mages in the same outfit she'd been wearing for the previous week. The taxi ride to the Obelisk had been full of fear and concern.

Now look at her.

She scanned the furnished apartment with expensive paintings on the walls. *Nandi Defends the City* had a prominent place above the faux fireplace. The coloring caught the time of day perfectly as Zuri's older sister defended a group of city dwellers from a horde of murderous demons. The work was commissioned by their parents; a famous artist Iona had never heard of, but who supposedly had paintings in the Louvre, had taken the job.

There were others as well, but that painting was Iona's favorite, because it told her that no matter the brutal schooling techniques of Coterie, the students could still go on to positively affect the world. That no matter the stories she'd heard about Nandi's time in the Obelisk, she hadn't lost her soul.

"Breakfast is ready."

The plate was covered in pink juices mixed with the runny eggs. A sugar-dusted croissant from the nearby bakery sat on its own small dish, but Iona only had eyes for the steak. A sharp knife revealed a purple-red interior.

"You could have taken it off earlier," said Iona as she shoved the first piece past her waiting lips.

Zuri removed her apron and carried her own plate over.

"My apologies, next time I'll toss the raw meat directly onto your plate," she said in that way that sounded like she was British royalty.

After the savory meat slipped down her throat, Iona sighed with relief.

"I don't mean to complain about a well-cooked meal, just, you know. For next time."

As Zuri was cutting her steak, she raised an eyebrow.

"This obsession with uncooked meat is going to make you sick. We cook food for a reason."

Iona put her knife to the steak, sawing away another piece.

"I know, but the burning takes away the flavor, and makes me a little ill."

Further conversation was cut short by a heavy bang from Justine's room. They both stared at the door for a long moment.

"Do we want to know?" asked Zuri.

"I'm sure it's innocent."

Zuri pursed her lips and gave her a look.

"Yeah, I know, living with a two-foot puppet that holds the soul of our friend has been strange, but not the strangest thing that's happened to us."

"I beg to differ," said Zuri as she popped a piece of meat into her mouth.

"She's still the same Justine, but, you know, smaller."

Zuri dutifully finished chewing her meat. Iona could imagine that her parents would yell at her if she ate too quickly, which was the opposite of her own problem. The food was gone before she really realized she was eating, especially if there was meat involved.

Her friend and classmate leaned over conspiratorially, speaking in a low whisper.

"You and I both know that she's not the same. Justine was a strange bird before, but now, I worry that the transformation has broken something in her. Or that that's not Justine at all—"

Another loud bang, followed by tinny laughter, had them both sitting up straight.

Iona finished her meal in silence, contemplating their diminutive roommate while enjoying the steak and eggs.

While she was cleaning up her plate and the rest of the cooking mess, Justine came ambling out of her room with white powder splashed across her face, wearing the same black smock she'd been in the day her soul had entered the puppet.

"Did you make some for me?" came the gravelly voice as the puppet grinned.

The sour smile made Iona grimace inside, but she didn't want to let her friend know how unnerving she could be in both voice and appearance. The poor girl had survived so much already.

"We got you a nice bowl of wood chips," said Iona as she shoved the plates into the dishwasher. "How's the… whatever you're working on in there?"

Justine ambled through the apartment and climbed onto the couch. She sat back and stilled, which made her look like an inanimate object again, until she turned her head suddenly.

"Is today the day?"

Iona hid her internal flinch.

"Tomorrow. We're headed to the Obelisk tomorrow."

"Which means we need to test the cubes again," said Zuri, rising from the table.

"We did that a week ago."

Zuri gave her a look.

"We both know that the moment the Obelisk opens, there's going to be a race to the level-four portal. I'm sure they figured it out over the summer just like we did. Blake and his minions are going to try to cut us off, keep us from passing. Or just kill us outright. If we don't get to the fourth before them and either get through or make sure we're ready for them, then why even bother going back this year?"

The cube testing was one of the more boring things Iona had done since she'd come to the City of Sorcery. It felt like real work, not the awesome surprises that came with the proliferation of magic. With the warding cubes, she felt like she was an electrician trying to find a faulty wire.

"Iona!"

"What?"

"You're not paying attention," said Zuri, stomping her boot.

Iona tried to ignore the way heat was rising in her chest, but it was hard.

"Sorry." She performed the little spell that made the cube light up. "There. It's working."

"You're distracted. We can't be distracted in the Obelisk."

Zuri had turned her back, so Iona made a face at Justine, who was weaving spell wire on the couch. The puppet giggled.

"Have you given my question any more thought?" asked Iona when it grew silent again.

"What question?" asked Zuri with a turn of the head.

"The Second Year Games."

"That's for the other Halls. We have more important things to accomplish in the Obelisk."

"It's for *all* the Halls," said Iona. "Or is supposed to be, anyway."

"It's optional, and frankly, we don't have the time."

"It sounds fun."

"Don't you get enough challenges in the Obelisk?"

"The challenge of not dying? It's great."

Iona rapped her knuckles on the cube.

"You know you get grouped with a bunch of normies from the other Halls."

"I was a normie last year."

Zuri sighed and hung her head.

"You know what I mean."

"No, I don't actually. I didn't grow up with an inflated sense of self or the wealth and privilege to fool myself into thinking I was."

"That's a low blow," said Zuri.

"Not as low as yours."

Zuri opened her mouth, then tilted her head as her jaw worked at the empty air.

"You're right. That was a low blow. I was just thinking about how those other Halls might not be up to the standard that we expect in the Obelisk. None of them have to live with life-and-death situations on the regular."

"Which tells you how fucked up our lives are," said Iona.

"You're not wrong, but it's the life we chose. Now let's get these cubes finished so we can start packing. I want to be through the door first thing when the Obelisk is open to students tomorrow morning."

"Aye, aye, Captain."

Iona gave her a salute, and when Zuri turned around, she stuck her tongue out. Childish, she knew, but it wasn't like she'd had a chance to be one. Iona checked back to Justine on the couch, but the puppet was unmoving, staring into space with her hands in mid-gesture. The stillness lasted for about twenty seconds and then Justine continued her weaving work. It wasn't the first time that Justine had locked up. Iona had asked her about it once, but she claimed that nothing had happened. Despite what she'd said to Zuri earlier, Iona was concerned that having her soul shoved into an inanimate object, no matter how many spells and enchantments had facilitated the transition, wasn't the best thing in the world for Justine in the long term.

Something to keep an eye on, she supposed. Iona just hoped that Justine didn't cause any complications in their already complex lives in the Obelisk.

THREE

Zuri woke at three in the morning and couldn't go back to sleep. They had to be at the Obelisk, seven a.m. sharp, ready to go with all their gear. It'd all been packed already, but she spent the time before her roommates woke double-checking.

Roommate, she reminded herself when she heard Justine shuffling around in her room. The odd puppet was awake at all hours of the day and night. Zuri wasn't completely sure she slept except for those strange moments of stillness that were completely unnerving.

When Iona awoke at five, bleary-eyed and with pale blonde hair sticking in all directions, breakfast was waiting: a plate full of pastries from the bakery, since Zuri didn't want to have to clean up before their big day.

"Everyone have everything?" she asked when they were in the back of the SUV.

"The early worm avoids the bird," said Iona with a lazy smile.

Justine was in the backpack in Iona's lap. They were the only ones that knew she was alive. Well, if a soul existing in a puppet could be called that. The funeral this summer had been a somber affair with her mother sobbing the entire time and her famous father, Justice Thornlock, staring solemnly into the distance, his jaw pulsing with anger or grief, it was hard to tell, the entire time.

Iona had argued with Justine about telling them, that it was only right that they knew she was still with them, even if it wasn't in the form they expected. But Justine had been adamant that they wouldn't like her new form and she was content enough that they'd even bothered to grieve her.

Their SUV was the first through the gate. No one else had arrived. Technically, they weren't supposed to be in the upper levels of the Obelisk until they'd met with their Patron, but no one really considered Professor Sinclair as the real Patron, even if he was acting as it on a daily basis.

Zuri almost expected to find Blake and his crew at the portal to level four. It would have been just like him to find a way around the summer restrictions and have already set up an ambush, but she was relieved to find it empty.

The tunnel beneath the unfolded pyramid led to a wide chamber filled with ancient Kemetic runes. Zuri pulled out the schematics and got to work directing her friends as they set up the warding cubes. Iona set the small glowing boxes while Justine ran the wires. It took three minutes longer than she'd timed in the apartment, but thankfully no one interrupted them.

"Are we good?"

"I think so," said Iona with her hands on her hips and her hair a little sweaty.

"Justine, you're on watch."

The puppet ambled up the ramp to the upper portion while Zuri pulled out the book of runes they'd been working on the entire summer.

Zuri was fairly certain that they had the correct solution, but she didn't want to rush to failure. They would confirm their answers as they worked.

The two of them took position at the far end of the room where they assumed the portal would form on the blank wall once they entered the proper solution to the puzzle.

"Jackal with feather and bones."

"Check," said Iona, pressing the sandstone.

It glowed faintly.

"Three stones and a bird."

"Done."

They worked like this for over an hour, pressing stones and confirming they were properly lit up before moving onto the next. They could have gone quicker, but Zuri insisted they stop and check the Kemetic circuit in the room after each rune.

When it came down to the last one, Zuri called out the pattern, "Vulture warrior with spear."

"Let's get ready to rumble!"

Iona touched the appropriate rune, which lit up as expected. There were no reverberations of a door opening or anything like that. Instead, the portal to the fourth level swirled into existence on the blank sandstone wall.

"Oh, thank Merlin."

"You want me to pop over and come back? Get the lay of the land? Then we can start moving our gear through."

"Together," said Zuri.

Iona checked back to the ramp and shrugged.

"Let's do this."

They approached the portal. Zuri had traveled through them countless times, but this one was making her stomach ache. Maybe it was the idea that they'd be back to knowing nothing and having to work out the dangers of the new level.

"On the count of three. One, two, three—"

Zuri extended her arms in unison, and the moment her hands brushed through the swirling portal, she was thrown backwards. Landing on her back knocked the air out of her.

"What in the actual—"

Iona was next to her, rubbing her head as she climbed to a sitting position.

"I don't get it," said Zuri. "We summoned the portal. Did we do something wrong?"

"No offense, Zuri, but you're way too annoying for us to have done something wrong."

Further conversation was interrupted by the rapid tapping of little wooden feet coming down the ramp.

"They're here! They're here!" came the rough puppet voice. Justine hurried down and hid behind the pile of bags. Her little feet made clacking noises on the stone as she ran.

No one needed any explanation of who "they" were. Zuri dusted herself off quickly and took position near one of the cubes as Blake, Scarlett, and the rest of the group came sauntering down the ramp.

He looked taller in her estimation. Tanned with the tips of his brown hair frosted. He wore the same arrogant countenance that he always did, the one that she'd seen him practice in the mirror when he thought no one was looking. The rest of the group had taken on his same demeanor. Arrogant, self-important, and completely oblivious.

"I figured you'd try to rush up here and get through before we arrived. Shame you're too slow, or maybe you didn't figure out the answer this summer."

Zuri checked behind her to see the wall had returned to its normal, flat sandstone version.

"Do you know what I don't understand?" she asked, reaching down and grabbing the trigger rod.

"What's that?" responded Blake.

"How you can be so stupid that you'd just walk right into my trap."

"What?"

The rest of his group took a few steps back. He tried to act like he didn't care, but she could see the fear in his eyes, especially when he noticed the pulsing cubes littered around the entrance.

"You're so damn predictable. Too lazy to get through the door when it opened, but absolutely sure that you'll have the advantage of numbers when you arrive. You didn't think we would be prepared? How stupid do you think we are? But I guess it's hard for someone with your intellectual deficiencies to understand someone who is actually smart."

"Blake, I told you," said Scarlett, glaring.

"Shut up, Scarlett. Now's not the time."

Zuri held up the trigger rod.

"I could blast the lot of you right now. Might not kill your entire group, but I figure I'd get at least half of you. But I'm feeling generous, and how would that look to start off our second year like this?"

She stomped her foot, making them flinch. The two in the back scurried up the ramp.

"It's just the two of you," said Blake, holding out his forefinger and pinky like a pair of horns. "You won't be able to avoid us forever."

"Why don't you do us both a favor and focus on your group. As we learned last year, your obsession with me proved disastrous."

"I'm not obsessed—"

Scarlett grabbed his arm, yanking him backwards.

"Let's get back to the lower level. I'd like to unpack."

He didn't move, so she shrugged and followed the rest of the group out of the chamber. Then when he was alone, Zuri held up the trigger rod, and he jogged away.

When they could no longer hear voices, Justine ran up to check, confirming Blake and his group had left the level. It was only upon knowing he was gone that Zuri allowed herself to relax.

"Maybe he finally got the message," said Iona.

"No. Not a chance. Not Blake. If there's one thing he is, it's persistent. It's one of the reasons he's actually made it this far. When we first started dating, I was surprised at how much he struggled to learn new things. But he doesn't give up. He'll work all night to learn a spell if he has to. Combined with his numbers, we're at a massive disadvantage."

"We could try recruiting others again."

"No one's going to join us. Not after last year and not while he still draws breath."

Iona gestured towards the trigger rod.

"You could have taken care of that."

"No, I can't. I can't be like him. The world doesn't need two of him."

"Shall we try again, then?"

Zuri checked to the pulsing cubes and equipment, then back to the blank sandstone wall.

"No, we need to get to the meeting with the Patron in a few hours. It'll take us that long to tear all this down, and then I want to recheck our calculations and try again at another time."

"Yeah," said Iona, scratching the back of her head. "I really thought it was going to work."

"I would have bet anything that it would, which worries me. We're missing something. Something big. And I don't like it."

"You're just not used to being wrong is all. It's okay, it happens."

"I'm not wrong. I know I'm not. We went over this all summer."

A strange little laugh had them both turning towards the puppet.

"Maybe we're not meant to get through," said Iona.

A pit formed in her stomach. It was what Zuri had been thinking.

"What do you mean?"

"We haven't had the meeting yet. Professor Sinclair has the portal blocked until we speak to him."

Zuri didn't believe that. Not based on what her sister had told her about coming back from summer break in the Obelisk. But she didn't want to worry her friends. They'd figure out the reason soon enough and then they'd be through and on to the next challenge.

"You're right, Iona."

"About what?"

"Let's pack up and get down to the meeting early. We should try to find more allies."

FOUR

Justine had the entire level to herself. No one to bother her. No one to remind her that she wasn't like them anymore. It wasn't like she couldn't see the glances or hear their hushed whispers as they talked about her, but if only they could understand this was the real her.

She turned sideways and slipped through the gap between the stones on the mausoleum. The building had been of great interest when they first came to the third level, but after disarming the traps, they'd learned it had nothing they needed.

But Justine knew better.

Zuri and Iona had given up too early. The building held more secrets than anyone knew, and she'd been waiting all summer to return. An interior space was filled with ancient writings, spells and runes dedicated to the realm between the living and the dead. The Veil.

The stuffed animals she'd left in the cubby remained. Justine threw herself on them, enjoying the way they cushioned her small body. She didn't feel the soft fur like she had when she was made of flesh, but the wooden body gave her a different sensitivity that made it pleasurable in a new way.

Justine pulled out her little book that was filled with drawings, secrets, and spells. Iona had found puppet-sized writing materials at a doll shop in the second ward. Holding the pen had required roughing up her fingers because they'd been too smooth before and the writing utensil kept slipping out.

She hadn't had much time in the necropolis before the semester had ended, so she got right to copying the spells. Magic was both harder and easier since she'd gained her new body. The finger gestures using her wooden digits left her frustrated and having to perform the same spell multiple times—even the easy ones—to get it right, but her connection to her conduit of faez was stronger than it'd ever been.

It no longer came through the base of her skull and it didn't have that chilled air feeling. Using magic in her puppet body, the raw stuff of magic, was like tapping directly into the feed. And it was warm as if it'd been traveling through sunlight before reaching her.

There was something else too. A hungry knot in her chest that she hadn't quite figured out. It was like there was still more to unlock, that the transformation into her puppet body was only part of what was to come. Whenever she thought about it, she became giddy with excitement. It was like staring at a box under the Christmas tree, hoping that it was exactly what you wanted, even if you had no idea what it was.

Justine was finishing up recording a section of runes when she heard the thump of something heavy being dropped. She climbed out from her throne of stuffed animals and slipped through the gap.

The strange dusk light that permeated the level made seeing beyond a hundred meters difficult. She saw two things moving at once. The first was further out to her right, near the back of the level at a cluster of buildings. The movement was slight and she lost sight of it right away.

The other thing moving was more obvious and made her forget the first. Justine hid behind the wall as soon as she saw him. Orion Dreadmarsh. He'd been a towering figure when she had a human form. Around six foot six, if she recalled, but either he'd grown a few more inches during the summer, or her diminutive form made him seem giant sized. The fact that he was as wide as two normal people made him seem impossibly big.

He'd dropped a big crate outside the unfolded pyramid. It looked like it would have taken two or three normal-sized people to carry it, but he'd done it himself with a huge pack on his back, which he let slough off his shoulders before heading down the ramp.

It'd be like him to not bother with protections or wards. Justine knew she should get back to her own work, but she was curious if he'd solved the final puzzle like they had.

She crept down the ramp, reminding herself that she should find rubber-soled shoes to keep her wooden feet from being so loud. He was talking to himself. He had a notebook open and was already touching the runes in the same order they'd uncovered. It wasn't sloppy or haphazard like she might have expected, nor was it filled with the constant double-checking that Zuri had required; it had a straight, direct to the point kind of feel. Like a martial artist using no more energy than was required.

Justine was mesmerized.

She stayed at the bottom of the ramp, clutching the scrolled pillar, listening to Orion work. She'd never heard him talk so much, but he had a constant banter going as he worked the runes. But then again, it wasn't like she'd spent any time with him either.

When Orion touched the final rune and the portal swirled into existence, Justine remembered that he'd left his gear outside and worried that he was going to turn around and spot her. With his long strides, he'd easily be able to capture her and then she'd be screwed.

To her utter relief, Orion strode towards the portal like an arrow shot straight to the target. He didn't slow when he reached it. Not a hint of self-doubt in that massive frame.

When he was thrown onto his back, she let out a snort of laughter. The portal had rejected him too and Justine found it hilarious. She held a hand over her mouth to contain the mirth, but when it grew too much, she had to run up the ramp.

Orion must have heard her because he came flying after her. She slipped into a gap between the stones of the pyramid before he could catch sight of her. The big second year scanned the area for intruders and after a long, tense minute, he returned below.

Justine made her way back to the interior of the necropolis, where she burst out laughing once she was safely inside. She couldn't figure out why it was so funny, but she didn't stop laughing for at least two minutes.

When it was over, she climbed back onto her throne of stuffies, pulled out her notebook, and got back to work transcribing the spells. The Obelisk held more mysteries than anyone knew, and she wanted to be the one to discover them all.

FIVE

I can't believe we're being forced to go to the Second Year Games," Zuri said for the fifth time since they'd climbed into the back of the SUV. "This is such a waste of time."

She knew what she sounded like, but she didn't care. Besides, Iona was curled into the corner of her seat, smirking behind a cupped hand.

"I know. But don't get too excited. We're showing up, getting put into a team, and then coming back to the Obelisk. We need to figure out why we couldn't get through the portal."

"I'm not laughing at you," said Iona, tongue resting on the bottom of her teeth.

Zuri extended her middle finger and made a raspberry with her lips.

A playful smile was returned. Iona stuck her face against the window.

"I'll never get used to these buildings. The tallest thing in Licking was the water tower and that was probably only eight stories high."

"So the magic and weird shit that's happened to us in the Obelisk is normal, but these regular skyscrapers are what blow your mind?"

"I grew up with a fanatical warlock and helped him with rituals on the regular. Magic seemed normal, even if I knew no one else in town could do it."

"I guess."

Iona turned her head. "What do you make of Orion not being able to get through the portal either?"

She tapped her fingernails on her pleated black slacks.

"I'd been afraid that whatever had happened last year with Fenris was interfering, like when he'd blocked the portal so we couldn't leave. But that couldn't be the case if Orion didn't get through either."

"Maybe we just both got the riddle wrong."

Zuri shook her head.

"I know we got it right. I know it in my soul, but we're missing something and I don't like what it suggests."

"What's that?"

The SUV lurched to a stop.

"We've arrived, Miss Musa."

"Thanks, Gentry."

Unlike the day of their Trials, they couldn't ride the gondola as it was reserved for faculty and fourth and fifth years, so they had to park nearby and walk the final stretch. The wide sidewalks were packed with other second years. A few recognized Iona, though she was surprised, since she looked nothing like the backwater yokel that had stumbled into the auditorium to laughter. But her pale blonde hair stuck out. It was white like pure snow, a contrast to her own lustrous black skin. There was a feralness about Iona too, which made her even more striking.

They were led to a theater with angled seats that went all the way around. Zuri led them to a spot near the first exit. She wanted to leave as soon as possible. There were at least three books she needed to track down that might help with the portal problem.

After a bit of pageantry with representatives from every hall carrying a flag with their badge through the chamber, a slight figure entered wearing a flowy dress in deep purple. Head Patron Pythia Silverthorne. The sleeveless outfit showed off the tattoos on her arms and the spiky black hair made it seem like she was about to break out in song, rather than address them about a magical competition.

Every time Zuri saw the Head Patron, she thought about how her sister had worked with Pythia to thwart the Infernal Invasion. It didn't seem real. The Head Patron was a mythical figure while Nandi was just her older, wiser sister.

"Greetings, Second Years!"

The magically aided voice boomed throughout the chamber, which erupted in applause and cheering. Zuri had been so determined to avoid the Second Year Games, she'd forgotten how much the other students looked forward to it.

Iona was leaning forward and applauding enthusiastically, occasionally putting her fingers in her lips to make a high-pitched whistle. If they'd had a normal-sized group, Zuri probably would have wanted to do the games too, but with only two and a half of them, they needed to stay focused on the portal problem.

"Before we get into the details of the Second Year Games, I have a few announcements. It's not often I get to speak to an entire class of students across all the Halls.

"I know it's exciting being a member of the Hundred Halls, learning magic, practicing your spells. But I want to remind you that what we do here is dangerous and that we should treat magic with respect. Attempting big, splashy spells before you're ready is a recipe for disaster. I say this because accidental deaths due to magical mishaps have risen sharply these last few years, and your class is no different. We won't be able to defend ourselves from the next Invasion if there are no more mages left."

Nervous laughter followed as she turned, facing each part of the auditorium in turn.

"I would also remind you that while the Undercity is not off-limits, it has become extremely dangerous these last few years due to the consolidation of the criminal gangs and the proliferation of faez crystals, which has made them more potent. Mages, even experienced ones, should not expect to have the advantage in the Undercity, and for you wet-behind-the-ears second years, you'll find yourselves woefully outclassed."

Iona spread her hands questioningly, so Zuri shrugged. She had no idea either.

"Finally, I would like to recommend that you stay out of the way of the Invictus PD. Not every strange thing that happens in the city is the result of some nefarious supernatural being or a loose magical creature."

"What's that all about?" asked Iona.

"No idea."

"If you ask me, more kids are going to be going to the Undercity and interfering with the police now," said Iona.

"Now for the big event. The Second Year Games. I won't be telling you anything about the actual event, that will be yours to discover, but I can assure you that our Gamemakers went to great lengths to create a memorable challenge for you.

"Remember that these games aren't just about creating a problem for you to solve. They're a way to get to know your fellow Hall students, and more importantly, yourselves. The further you get in this challenge, the more you'll find the contest is about discovering the best, or worst, version of yourself."

Head Patron Pythia offered a pinched smile to the auditorium, but Zuri didn't get the impression that it was a lighthearted statement. To the contrary, it sounded like a warning, one that most of the students wouldn't get.

"But the challenge isn't why you're here, but the prize. This year, we have a special reward courtesy of a collaboration between Patron Celesse D'Agastine, who personally brewed these potions, and the Oculus Hall."

An older student pushed a cart filled with small vials onto the platform. He left it near Patron Pythia before leaving. She picked up a glass of light green liquid and held it up so it caught the light. Even from a great distance, Zuri could see the swirling golden hue within the green.

"Whichever team wins the Second Year Contest, they will each be given one of these vials. The liquid within is called the Elixir of Foresight. After drinking it, you'll find yourself capable of understanding even the most complex subjects and finding answers to challenging and thorny problems. The divination side of the potions will even allow you to anticipate things that may or may not happen in the near future. One of these potions might just be the reason you become world-famous, or a titan in the industry of your choice. And before you think you can do this on your own, know that the reagents required for these potions are nearly impossible to find, so don't think you'll acquire them any other way than winning the contest."

A hushed silence was followed by scattered applause.

"Now that you know the stakes, it's time to get started. Follow the floating mage lights into the corridor, where you'll take your Second Year Games test. Based on your scores, and your Halls, you'll be placed in a team. Remember these games are a chance to work together across Halls and learn the value of our diverse magics. We couldn't have stopped the Infernal Invasion without all the Halls working together."

Zuri got a little shock when the Head Patron's gaze was sent directly at her. It was brief, and Pythia turned away before anyone else noticed, but she sensed the intentionality of that look.

As the auditorium full of second years rose to their feet, Iona tugged on her arm.

"You heard that, right?"

"Which part?" asked Zuri.

"The Elixir of Foresight. We could use that to figure out the portal problem."

"Even if one of us managed to win, beating out two hundred something other teams, we wouldn't get our prize until the end of the year. If we're not through before then, we're screwed."

"Then it would help us with the next level, or whichever one gets us stuck," said Iona.

"Or we could put our noses down and work hard and never have to need the stupid elixir in the first place. My parents always taught me there were no shortcuts. The Second Year Games would be a major distraction."

They filed in behind the lines of students. The wait wasn't as long as she thought it would be. The test, whatever it was, seemed to take a few minutes max for each student, and there were dozens of doors.

"Good luck," said Iona as she went through a door, bright-eyed and cheery.

It reminded Zuri how different their backgrounds were. Iona looked forward to the drudgeries of school because she'd never experienced anything different, while Zuri was overly cynical due to her history.

"Have a little fun for once," Zuri told herself as she entered the testing room.

A rainbow ball was resting on the floor in the middle of a slight depression while there were five colored discs on the four walls and the ceiling.

A disembodied voice came over a speaker: "This is a test of your mastery of the five elements and your faez endurance. The goal is to keep the rainbow ball in the air by hitting the discs with the appropriate element when they light up. The stronger your hit and the shorter the delay, the longer your ball will stay in the air. The test will grow more difficult as time goes on. The current record is one minute and thirty-eight seconds. You may start when ready."

Loosening up her fingers and shaking out her arms helped Zuri get in the right mindset for the contest. While she had no plans on continuing in the Second Year Games, she couldn't back down from a challenge. She memorized the locations of the elements: air to the left, earth to the right, fire on the far left, with water on the far right, and spirit on the ceiling.

Fire was her slowest element, so she started with that. The ball leapt into the air, hovering at the center of the room, as the counter started ticking upward. The spirit disc lit up with light purple, so she blasted it with a quick force bolt. A few seconds after that the fire disc glowed and she hit that. Zuri got into a rhythm as the lights sped up, occasionally glancing at the timer to see her progress.

When thirty seconds passed, the pace increased until there was no resting between elements. By the time it hit a minute, she was firing the next one by the time the light on the previous had gone out. Up, left, right, right, far right, far left, up, up, up—

Sweat dripped from her nose as her arms and fingers worked the magic like a drummer on their solo. As the time neared the record, she didn't think she could hold on anymore. Her head felt like it was being squeezed by a vice and the faint sparkles of unused faez in the air were making her dizzy.

The test ended when she missed the earth disc and the ball dropped to the floor. One minute, thirty-nine point eight seconds. A new record.

Zuri sunk to the floor, breathing as if she'd just finished a marathon. She clucked her tongue since she was too tired to speak. She hadn't intended to try so hard, but once it got going she didn't know how to stop. A door on the opposite side appeared and she trudged through it, wishing she hadn't eaten so much that morning.

The hallway led to a dead end with an obsidian pillar sitting in the center. A portal. Zuri checked around, looking for hidden doors, but there were none. The lack of an exit was a bit disconcerting, but then again, she'd been near the end of the test, so it was possible she was getting sent to her group.

Zuri was about to test the obsidian portal when the same voice from the testing room spoke: "You may enter the portal and discover your Second Year Games team. Good luck."

She hesitated before she placed her hands on the obsidian, thinking about what she was going to tell her group about not being able to compete with them.

"They'll just have to get over it."

The stone pillar was cool to the touch. She closed her eyes and sent faez into the stone.

The sudden catapult vertigo left her dizzy upon arrival, right as four other students appeared in the space. At first she thought her mind was playing tricks on her, or that she'd been sent to the wrong place.

"Zuri?"

Iona was standing across from her, hands spread questioningly as she glared at the other three members of the team. Everything was wrong. Very, very wrong.

Orion Dreadmarsh.

Scarlett Calloway.

Blake Lockwood.

SIX

The shouting was rising to a crescendo while Scarlett stood back with her arms crossed. It was mostly coming from Zuri and Blake, with the occasional odd comment from Pig Girl. Not that she looked like the same backwater yokel that had wandered into the Obelisk last year. Iona had found a sense of fashion, or Zuri had dressed her.

Orion, on the other hand, looked completely bored, standing to the side sipping from an energy drink he'd pulled out of the refrigerator. The bottle looked like a tiny teacup in his massive hands. Scarlett was sure that he'd grown since last year, a worrying prospect as he was already an enormous, menacing figure. Though as she stared at him quietly enjoying his drink, she wasn't as frightened of him as she normally was.

"Will you two shut up," said Scarlett when she couldn't take it anymore.

The screaming petered out with both combatants slowly turning towards her.

"None of us want to be here, and especially not in this group, so I don't know why you're both trying to give yourselves heart attacks."

Blake glared back with his arms crossed while Zuri had self-awareness enough to take a deep breath as if she was trying to calm herself.

"Great. Now that we're going to act like adults—"

The words died on her tongue the moment a sixth person entered the room.

Zuri was the first to blurt something out: "Head Patron Silverthorne..."

Scarlett was struck by how small the head of the magical university was, and how young she looked, but that lack of size or age didn't change the intensity of her presence. It was like standing next to high voltage power lines without any protective gear.

"Zuri Musa," said Pythia. "How is your sister doing?"

"I...thank you for asking, Head Patron. She's bored of foundation work and wishing she'd taken a different specialty in Coterie."

"I for one am glad she was a demonologist. Her expertise came in handy when things got bad."

Scarlett had always been aware that Zuri's sister had known the Head Patron and even fought beside her during the Invasion, but knowing that and seeing evidence before her eyes were two different things.

"Hello, Patron Silverthorne," said Scarlett, extending her hand.

"Scarlett Calloway. I knew your cousin Simone. Is she still with Derek Kensington?"

"They got divorced a year after they married."

"That's a shame, they seemed like a good couple." The Patron turned towards the big man in the corner. "Orion Dreadmarsh. I see you're carrying on the Dreadmarsh name quite well. You're one of Leo's brood?"

He shook his head tightly.

"My mother was Etienne."

The Head Patron gave a slow nod as if she were considering this news. Scarlett was confused as well. She'd always thought that Orion was part of the main trunk of the Dreadmarsh family, not one of the offshoots. Not that it mattered. Any Dreadmarsh was inherently dangerous and even the Head Patron seemed wary.

"Oh yes, I believe I might have met her at a charity event last year?"

Orion stared back without answering until the Head Patron turned towards Iona.

"Miss Storm. It's lovely to meet you. I'm pleased that our new scholarship system worked out for you. I was a little worried about an outsider joining Coterie, but you seem to have fit in quite nicely."

"It's had its challenges."

"I can see that."

"Are you here to fix this mess?" asked Blake as if he were addressing a waiter about his undercooked steak.

Scarlett wanted to yank him by the ear and remind him who he was talking to, but that was one of the curses of her boyfriend. He spoke his mind no matter who the audience.

The Head Patron was not amused. Her lips were flat and she stared back with the intensity of an angry lioness.

"How is Alton?"

Blake swallowed heavily.

"You knew him?"

"He was an upperclassman when I was in Coterie."

"Oh." Blake looked away from her heavy gaze. "He lives in a home since the accident."

Scarlett was almost sure the Head Patron was going to say, "Good," but then she turned towards them all, a pained smile on her lips.

"As you can tell by your existence in this room, there seems to have been a mistake. There should be five students from different Halls, not all from Coterie and not five with a clear history with each other."

"We're as confused as you are, Head Patron," said Zuri.

Scarlett had to resist the urge to roll her eyes. Always the teacher's pet, that Zuri Musa. That they both had been with Blake didn't bother her as much as the goodie-goodie act that Scarlett knew was complete bullshit. The girl was as ruthless as her sister.

"Yes, this is unusual, though not the first time it's happened," said the Head Patron with her hands clasped behind her back. "But maybe it makes sense. The contest is meant to bring together differing viewpoints, and while usually that means different Halls, it appears that the sorting spell thought that the five of you were meant to be a team based on your past interactions."

"That might make sense, except for him," said Iona, gesturing towards the towering figure of Orion Dreadmarsh. "Neither side interacted with him much during our first year."

"Perhaps the spell sensed you needed to come together. Zuri might know this, though it's not common knowledge, but her sister and her friends were trying to kill us at the beginning of the Invasion. It was only when we realized we had a common enemy that we came together."

"I'm not grouping with them," said Blake.

"I didn't think Coterie really ever joined the Second Year Games, so maybe it's best you're in a team together—that way none of the others are handicapped with a missing member."

"We weren't planning on staying," said Zuri. "We only came because Professor Sinclair requested it."

"And I thank him for it. Once you've missed the sorting test, there's no way to get you on a team, and you never know when you might decide to give the contest a chance."

"No way in hell. I'd rather eat a bag of bees," said Blake.

"I can make that happen," said Zuri.

Before Blake could respond, the Head Patron held up a hand.

"Alright. I've made my decision. The five of you will stay a team. Whether or not you choose to compete is up to you, but let me remind you that our fellow Halls or students are not our enemies. The world, the realms, is a dangerous place and while the infernal threat is no longer a big risk, there are other issues on the horizon that might require us to put aside our differences."

Blake looked ready to blurt out something rude, when the Head Patron snapped her fingers and his lips clamped shut as if held by invisible fingers.

"Don't try me, boy. Unless you'd like to end up like your brother."

The Head Patron strode to the portal and disappeared.

"You bitch," said Blake once she was gone.

"Shame keeping you shut up like that didn't last," said Zuri.

Before he could restart the argument, Scarlett hooked her arm around his waist.

"Come on, Blake. Let's go. We weren't going to do the games anyway. No reason to waste our time with them."

"Fine."

She led him through the portal. Other second years were appearing at the exit at the same time, laughing and joking with their new teammates.

"What do you think that bitch meant when she said that?" asked Blake, scowling.

"Zuri or the Head Patron?"

"That imposter."

"I have no idea, but let's worry about our more immediate problems before you start a feud with the most powerful woman in the world."

"She insulted my family."

Scarlett put up a smile and rubbed her hand along his back.

"Come on, babe. Let's not ruin things after a wonderful and sexy summer on my parents' yacht. If you're good, I'll let you do that thing you've been wanting for a long time."

The offer broke him out of his anger, which it usually did. She shifted her hand down the back of his pants, squeezing his ass and reminding him of what she could do later. He was annoying when he was angry, but he was also easier to manipulate.

"Nothing makes sense," he said, shaking his head. "Not the stupid portal, not the contest, not whatever that bitch had to say about my brother."

"Well, if she did something, babe, it's much better to hold your tongue and get your revenge when she's least expecting it. Telegraphing your intentions isn't going to work on the most powerful woman in the world."

"I wanted her to know how I felt."

She patted him on the ass.

"She felt it. That's for sure. But you might want to consider a little subtlety."

"I don't like being subtle. That's weak. I'm not weak."

"No, you're not, babe. But we've got to figure out why the rest of our team got through the portal, but we can't, or our little spats with Zuri and the Head Patron aren't going anywhere."

"What are we going to do?" he asked.

Scarlett gave him a sweet smile.

"Maybe whatever happened last year with that warlock is still interfering with the portal."

"But he's dead."

"That ritual was focused on Iona. Maybe we need to take her out so we can go through."

"And Zuri. Don't forget Zuri."

"I would never do that, babe. Do we have a plan?"

Blake stared into the distance before giving a nod.

“Great,” she said, then whispered something in his ear that make him squirm with delight.

“You promise?”

She grinned.

“I promise.”

“Then let’s kill those bitches.”

SEVEN

A crowd stood outside the Aquarius gawking at the massive saltwater tank that took up the entire front window when Zuri's SUV pulled up to the valet area. Kids were laughing as the octopus signed innocent jokes while the parents glanced around nervously.

Zuri smiled at the display, even as her stomach was twisted in a knot. She'd been nervous about the visit since Ana had texted a week ago.

The hostess led her to a private booth in the back of the busy restaurant where Ana was already waiting. She wore a tight-fitting red dress that showed off her curvy body and accented her auburn hair and freckles.

"Zuri!"

The long hug broke loose some of the nervousness.

"It's been too long," she said as she sat across from Ana.

A waiter appeared and they gave their drink orders.

"What brings you to town? I'm sorry if you already said so in our texts, but things have been crazy and we don't get much reception in most of the Obelisk."

"I bought tickets for The Durge at the Bastille Charity event last month."

"The Durge?"

Ana made a random gesture with her hand.

"Some hot new band that people are saying are the next Garbage Kings. They've sold out the Glitterdome. I don't know any of the music but I hear they put on a good show." Ana rolled her eyes. "That's why we're eating here, by the way. A private dinner came with the tickets. I hope you don't mind. This isn't exactly our normal kind of eating establishment."

"Of course not. It's good to get out. How are your parents?"

Ana exhaled heavily as she ran a fingernail around the top of a water glass and looked away with a pained expression.

"They're a wreck. I thought they'd get better with time, but it's been over two years and they look like they're waiting for Gemma to get home any minute. They haven't touched a single thing in her room."

Zuri reached out and took Ana's hand.

"Not a day goes by that I don't think of her. It's been so hard. I can't imagine how it must be for you and your parents."

The sudden removal of Ana's hand startled Zuri.

"Then why are you working with him?" came the angry retort.

"What are you talking about?"

"Blake. I heard from some other St. Jude's alumni that you were working with him in the Obelisk last year and now you're grouped with him in the Second Year Games."

"It's not like that. We didn't work with him. I didn't work with him. He tried to kill me multiple times last year, and as for the Second Year Games, we don't know how that happened, but Head Patron Silverthorne left us that way. But don't worry. We're not doing the games. Especially not with him."

"Why haven't you taken care of him? For Gemma?"

"It's not that simple."

"The hell it is. You said it yourself. He killed Gemma, but then you let him get away with it. My family is ruined. My parents are shells of themselves and nothing is right anymore. If you have a chance, you take him out. That's only fair. Unless you're lying."

"I'm not lying."

"But you said you'd take him out."

"He has a big group. It's only the two of us."

"The Zuri I know, the one that my sister worshiped, could get him, or are you too afraid to do it?"

Zuri opened her mouth to respond, but she remembered last year when she'd had a chance to kill Blake, but had let him go.

"I knew it," said Ana, shaking her head. "You're afraid."

"I'm not afraid, but..."

"You promised me that you'd take Blake down. Don't you remember that? After the funeral. I wanted to know that some of the pain was going to go away, and you promised me his cold lifeless body, but he's still alive and I still hurt."

Water in her eyes pooled at the corners. Zuri was gutted. She had no idea what to say, but then the waiter appeared, oblivious to the undercurrents, and took their order. Zuri wasn't going to eat anything, but Ana ordered a special meal for two.

"I know you don't want to hear this right now, but I'm barely surviving. When the trial was over, everyone thought I was lying, that I was just the jealous girlfriend who wanted cheap revenge for his successes. That he was the boy with a bright future, and how dare I try to take that away from him for something that *I* probably did. My own parents didn't show up when I joined the Halls because they were afraid of being seen with me.

"I'm sorry, Ana. I really am. I loved Gemma like a sister, but nothing I can do will fix the fact that she's dead."

Ana sniffed and dabbed her eyes with her napkin.

"I'm sorry, Zuri. I shouldn't have come at you like that. I've just been under a lot of stress. The family business isn't doing well, especially with my parents being so distracted."

"What's wrong?"

"It's nothing..."

"Ana. Tell me. If there's something I can do to help, I'll do it."

As soon as she said it, Zuri cringed internally. She'd promised revenge on Blake and hadn't delivered that.

"It's the Siren Sisters. Well, not them, but their family. They're trying to move into our side of business."

"I don't understand, I thought they worked with entertainers. Career management and stuff like that."

"It's really not so different from the business management we do, but with the reputation hit from the trial, we've been losing clients. The Siren Sisters are our biggest threat. They have the size and background to sway the nervous away from us. They're saying if we couldn't defend Gemma at trial, then how can we help them with their careers?"

"That's bullshit. How can they be so callous?"

"Zuri, come on..."

The conversation was interrupted when three waiters appeared. They were carrying a steaming cauldron ringed in runes using a pair of long two-person tongs while the third brought a tray of vegetables and meats. The cauldron was set in a hole in the table while the waiter explained how it all worked.

"The cauldron is enchanted to cook your food perfectly. Throw anything in, veggies, meats, you could throw in your shoe if you wanted, and when it's done, it'll rise to the surface where you can scoop it out and eat it freshly cooked. There's a color chart on the tray to show you how long each thing takes to finish so you don't have your entire meal ready at once."

After the waitstaff left, Ana smirked as she grabbed a handful of mushrooms and tossed them into the steaming cauldron.

"Sorry. I had no idea that we'd have to cook this ourselves. Hard to believe there's a line of people trying to get in this place with *this* kind of service."

"It's not all bad. Cooking for yourself, that is. I did a bit of cooking this summer and I'm not terrible."

"Gemma liked to cook."

"She wasn't very good at it," said Zuri, which got a laugh out of Ana.

"No," said Ana, shaking her head. "Despite what she always said, hot sauce does *not* go on everything."

"She put it on her cereal once just to prove a point."

"Seven hells, she did?"

Zuri smirked.

"It was disgusting, but she didn't want to admit she was wrong, so she ate the entire bowl without complaint."

"That makes my stomach hurt just thinking about it."

Zuri threw some random meats into the cauldron.

"She'd love this place."

"She would. It's just cheesy enough for her to enjoy. She never liked the uptight restaurants our parents would take us to."

"I miss her."

"Me too," said Ana. "But at least she won't have to be around when the family business fails."

"Is it really that bad?"

"We've already lost some of our best employees. Poached by the Siren Sisters. Which isn't helping after all the legal bills. Our lawyers don't think the libel suit will stick, but I don't think the Lockwoods care. They're just trying to bankrupt us through the legal system."

"I'm sorry, Ana. I didn't know."

"It's okay. There's nothing you can do."

Zuri knew *that* wasn't true, but she also knew that Ana would never ask. Directly. In fact, she was pretty sure that's why they were meeting in the first place.

"I can't promise anything, but I can dig around and see if there's anything interesting with the Siren Sisters."

"Anything would help. Anything to put them on their back foot, give us room to climb out of this hole. If my parents had their minds right, this wouldn't be a problem, but they've just never..."

"I know, I know. I'll see what I can do."

A mushroom stalk plopped to the surface.

"Dinner's ready," said Ana, laughing.

"I hope we don't get too full," she said, matching her mirth.

As if summoned, other pieces of mushrooms, veggies, and bits of meat appeared like divers after a long time beneath the surface.

The rest of the dinner they stayed away from serious talk and instead spent their time making fun of their dining experience, but generally enjoying the meal. The entire dinner, Zuri couldn't help but think about Gemma's parents and their business and how she might be able to help with the Siren Sisters. She had nothing specific in mind but vowed to keep her options open. She owed Gemma that much.

EIGHT

Iona's stomach rumbled despite her leaving a corner diner where she'd had a very rare and extremely greasy burger. She pushed away the annoying sensation and focused on the group of students ahead of her. They sounded like first years based on their conversation, though she thought they'd come from different Halls. Maybe they'd made friends in the third Trial.

What a different experience they were having: wandering the streets carefree, learning magic with professors that actually cared, and having fellow students that weren't trying to kill them. Their attitude showed up in their choice of clothing. Hoodies and T-shirts with half of them with Hall logos. Much different than the expensive slacks and silk shirt she was wearing, but fitting in at Coterie required a completely different wardrobe and mindset.

Iona adjusted the backpack full of tomes. She'd been scouring the various bookstores for books that might help them with the portal problem. The weight was putting pressure on her shoulders, but she'd given herself a little endurance charm to make it back to the Obelisk.

A pair of kids ran by with novelty wands, controlling illusionary dragonlings above their heads while their parents shouted to slow down and watch out for strangers. She dodged around them, stopping behind the other students as they waited to cross the busy intersection.

Iona glanced into the park at a group of pigeons pecking at thrown seeds. Her stomach grumbled in response.

"Stop that," she muttered, holding her gut.

But she couldn't help but stare at the pigeons and wonder what they would taste like.

"What is wrong with me?"

A girl in the back of the group checked back, curious, but then the light changed and everyone surged to cross.

Iona didn't understand it. Every meal she wanted to eat almost raw and even then she didn't feel sated. It was like her stomach was a bottomless pit.

When she reached the other side, Iona turned in the direction of the nearest station and saw a woman that made her stop in her tracks. Pale blonde hair. Elegant. Dressed similarly, but yet…better.

The urge to flee filled Iona's chest. The woman's approach made her claustrophobic. Panicked.

I don't even know this woman, she reminded herself.

But she felt like she did. And that she wanted to know more. Maybe this was someone who had answers for who she was. But answers came with danger, especially if they'd known Fenris, and Iona certainly felt like this woman might know him since she looked like they could be half-sisters.

She summoned her resolve and continued forward as the woman

closed the distance, clearly headed for Iona.

They stopped ten feet apart as the crowds flowed around them.

"Hello, Iona."

A memory of the letter fragment from the destroyed farmhouse came back.

"You must be Ilyana."

This seemed to surprise Ilyana, who tilted her head.

"He mentioned me?"

"Not directly."

Ilyana's gaze darted towards a nearby coffee shop. Iona followed her inside. They didn't bother with drinks, but took a booth in back. The privacy bubble that flowed from Ilyana's hands was smooth and effortless, telling Iona that she was an expert practitioner.

"Where is Fenris?" asked Ilyana after a long, uncomfortable silence.

Iona detected an accent. A little Eastern European with a touch of French? She was no expert but that's what her mind said.

"I don't know."

"What do you mean, you don't know?"

"He went out one day and never came back."

"Never came back..."

"He'd been eating so much. Going out frequently. It was unlike him."

"You're lying."

The accusation put Iona on edge. She sensed that Ilyana would have no problem killing her in the busy coffee shop if it came to that.

"I'm not."

"Fenris doesn't get lost."

"I didn't say he got lost. I said he never came back." Iona tried to remember if the letter she'd seen had a date on it. "Not quite two years ago. After months of his absence I came here."

"But you said he mentioned me."

"I didn't say that. I said that I know who you are. Or guessed, really. I read one of your letters."

"This doesn't sound right. Fenris wouldn't move on without taking his stuff. Without taking you."

"So you already knew who I was?"

"I did."

"What did he say about me?" asked Iona.

"He said you were his brightest pupil."

Pupil. The word didn't sound like Fenris. At least he'd never said anything like that to her. But he'd also claimed in the moments before his death that he was preparing her. That he wasn't going to kill her. She'd never quite decided if that was true or not.

"He didn't talk to me much."

This also surprised Ilyana.

"I'm having trouble believing you."

"Believe what you will, but I was his assistant. I helped him with the rituals and if I screwed up, he beat me. Or locked me in my room. Even when I didn't screw up, he ignored me, so I tried to stay out of his way and learn everything I could so I wouldn't mess anything up."

"Then what about the tattoos?" asked Ilyana, gesturing towards the ink sticking out from her shirt.

"I know a little about them. But not all."

Ilyana tapped her fingernails on the table impatiently. Her jaw pulsed as she stared out the window.

"You're a member of Coterie," she said with a sneer. "That seems highly unlikely."

"I won a scholarship. You can check the records. I sent in a video."

Ilyana seemed angry that she couldn't catch Iona in a lie. It was clear she suspected that Fenris hadn't just disappeared.

"Why did you burn down the farmhouse?"

"I didn't. It was like that when I returned last summer. I suspect the townsfolk figured out we were both gone and burned it. I'm glad I wasn't around, as I doubt I would have been able to stop them." Iona grimaced. "Are you his daughter too? Or are we related in another way?"

Ilyana raised her eyebrows.

"He didn't say?"

"I only learned I was his daughter from his notes. The ones I could read anyway. He always told me that he'd got me in trade for drugs from my real parents. Well, I guess she was my real mom, but I didn't know he was my father."

"He was my father first."

"Are there...a lot of us?"

The question made Ilyana scowl.

"It appears there's a lot for you and I to discuss."

"I have many questions."

"As do I. But I have an appointment that I cannot miss. Let's meet again. Soon," said Ilyana.

"Agreed. But things are a little crazy in the Obelisk. I'm not easy to get ahold of."

Ilyana pulled out a card and scribbled on the back.

"Call this number when you can meet. I'll make sure I'm available."

"Thank you," said Iona, putting the card in her purse.

Her stomach grumbled loudly, which Ilyana noticed, but she was kind enough not to say anything.

The privacy bubble disappeared as Ilyana stood and strode from the coffee shop, leaving Iona by herself. A few people glanced over.

Iona exhaled, finally allowing herself to relax. The entire interaction had been tense. Ilyana clearly suspected something had happened to Fenris. If she found out that she'd killed him, Iona didn't think Ilyana would take that lightly, especially based on the letter she'd read.

But Iona had questions too. Fenris had told her nothing about herself, her family, or why she was always hungry. Ilyana provided an opportunity for answers. She might not like the answers, but better to know than to wonder.

As she left the café a new thought intruded.

I have a sister. That I might have to kill.

NINE

Gray October skies covered the city, erasing the top half of the Spire and blowing brisk winds through the streets. The clouds reminded Zuri that they were rapidly running out of time. The semester was nearly half over and they had yet to discover the reason they couldn't get through the portal.

It had to be something that Fenris had done last year, because Blake and Scarlett were stuck too. The rest of their group had gone through the portal. Fenris' ritual was the only thing that made sense.

Zuri was about to cross the street when a voice startled her.

"Your debt is unpaid, Zuri Musa."

A woman with silky black hair and one gray eye was standing off the sidewalk. No one else seemed to notice the woman. The other side of the street was faintly visible.

"Debt?"

"Did you think that book was free?" asked the half-maetrie woman named Murder.

Nandi had warned her. She should have expected this, but the trials of the first year had buried this inconvenient fact.

"Come see me. Now. I know you're only a few blocks away."

The illusionary projection winked out, leaving Zuri with a stone in her gut.

"Seven hells."

Zuri had other business to attend to. She didn't have time for dealing with the owner of Grimoire & Gold, even if she did owe a debt. She headed the opposite direction, making it half a block before she found herself back where she'd been right before.

She growled under her breath and marched back in the original direction. The dislocation happened much sooner and this time she found herself staring at the spot between the ice cream shop and haberdashery. The hidden door revealed itself a moment later.

Nandi had warned her not to use Grimoire & Gold, that the more you relied on the owner, the worse things would get. Now it didn't look like she had a choice, so she went down the stairs.

The strange and crooked bookstore was filled with musty books and glass cases. She maneuvered down the angled passages in search of the owner, occasionally spotting interesting titles like *Noble Arcana*, *The Secret Lives of Pottery Ants*, or *The Value of Souls to the Fae*. The urge to read was tempered by the fact that her visit had been required.

A pungent rich smell led Zuri to a side room where she looked through a gap to see a slim woman wearing a leather apron and wielding a butcher knife. The strike of the heavy blade separated a piece of the small body, and once struck, she glanced up, a grim smile lurking on her lips. The one gray eye looked into her soul.

"Come in, Zuri Musa."

She approached apprehensively. The owner seemed different than last year.

Zuri examined the mess on the wooden table. It was scarred with butcher knife blows. At the center of the bloody pool was a small figure with fur that had been dismembered into four pieces. It was unrecognizable to Zuri, who stared back at Murder rather than the dead thing.

"I'm sorry I didn't—"

The words died on her lips as she examined the room, filled with bones and stuffed creature heads including a bat-like one the size of a human's. A scapula and rib cage were spread out on the wall with black runes drawn over the bones.

Zuri caught herself when she realized she wasn't under the effect of the maetrie charm. The owner, Murder, was half-maetrie and last time it'd scrambled her thoughts. She examined her to find the silver leg beneath the knee suggesting that it was the same person.

"Do you think I'm a library?" asked Murder, pointing the bloody butcher knife at her. "Do you think you get to come in here and make a request like I'm a fast food window and do nothing for me in return?"

She slammed the knife into the wooden table and grabbed a towel to clean her hands. The look made Zuri wonder for her safety.

"I'm sorry. I didn't—"

"You didn't what?"

Zuri swallowed. She'd already stuttered that out once and she knew how stupid and young she sounded. The half-maetrie woman outclassed her and she felt small in her presence, much like the moment that the jury had revealed their not guilty verdict.

"I...I don't know how this works."

The owner tossed the bloody rag on the ground.

"I gave freely last time. Now it's your turn."

Zuri was reminded of a drug dealer's motto: the first one's free.

"Of course."

"Follow me."

She followed the owner through the stacks. Along the way, they passed a figure slumped over in a corner. Zuri opened her mouth to ask about them but then realized it was a bad idea. She was on unfamiliar turf.

The space they stopped in was dominated by a working fountain with what suspiciously looked like the owner as the central sculpture. A ring of shelves surrounded the fountain. Murder climbed up a rolling ladder and grabbed a tome off the top shelf, handing it to Zuri upon return.

"I don't understand. It's empty," said Zuri, after paging through it.

"Exactly. There's a book in the possession of Professor Cornwallis. A diary of sorts. I need a copy of it. Bring me that or I'll exact my payment in another way."

"Professor Cornwallis?" exclaimed Zuri.

"Did I stutter? Or are you a middling mage with little or no ambition?"

"How will I know which one it is?"

Murder's eyes turned to slits.

"It has a golden eagle on the front. She keeps it in her office on the third shelf, next to the bust of her father."

The idea that she could sneak into the office of one of her professors—a Coterie mage—and come out with one of her prized books seemed ludicrous, but Zuri wasn't about to admit that in front of a woman she knew very little about.

"How do I copy it?"

"The book will do the work. It's a Libri Tempus."

"I guess I'll figure it out."

"If you can't then you're not much of a mage." Murder looked into the distance. "I have other business to attend to. You can let yourself out."

The owner marched through a gap in the stacks that Zuri didn't see. Clutching the copy tome, she headed back to the exit. By the time she was back on the street, the whole thing felt like a dream. She might have thought it a hallucination except for the book she had in her hands.

"What have I gotten myself into?"

As Zuri headed back to the Obelisk, she wondered if she'd try to steal the book from Professor Cornwallis. It seemed extremely dangerous. The professors were not like the ones from the other Halls. She would kill her if she found out, that much Zuri was sure of.

She shoved the copy tome into her bag and vowed to herself that she would find another way out of the problem. Stealing from a professor was a step too far. But then again, the half-maetrie woman, Murder, seemed like she might be worse than Professor Cornwallis. Caught between an immovable rock and an unstoppable force, Zuri had no idea how to escape the trap.

TEN

The subject of the lecture, how to deal with supernatural beings from the Veil, had been less than exciting. Professor Horace Green, while knowledgeable, taught his classes as if he'd never been a teacher before. He had unreasonable expectations for the students and tended to get angry when someone didn't perform a task perfectly.

"I don't know how many more of his classes I can sit through," said Iona as they crossed the residential part of the lowest level on their way to the portal.

Zuri was busy on her phone as she had been all class. The screen showed a series of diagrams and arcane formulas.

"Zuri?"

"Oh yeah, sorry." She sighed. "I had an idea, but it's not coming together. I thought we might be able to short-circuit the pyramid and reset the portal, but it would probably kill us instead."

Zuri might look like a runway model, with glossy black skin and a look that exuded confidence and poise, but she was also the smartest, nerdiest mage she'd ever met. Not that she'd met a lot, but she was much different than the other students in Coterie.

"You would have been a great fit for Arcanium," Iona blurted out before she thought about it.

Zuri turned on her, forehead crinkled with anger.

"Why would you say something like that?"

Iona swallowed and prepared to apologize when something caught her eye in the side passage near the statue of Malden Anterist. Zuri followed her gaze.

"What the…?"

A bloody, mangled body lay in the middle of the hallway surrounded by a pool of blood. Iona approached with a sick feeling that turned to hunger the closer she got. The gruesome scene should have been horrifying, but she found herself drawn towards it like a moth to flame.

"Can you tell who it is?" asked Zuri.

Iona crouched on her heels, spotting a little trail of tiny footprints leading away from the pool towards a side passage. She was about to mention it when a second group came from the other direction. Fourth years.

A blonde girl with a high ponytail screamed when she saw the body. She threw herself on her knees before the bloody scene.

"Anton!"

Zuri leaned in her ear.

"Jessica Goodheart."

Iona had heard the name but didn't know much about her other than she was a fourth year and a member of one of the more ruthless upperclassman teams.

When glares were sent their way, Zuri held her hands up.

"We stumbled upon this the same time as you did."

A tall fourth year with mellow brown skin stepped forward.

"Pig Girl and the Traitor."

Iona grabbed Zuri's arm, whispering, "We should go."

Her friend seemed to agree, but before they could turn, the tall guy said, "Neither of you are going anywhere until we say so."

Not only was it four against two, but they were outclassed in ability.

"Fine," said Zuri, more defiant than Iona would have advised, but she knew these people better.

"What happened, Jack?" asked Jessica as she was sobbing and thumbing away tears.

The tall fourth year crouched down.

"It looks like something was eating him."

A loud gurgle erupted from Iona's stomach. So loud the others heard it and glared. Zuri elbowed her in the side.

"I couldn't help it," she whispered back.

"Let me check something," said Jack, pulling back his sleeves.

Iona had no idea what the spell was but she was mesmerized by his smooth motions and absolute command of his craft. The magic flowed from his lips like a soliloquy on the stage and when he was finished the body lit up with strange, pale gray light.

She was expecting to see the light follow the little footprints, but instead a tendril undulated from the gnawed corpse and eventually split into multiple sections with most pointing to other parts of the Obelisk, but then the two largest connected to both her and Zuri.

The other group bristled, appearing on the verge of combat.

"You did this."

"We had nothing to do with this," said Zuri, holding up her hands. "We were in Professor Green's class and before that we were out of the Obelisk. This looks too new. It can't be us. Someone's setting us up."

"No," said Jessica, standing and stretching her fingers. "No. You don't get to lie to us like that. Neither of you should be in Coterie. Never should have been let in. And now you had the nerve to kill my boyfriend. We're gonna make you pay."

Zuri looked like she was ready to defend herself while Iona knew it was time to flee. The four upperclassmen were starting their spells as a new person arrived.

"What in Merlin's name is going on here?" asked Professor Green.

Upon spotting the mangled body, he pushed past Iona and Zuri, unknowingly protecting them from attack. The others let their spells drop, which left golden sparkles of unspent faez in the air.

"Is this…?"

"It's Anton."

The professor muttered something in a language Iona couldn't understand.

"They killed him," said Jack, extending his arm.

The professor turned his head, raising an eyebrow.

"I seriously doubt it. This boy was attacked a short time ago, not longer than twenty minutes, this blood is fresh and the body is still warm and they were in my class during that time."

"I cast the Inquisitor spell. It connected with these two."

Professor Green cupped his chin in his hand.

"Curious, but that doesn't mean they did it. The Inquisitor spell only suggests a connection. It's not admissible in court, not that we're involving the legal system." He glanced to Zuri. "But this is a tragedy. Anton was an excellent student and your friend. I grieve with you."

"I don't want grief, I want revenge," said Jessica, flexing her hands and looking ready to resume the fight.

"It's not my business to get involved, but I should remind you that attacking a professor, even on accident, is a capital offense in the Obelisk."

Jack put his hands over Jessica's arms, making her end the spell. The professor turned his head.

"Now is a good time."

"Thank you, Professor," muttered Iona as they jogged away, headed to the opposite side of the level.

"As if things couldn't get any worse," said Zuri, shaking her head. "That's the last thing we need. A bunch of upperclassmen out to get us."

"Hopefully they'll be too busy with their challenges to go after us. It's not like we're in the same area."

"Yeah, but we're stuck and everyone knows it. I hated going back to the pyramid already, now, I don't know how we can manage it without exposing ourselves. We might just have to stand down for a while until they get bored and move on."

"You don't look like you believe yourself," said Iona.

"No. No, I don't."

Iona checked behind them to make sure no one was listening.

"I didn't mention it back there, because, you know, but there was something else wrong at the body."

Zuri arched an eyebrow.

"Two little footprints leading away."

"What? Really?"

"Yeah," said Iona despondently.

"You don't think Justine was involved? Or did it?"

Iona rubbed the back of her neck.

"Would she do it? Yeah. I hate to say it but I feel like we don't know her anymore. That having her soul shoved in that puppet changed things. On the other hand, I don't know how she physically could have managed it. And the chewing? That couldn't be her."

Zuri made noises in the back of her throat.

"We have to figure out why we can't get through the portal."

"No shit," said Iona.

"I have an idea."

"Don't hold back. It's not like we're flourishing here."

"It won't fix everything, but it'll at least tell us if our method for getting through the portal works. Let me set up a meeting. I'll let you know when."

"Who are we meeting with?" asked Iona.

ELEVEN

The eleventh ward was nothing like Zuri remembered from when she was younger. Her father had gotten lost in the third and accidentally ended up in the Enochian district where a guy with tentacles for arms had chased their vehicle down the street.

Now it was a gentrified area with high-end shops, award-winning restaurants that served such delights as fried speckled locanath or sautéed ghost-eye stalks, and late-night dance clubs that only allowed those that could use magic inside. The value of the vehicles on the street was probably more than the entire area was worth a decade ago.

"Welcome to Lilith's, Miss Musa," said the hostess. "I'll lead you back to your table right away."

"Thank you," she said as Iona leaned in her ear.

"How did she know?"

Zuri whispered back. "The top places have a lookout to spot guests when they arrive."

"Wow," said Iona, adding a whistle. "When I think things couldn't get any more pretentious."

When they reached the sliding doors of the private room, the hostess turned with a pained expression.

"Your guests have already arrived."

Zuri cursed under her breath. She'd showed up fifteen minutes early just to beat them to the table.

"Candi, Coral. So lovely to see you," said Zuri when the paper door slid wide, revealing a pair of women with stringy brown hair and black, shark-dead eyes.

"We've agreed to this visit. Don't waste our time with bullshit," said Coral.

Zuri slid into the booth opposite. The waiter appeared and took drink orders for the four of them.

"What do you want?" asked Candi, the allure of her voice tapping on the windows of Zuri's mind, but failing to penetrate due to the amulet she and Iona wore.

"You both look lovely tonight," said Zuri. "Can't we enjoy ourselves outside the Obelisk without resorting to insults and violence?"

The sisters shared a glance.

"The rest of our team is at a bar across the street," said Coral.

Zuri held up her hands.

"We came to offer a deal."

"Like the deal for the onyx heart-seed which you dangled before us before giving it away?" asked Candi, staring directly at Iona.

"Maybe you should have sweetened the deal more. Or maybe it just made sense to give it to our teammate."

"Who died and presumably lost the onyx or you would have brought it up again."

"Yes, Justine's death was tragic. As was Melanie's and Marcus' but we must go on. It's the Coterie way."

A tray of drinks was set on the table. Everyone grabbed their drink, lifted the glass slightly, and took a sip. Orders for dinner were given right after.

"Get to the point, Zuri. We didn't come for small talk," said Candi.

"Fine. Here's the deal. You haven't figured out the pyramid problem yet. We can offer you that solution in exchange for a favor."

The twins bristled.

"Why would you do that?"

"Why does everything have to be so cutthroat?" asked Zuri. "There's no reason we can't work together in larger groups. Why not pass as a class rather than pick each other apart?"

"Bullshit, Zuri. This isn't charity or about class teamwork. What do you want?" asked Coral.

"I want to help my fellow classmates. And I want some help with the upperclassmen. I believe your brother is good friends with Jack and Jessica's group."

"No way. We're not involving our brother in your screwup," said Candi. "It's not our fault you can't stay out of trouble."

"Well, you could always flounder away at the pyramid problem. You're practically the only group left that hasn't moved on. Be a shame to not pass second year because you were too stubborn to make a great deal," said Zuri.

The Siren Sisters shared a glance. Zuri didn't know if that "twins know each other's minds" bullshit was true, but for Coral and Candi she had no doubt.

"Even if we agreed, we can't guarantee that they would listen. Jessica is convinced you were behind Anton's death."

"We were in Professor Green's class when he died, and why would we draw even more attention to ourselves when we already have Blake to worry about? It makes no sense and is likely a setup," said Zuri.

The waiter returned with an enormous tray of exquisite sushi. The Siren Sisters were distracted and picked up their chopsticks.

"Try the Cthulhu jelly rolls, they're divine," said Coral with a quirk to her lips.

"Are there any less gooey rolls?" asked Iona, frowning at the tray.

The four of them dug into the meal. The Siren Sisters, despite their seaweed thin bodies, devoured more sushi than Zuri thought possible while Iona barely ate, picking at the less adventurous rolls.

Candi hid a belch behind a cupped hand.

"Excuse me. As we were saying before, we can't guarantee that our brother can do anything to dissuade them of your guilt."

"Anything can help. And we're not making that a condition of the information."

Zuri pulled out a small notebook and slid it over the table.

"Here's a copy of all my notes on the pyramid problem. I'm just asking you to try."

The sisters both reached for the notebook, resting their fingertips on the cloth binding.

"We'll try. That's all we can promise."

"Fair enough."

Coral put the notebook in her carryall as the sisters rose from the table.

"See you around."

When they were gone, Zuri leaned against the booth and massaged the bridge of her nose with forefinger and thumb.

"Those girls sure can eat. I thought I was watching a pair of orcas cull an entire pod, or whatever you call it, of seals."

"You barely ate. That's unlike you."

Iona pushed her plate away.

"I'm not hungry," she said as her stomach gurgled. "Do you think they'll get through the portal using your solution?"

"Unfortunately yes, which means that it's not our answers, but something with the portal."

"Or Fenris."

"He's dead."

"Doesn't mean he didn't screw us up before he bit the big one. But if they do get through, what do we do then?"

"It might be time to revisit the Second Year Games. As much as I hate to say it, the Elixir of Foresight might be our only chance of figuring out how an ancient warlock cursed us to not get through that portal."

"I mean, that wouldn't be all bad. Minus the Blake and Scarlett part, of course."

Zuri paid the exorbitant bill, and when they reached the street filled with expensive vehicles, Iona stretched her arms.

"Think we could grab a burger somewhere? Extra rare?"

TWELVE

Iona was standing outside the cage of the carnivorous dragonswallow plant when she spotted a bushy-tailed squirrel run down the inside of the wrought iron fencing.

"No, no, little buddy," she said, even as part of her was hoping the critter would get too near the big plant.

The colorful red-orange flowers looked like the mouth of a dragon and the sign on the enclosure said that the interior was hot like dragon breath. The plant lured insects and creatures near it with the promise of warmth.

The approach of footsteps had Iona tensing, but she tried not to show how nervous she was.

"Have you ever seen a dragonswallow plant feed before?" asked Ilyana.

"Until I came here, I only knew the farmhouse and a few select places around Licking, Missouri. Any greenhouses in the area were probably filled with illegal drugs, not carnivorous plants."

"I was quite pleased to learn about the greenhouse. While I'm not a fan of the Halls and all they stand for, if I'd had to join one, this new Hall would have been my choice," said Ilyana.

"You...like plants?"

Ilyana leaned forward, an excited grin perched on her lips.

"Watch."

The squirrel was sniffing around the base of the plant. Iona flinched when the flower rotated towards the critter. The opening was as large as a bucket. The squirrel raised itself on its hind legs, sniffing towards the warm, pungent flower, when it snapped forward, grabbing the creature. Struggling legs disappeared into the closed flower, which pulsed movement.

"Merlin's hairy legs..."

"Quite exciting, isn't it?"

Iona didn't want to admit it, but she was suddenly hungry again, even though she'd eaten a big rare steak before arriving so she wouldn't be tempted by anything Ilyana had to offer.

"It is."

"Why have you been avoiding me?" asked Ilyana.

"Not avoiding. Busy."

"You don't need this."

They walked the paths beneath the arched botany dome until they came to a glass case filled with wavy blue-green plants that moved on their own. The tips had a bulb covered in milky dew. When Ilyana didn't move on, Iona examined the sign.

"Thieves' Milk. From the realm of Harmony. I wonder why they included this plant in the dome. Doesn't seem to have supernatural properties like the others."

"What the sign doesn't say is that milky substance can knock even the most powerful creature out with only a few drops. A thimbleful can stop a heart."

The way Ilyana stared suggested she was expecting a reaction. A clue that she'd somehow acquired the plant to kill Fenris. After an uncomfortable silence, Ilyana gestured to continue.

"You know," said Iona, "I didn't know I had any other family until you showed up. As far as I knew, it was just me and Fenris. And once he left, I had to figure out my own path."

"But now you know you do. Why stay in Coterie?"

"I don't know you."

"We're half-sisters, darling. That's all you need to know."

For the next hour, conversation turned back to the unusual plants contained within the dome, including a thorny vine plant that undulated to music, a bush that secreted a bloodlike substance, and a young nekyia tree that was being pruned to keep it from connecting to the Veil. Ilyana surprisingly knew a lot about the plants, which made it easier to relax. When they'd had enough of the greenhouse, Ilyana suggested they grab a drink nearby.

"Are there others like us?"

"Like what?" asked Ilyana with her hands behind her back as they cut through an alleyway, dodging around rusted old garbage bins and a couple of homeless sleeping in cardboard boxes. The way Ilyana looked at them made Iona feel like she was sizing them up as a meal.

"Fenris'."

"There are."

"How many? Do any live in the city?"

"Oh no. Not in a place like this. Too bright, too many curious mages. We live in other parts of the world where rules are less confining."

Iona didn't like the sound of that, but she tried to keep her face neutral. She wanted answers, and knew that insulting Ilyana wouldn't get them.

"My turn," said Ilyana. "What really happened to Fenris?"

"I told you," said Iona, looking directly in her eyes.

"I'm not certain I believe you."

"You really think that I could somehow kill Fenris? I appreciate the vote of confidence, but I've seen what he can do. His rituals. The tomes. Especially now that I've had a year of schooling in Coterie. The things he could or can do, they're frightening."

Ilyana made a noise in the back of her throat.

"Well, there is that. But it's unlike him. He moves from time to time, especially when his hungers start to get noticed, but he usually brings everything with him and leaves a trail to make it easy to find him again."

"Speaking of hunger."

Ilyana smirked in her direction.

"I see you suffer from them. We could make a detour and take care of them for you."

"I'd like to understand them first."

"What's to understand?" asked Ilyana, gesturing towards a homeless woman in dirty rags who was feeding a small, ratty dog in her lap. "We hunger. We eat. That's all there is to it."

"But normal foods no longer sate me. I have cravings."

Ilyana reached over and ran her fingertip across Iona's jaw. The intensity in her gaze was unnerving.

"Then eat."

"I—"

Iona heard the guttural words at the same time that Ilyana pushed her out of the way. She crashed into the side of the dumpster as sorcerous energies filled the alleyway.

As Iona climbed to her feet, Ilyana threw up a shimmering barrier that blocked the multiple lines of elemental magics that had intended to kill them. On the other side of the alleyway, the upperclassmen who'd accused her and Zuri of killing their teammate were lobbing brutal sorceries that would have annihilated Iona if she'd been alone.

"Get ready when I drop the shield," said an eager Ilyana.

"Ready for what?"

The words had barely left her lips when the shimmering barrier winked out of existence. Ilyana shot across the gap like a lightning bolt, appearing in their midst. Two of them flew into the brick wall, while a third was suddenly screaming as she had him around the neck. It was Jack Townsend.

"Stop!" she yelled before Ilyana could kill him.

The blow never came. She glared back.

"If you kill him the entire class of fourth years will come down on us. It'll be a death sentence."

Ilyana gnashed her teeth and tossed the stunned Jack onto the ground. The others were climbing to their feet, shaken and mystified by the reversal.

"Go on," said Ilyana. "Before I change my mind and rip your throats out."

The upperclassmen scurried away, glancing backwards as if they were being chased by psychotic ghosts.

Ilyana strolled back, knocking the dust from her hands.

"You should have let me kill them. That would have taught them a lesson."

"I think they'll be less likely to come after me again after that. Thank you," said Iona, hating that she owed a debt to her half-sister.

"Anything for family."

"That was impressive," said Iona, gesturing randomly.

"Gifts from Fenris."

"He didn't give them to me."

Ilyana frowned.

"Of course he did, darling. You're his flesh and blood. But you have to give in to the hunger. Let me teach you, sister. You could be unstoppable."

"And what does that—"

A buzz in her pocket had her pulling out her phone. Zuri. She turned away from Ilyana.

"What's wrong?"

"Two things. The first is that Jack and Jessica's group is in the city looking for you, so keep an eye out."

"Already ran into them. I'll tell you about it later."

"What? Okay. Glad you're fine."

"What's the second thing?"

"The Siren Sisters got through the portal."

Iona put a hand to her forehead.

"I should be happy, right?"

"It means we're not idiots, but..."

Iona paced away.

"What are we going to do?"

"I already reached out to Blake and Orion. They've agreed to meet us at the Second Year Games portal in an hour."

"Are you sure this is safe?"

"It'll never be safe, but this is the only way."

"Right."

Zuri sighed.

"One more thing."

"What's that?"

"I want you to make friends with Orion."

Iona recoiled.

"What? Why?"

"Because if Blake decides to backstab us, I want Orion on our side so that it's at least three on two. And we need to figure out why he was grouped with us. There has to be something that will help us figure out the portal problem."

"But why me?"

"Because as far as I know, you're the only person Orion has spoken to since he came to Coterie. Seven hells, probably since I went to St. Jude's. The guy is famously quiet."

"Oh. Okay."

"I gotta go. I'll see you in an hour."

Iona hung up with Ilyana staring at her.

"I'm sorry, I have to go."

Ilyana showed her a toothy grin.

"You don't have to, you know. That way is full of disappointment. Let me show you real power, the kind that doesn't require getting finger banged by a bunch of murderous rich kids."

A knot caught in Iona's throat. She wanted to know more, but she didn't want to know too much.

"I...I have to go. Can we catch up again later? There's so much I want to ask you."

Iona had to force herself to relax when Ilyana approached. She leaned over and kissed Iona on both cheeks, before winking and striding away, speaking over her shoulder as she went.

"You know how to reach me."

Once Ilyana had turned down the street, leaving Iona alone, she spoke softly to herself.

"That's what I'm afraid of."

THIRTEEN

Zuri was last to arrive in the Second Year Games portal room in the Spire. Iona was sitting in a chair near the mini-kitchen while Blake and Scarlett were conspiring on the couch. In the back of the space, Orion was staring at the glossy obsidian portal built into the far wall.

"Thank you for coming," she began. "I'm glad we could—"

Blake burst to his feet angrily.

"Who said you were the leader of this group?"

"What? I was just—"

"If there's going to be a leader, it has to be me or I'm walking out. Scarlett and I already decided before you got here."

Zuri ground her teeth as she considered calling his bluff. But she knew how stubborn he could be. Almost to the point of stupidity. Iona gave her a 'Who cares" gesture while Orion had barely acknowledged her arrival with a brief glance over his shoulder.

"Fine, Blake," she said through gritted teeth. "You have the lead."

"Everyone remember that. If we're going to win this stupid Games, you're gonna have to listen to me. None of this clever, namby-pamby bullshit that goes down in your stupid puzzle competitions. I've already done some intel with some other teams—"

Iona spread her hands. "I thought competitors couldn't talk about the event? That's what the charms during the welcome ceremony were all about."

Blake scoffed.

"Rules are for suckers. If you're not cheating, you're not trying."

Zuri returned the "Who cares" gesture, which had Iona shrugging.

"As I was saying," said Blake, cracking his knuckles, "this isn't a puzzle, but a knock-down, drag-out battle. If all of you suckers listen to me, we're gonna kick this thing's ass and come away with the elixir so none of us ever have to see each other again."

"I'm all for that," said Zuri. "What's the—"

Blake grabbed Scarlett's hand and marched to the portal. They went through, leaving the three remaining members of the team to stare at each other. Orion followed without comment, leaving just her and Iona.

"Are we really sure about this?" asked Iona.

Zuri forced a smile.

"Let's get this over with," she said before heading through.

The vertigo was minimal. Iona was bent on her knees, but quickly regained her form. Zuri barely paid attention because she was struck by the view they had from the spacious balcony.

"What is this place?" asked Iona.

They stood on a high place with an expansive, crowded city beneath, ringed by high walls the color of wrought iron and covered in crenellations and the occasional gargoyle. An inner wall split the city in half while a third wall protected the dome-like structure in the center.

It wasn't the crooked buildings or the dingy gray stone that gave her pause, but the hazy green mist that surrounded the city, covering the featureless plains. A large winged shape flew over the wall, making a horrifying screech.

Zuri wanted to answer, but the words were caught in her throat. This wasn't what she'd expected from the Second Year Games.

"Anyone? Where are we? And why does everything look like we just died?"

"This is the Veil."

Zuri didn't register the answer at first because she wasn't sure she'd ever heard Orion speak. The deep baritone with a hint of scratch was the voice of a villain's favorite henchman.

"Not really, right?" asked Iona. "This isn't really the Veil."

"Of course not, you dolt," said Blake. "It's the Second Year Games, none of this is actually real."

"Feels real," said Iona, rapping her knuckles on the balcony wall. "But I thought the Veil was a big, giant empty space. No one said anything about a city."

"I've never heard anything about a city, either," said Zuri. "Maybe it's something they made up for the Games. The Gamemakers might have just used the Veil as their inspiration."

"Mors Sepculatum."

Once again, Zuri didn't register the words right away since they'd come from Orion. She translated the Latin as best as she could.

"Death's Mirror?"

"It's a necropolis," said Blake, gesturing angrily forward. "A city of the dead. Nothing to get spooked about, or overthink. We've got dead people to kill."

"They're not dead," muttered Iona.

"Come on, everyone," said Scarlett brightly in a way that made Zuri grit her teeth. "We all agreed that Blake's the lead. Let's get to work. None of us want to be here any more than we have to."

Blake and Scarlett headed down the stairs at the back of the balcony while Orion continued to stare at the city.

"This should be fun," said Iona, following.

Zuri wished she had Iona's optimism about the competition. The creaky stairs led them through an old house. Iona gestured towards a painting on the wall that depicted the five of them looking like apparitions with haunted gazes and grayish complexions. The replications were creepy, but not scary as she thought the designers might have wanted it to be.

All five of them stood outside the building, staring down a cobblestone street while figures ambled around aimlessly. Zuri spotted a shopkeeper sweeping away dust from the front of his shop with a straw broom while a young girl sat against the wall playing with something at her feet. The scene had a melancholy air, which made her wonder if they—

"Okay," said Blake, interrupting her thoughts. "This is the deal. My intel tells me that as soon as you get past that third building, the dead will attack."

"They're not dead," said Iona, louder.

"This is the Veil. Of course they're dead."

"I'm just saying they're imprints of people that were once dead. Not the actual dead people. That might be important."

Blake mimed pushing glasses back onto his nose.

"There's that smarty-pants stuff I was talking about. I *said* it was a necropolis. A city of the dead. Stop overthinking things. This isn't puzzle club. We don't get points for being clever. The City of the Dead is going to test our ability to battle through endless waves of these assholes, not how well we can remember their backstories, or some bullshit like that."

"Tell us how we're going to win, babe," said Scarlett, patting his arm.

"Like I was saying before I was rudely interrupted, when we get past the third building that's when we need to start blasting. Zuri, you're in charge of warding. Me and Scarlett will focus on ranged. Orion, you smash anything that gets near, and Iona...I have no idea, what can a girl from Iowa do?"

"Milk a pig," she said.

"What?"

"She's kidding, babe," said Scarlett.

"Weird thing to kid about. But really, what can you do?" he asked.

Iona pulled up her sleeves, revealing her tattoos.

"Bend over and I'll show you, or did you forget about last year?"

Blake puffed up, but Scarlett whispered in his ear and he pulled back.

"Alright, kiddies," said Blake, clapping his hands together. "Story time is over. Now it's time to smash and blast! Follow my lead and we'll have this elixir faster than Orion can recite all one Hundred Halls."

"Shouldn't we put up protections first..."

Zuri ran to keep up as Blake marched to the middle of the street. The grand gestures were impressive and followed by a barrage of searing white shards of light that whistled through the air, impacting a group of city folk clustered near a shop front.

Half the targets remained standing. Zuri wondered what was going to happen next when the shopkeeper and a little girl in a dusty gray dress screeched in unnatural voices, their forms turning hazy as they shot at Blake.

A second and third illusionary Blake appeared on either side, confusing the dead, until they turned toward Scarlett as she tried to maintain her illusions.

Two sets of force bolts, one from her and the other from Iona, impacted the dead, turning them to dust, but every other humanoid in range reared back their heads and, after awful throat noises, came rushing towards the group.

The next two minutes were a blur to Zuri as she tried to keep up with the onslaught of the dead. Every time they cleared out the oncoming, Blake would surge forward, drawing more on them.

"We need a break!" she yelled a few times, but he ignored her and continued charging forward.

The group made it to the end of the next street before a large group of customers in an outdoor café flew at them in such a mass of dead that their spells failed to knock down enough of them. A woman with aviator goggles tackled Blake and then two others grabbed Scarlett. The loss of spells left them defenseless and the rest of the team was overrun. The last thing Zuri saw was a spectral mouth growing large enough to swallow her whole.

§

Zuri snapped awake in the portal room, arms flailing to push the bodies off of her, but it was over. They were out of the game. She was still processing the feeling of dying when Blake clapped his hands and gave a shout.

"Did you feel that? Wasn't that fucking balls? We slayed and slayed and slayed."

"What are you talking about?" said Zuri. "We got slaughtered."

"See? This is why we're not together anymore. You're not smart enough to trust me. That first attempt was further than anyone else's first time. Coterie gets it done."

He grabbed Scarlett and gave her a long kiss that Zuri regretted watching the entirety of.

"Hell yeah," said Blake, hopping around like he'd chugged an energy potion. "If you guys had my back like I told you, we could have gone further. Orion, not to complain, man, but you barely moved the entire time."

The big man stared back ambivalently. Zuri couldn't recall that he'd lifted a single finger during the fight.

"But you do you, man," said Blake, holding out his hands.

"Next time can we put up wards first? You did put me in charge of them," said Zuri.

"You should have been adding them during the fight. We're gonna have to learn to be quick about it." He clapped his hands again. "Anyway, good first attempt. Let's do better this time. Come on."

Before she could respond, he disappeared into the portal. Scarlett quickly followed, and then inexplicably, Orion lumbered through.

"I mean, it wasn't terrible, right?" asked Iona, before disappearing.

Zuri shook her head as she approached the portal.

"This is going to be a long year."

FOURTEEN

Silence never sounded so good to Justine. No one to bother her. No one to sigh with exasperation when she was making too much noise. A blank canvas for her to break.

"Never go alone. Or you'll go to the stone."

The words weren't exactly what Zuri had told the group about not exploring the other levels, but it was close enough to make her giggle. She never felt as free as she did when she was exploring by herself.

Everyone else from their year had moved on, and the first years were a long way from getting to the third level, leaving her with a huge playground. There were dangers, of course, but she knew how to avoid them and some didn't trigger at all on her little wooden body.

Justine skipped across the stone floor, frilly pink skirt bouncing around her waist while her wooden feet rung loudly. She'd taken off the little sneakers so she could feel the ground against her impervious feet.

The only reason she wore them was not to be so noisy around her friends, but no one was on the same level, so why bother?

The ring in her pocket was meant for a human finger, so she slipped it over two digits, bending them to keep the silver band on. Justine approached the smooth wall, holding the ring against a depression in the stone. A passage revealed itself. She giggled with delight.

With her friends busy in the Second Year Games, she'd been uncovering secrets on the third level. Acquiring the ring had required solving a shifting ward puzzle and then it'd taken her a few days to figure out what the ring was for.

The passage led to stone stairs, which brought her to a window high in the wall that gave her a good view of the pyramid level. The twilight that pervaded the level made vision challenging, so Justine added a spell that helped her see through the dim.

Feet hanging over the edge and kicking, Justine kept watch for movement. She'd been coming to this spot for the last three days.

She started zoning out after the first two hours and was considering a break when she caught something out of the corner of her eye near the entrance portal. Her magic-aided vision had a hard time penetrating the distance, but she saw something low, slinking through the buildings on that side of the level.

Justine popped to her feet and scurried down the stairs, ignoring the loudness of her wooden feet on the stone. Once she reached the main floor, she pulled the shoes out of her satchel, donned them, and continued towards the portal. Slow and steady.

Unlike some of the supernatural creatures that permeated the Obelisk, like the gloomrends or crystalline spiders, the thing she'd been tracking for the last month or so was able to move between levels, which was unusual, and suggested that it wasn't just a critter to be avoided. It was something else. Another secret. One that seemed more dangerous than the others.

The area around the portal was uninteresting at first glance, so she cast a *sanguine revelare* spell, which caused blotches on the stone to glow as if it were under a black light. The blood trail headed in the general direction of the pyramid. Justine crouched down and examined the smeared print, which almost looked like clawed feet.

Taste the flesh, whispered a voice that was not her own.

"Hush."

Travel to the second level was instantaneous and without the vertigo she experienced when she was made of useless flesh. A second spell revealed more blood. The creature had been hunting on the second level this time.

Justine followed the markings, which sometimes were absent for dozens of feet before reappearing, but the further she went, the more defined the blood smears were, which suggested she was nearing their origin.

Excitement built in her chest as she rubbed her finger in a coagulating blob of blood that had been left on the corner of a wall. Justine rubbed the sticky liquid on her cheeks like war paint, receiving a cheer inside her head.

The body was mostly eaten when she found it. Near the fountain at the mummy-mirror room. Justine couldn't tell the identity of the person, only that they were probably male by the single sneaker lying away from the carnage, and probably not one of her classmates. It was mostly a single leg and some hips that hadn't been eaten by the creature that had slunk back to the third level.

Justine shoved her finger into the bloody meat on the side of the hip, enjoying the squish. She giggled as she sniffed the still-warm flesh.

This is what I was before, a useless, bloody meat puppet.

Sometimes she wished her father could see her, but she knew he wouldn't understand. He only understood flashy masculine displays of magic and power. What she'd accomplished on her own—which was far greater than anything he'd ever done—would be lost on him.

Before she left the body, Justine found a runed gold bracelet that had fallen off, or been spit out, after the attack. It was too large for her wrist, but maybe she could modify it to fit. It wasn't as if the owner was going to need it anymore.

Justine returned to the third level, heading straight for her hidden home deep within a mausoleum, and threw herself on the pile of plushies that she used as a bed. Mr. Paws formed a comfortable pillow, while Andy the Aardvark was a leg rest. Near her head, a natural shelf had become a trophy case for her discoveries: an enchanted finger bone, a glass eye that could see heat spectrums, a coin that flipped itself when the command word was spoken, and a few other smaller trinkets she'd acquired.

She was rubbing the old blood off the bracelet when she heard scratching near the entrance. Quiet as a mouse, Justine crept to the gap, listening intently. The scratching had gone quiet, but was replaced with sniffing instead.

Justine held herself unnaturally still. The creature had tracked her to her hidden space. She hoped it was too large to fit through the narrow gap, or she'd get to learn what it really was soon enough.

She retrieved a slender knife from a box, holding it out like a miniature sword, ready to stab anything that tried to slip through the gap between the stones. She kinda hoped it would. The blood of the hunter would smell divine, she decided.

Eventually the sniffing stopped and she thought she heard the scratch of claws heading away. Justine slipped out of the mausoleum, but moved no further, like a prairie dog staying near its hole.

She saw no signs of the creature except for a few smears of blood on the wall where it had stuck its head into the gap. The idea that the creature knew where she was living wasn't lost on her. Additional protections would be needed. Maybe even an illusionary covering if she could manage it. Not that she feared the creature. After all, she was made of wood and magic. There was nothing left of her to eat.

But she really wanted to uncover how it was able to move between levels while hunting the students and if she could, watch it in action. The idea of watching it feed excited her. Justine returned to her cubbyhole and plotted her next moves.

FIFTEEN

Iona sat on the couch with her head between her hands, trying to erase the last death from her memory. She'd thought it a good idea to make a magic-aided leap to the roof of the corner building so she could spray ice across the cobblestone side street and keep the horde of parishioners from hitting the team at the worst possible moment. It's the spot they'd been stuck in for the last two days.

But she hadn't expected that the roof contained dead people too. She heard the scuff of a foot the moment before she was shoved off the three-story building. The fall broke her neck. The cobblestones were slick against her cheek as blood pooled around her.

Death took much longer than normal because the dead had ignored her. She only returned to the staging room once she'd bled out, but by then, only Orion remained. The others had gone for lunch with a promise to bring some back for the two of them.

"Thanks for waiting," she said, once she'd composed herself.

Orion sat on a stool that was too small for his enormous body. He grunted without making eye contact.

Iona went to the refrigerator and grabbed an energy potion to help clear her head. She took a long draw from the cool liquid before spinning the lid back on. The urge to lie on the couch and rest was strong, but she remembered Zuri's request to make friends with Orion in case of a Blake and Scarlett backstab.

"That was an interesting last attempt," she said, leaning against the couch. "I really thought we were going to get farther."

Orion squeezed his hands together while his jaw pulsed.

She sighed.

"You know it's okay to express yourself."

His heavy gaze caught her eye.

"It's okay to be quiet too," he said.

She snorted with laughter, which made the corner of his lips curl slightly.

"I saw that. Not that anyone would believe me. Orion Dreadmarsh laughing. Never happened, they'd say."

He lifted his chin, swallowed.

"They wouldn't say that."

The intensity of his gaze caught her. She tried to smile but he turned away before she could muster the response.

"You know we're similar. Everyone thinks we're monsters."

He hunched his forehead. "No one thinks you're a monster."

"Maybe I do," she muttered under her breath. "But—"

The door swung open revealing Blake Lockwood with a greasy bag in each hand, raised high in victory.

"Diner slop, just like you wanted." He threw the bags on the table. "Don't know how you eat that crap, but I don't want my teammates going hungry. We've got a lot more work to do."

Zuri came in last after Scarlett, frowning in Blake's direction, but Iona was too busy digging into her lunch bag. The burger was as greasy as advertised, with hand-cut fries that melted in her mouth. The meat wasn't as rare as she liked it, but the last death had really taken it out of her.

"Next attempt," said Blake, clapping his hands and leaning on his knee like a football coach in the huddle. "That was a great idea, Iona, trying to take the high ground. Shame it didn't work out that time, but do you think you could make it work on the next?"

"I, I guess. Yeah. I'll know to clear out the dead on the roof before bothering with the old church."

"Have you considered a Shock Glyph? It'll freeze them in place while dealing damage, giving you enough time to finish them off. I can show it to you if you'd like."

"Good thought, babe," said Scarlett as she cracked open an energy elixir.

"I actually know that one," said Iona.

"Great. Will that work?"

She nodded.

"I'm gonna hit the head and then let's get ready for the next attempt."

While he was gone, Iona raised her eyebrow in Zuri's direction, but she wasn't paying attention. That Blake was the leader of their group clearly bothered her, especially because he was actually doing a good job. Iona wouldn't have guessed it, but then again, Zuri had always said he had a sweet and engaging side. He seemed nothing like the sociopath from last year, or even from the first part of the semester.

"Let's go! Coterie gets it done!" yelled Blake when he returned and headed for the portal.

"Hell yeah," said Scarlett. "We got this!"

Behind them, Zuri went through the portal muttering profanities.

"Ready to die again?" she asked Orion.

The hulking mass rose to his feet. She was always surprised how big he was up close.

"Die quicker this time," he said in his normal deadpan voice.

She snorted and went through.

Zuri was layering enchantments on the others when they arrived. She looked like she was going to implode, having to play buff witch for the group.

"Everyone ready?" asked Blake when the spells were finished. "Let's do this!"

"Kick some ass!" shouted Scarlett as they moved into the street.

Iona stretched her fingers as she prepared for the nonstop fighting that would occur until they died again. She winked at Orion when she caught him staring, which made him turn his head away.

The first kills were the shopkeeper and the young girl. Iona hated how their attacks transformed the normal looking dead into shrieking apparitions. She felt a kinship with them from her time with Fenris and really wanted to ask these folk how they'd come to the city of the dead, even as she knew that it was all part of the game.

Iona fell into the groove once they got started. Fire force bolts at the dead people in the candy shop, a slick wave across the cobblestones in the alleyway when the bums awoke, then freeze the elderly couple in place with ice bracelets. The fight had a rhythm that felt like music.

The entire first year of her Coterie experience had been focused on solving complex arcane puzzles or unlocking secret doors, which had been great for expanding her knowledge of magic, but did little for the actual practice. The five elements, which were the building blocks of Hall magic, felt more natural due to the constant practice. When a shrieking apparition was racing to rip off your face, completing your spell quickly and efficiently became the norm. The Second Year Games were more than an exercise in teamwork, they were a way to practice magic in a practical and rapid manner.

When they came to the cross street that had gotten her killed last time, Iona hesitated before she cast the cloud jump spell. The memory of the slow death was fresh, but she didn't want to screw up the group. Jumping straight to the roof was impossible, so she hit the awning first, then hit the open window on the second floor, before making the final magic-aided leap to the roof.

She didn't see any dead people on the far side of the roof, but placed the Shock Glyph behind her and took position at the corner. The ice spray coated the cobblestones the moment before the mob of dead people raced around the corner, spilling onto their backs when they hit the slick section.

A burst of electricity startled her to spin around to see not one or two dead, but a dozen, all racing to kill her.

"Oh balls."

Iona prepared to defend herself knowing full well that she was outmatched, when something flew through the air to her right, slamming into the horde and tossing them away like bowling pins.

Orion rolled to his feet, throwing punches in every direction. The impact of his fists crackled with electricity and were like sledgehammers to the face.

The tide turned. Iona went from accepting impending death to a cheer of victory when the last dead was destroyed.

"Thank Merlin you came up. I really didn't want to die alone again."

Orion's mouth worked the empty air but nothing came out. An explosion startled them both as a brick wall collapsed from a nearby roof unleashing dozens of dead, which was significantly more than they could handle.

The big man prepared to face the horde, but Iona saw there was no way they could take that many on.

"Come on. We need to get out of here," she said, grabbing his calused hand to get his attention.

He stared at the contact as if he'd been lit on fire, so she quickly released her grip and extended her arm to indicate a direction.

"Orion. We have to go. That's too many."

"Where?"

"That other roof. Come on. You can make it."

Iona backed up to give herself more room to run as the dead piled onto her roof. As they raced to grab her, she burst into a sprint, working her fingers to time the spell's conclusion with her leap.

She flew over the twenty-foot gap between buildings, skipping off little puffy clouds that helped carry her the distance, and landed hard, rolling onto her back. Orion shook the roof when he landed, and to her surprise, he helped her to stand though he pulled his hand away the moment she was standing.

"Thanks."

Iona spied over the edge to see where the others were located. The sounds of battle and magic reached them from around the corner. The rest of the team was alive, but now the two groups were separated.

"Come on, let's see if we can circle around to find them."

As they worked their way across the rooftops, the occasional dead came rushing at them, but they were easy to destroy. The only problem was that the path was taking them further from the others.

Iona stopped when they reached the back of the line of buildings. They'd been working their way through the upper bowl of the city, but now she faced the interior section. At the center of the city was the great dome, and now that they were closer, she could see dark winged creatures circling the structure.

"What do you think that place is?"

"The Queen of the Veil's palace."

She hadn't expected him to answer. Iona turned her head sharply.

"How do you know that? I didn't think the Veil had a queen."

Orion stared ahead without acknowledging her question. The sounds of battle could no longer be heard.

The fact that they hadn't been attacked yet bothered Iona. She used the opportunity to study the way ahead. They'd only crossed a quarter of the city. Before they could reach the inner wall they had another section of residential buildings to pass through and then find a gate to reach the central region.

"Look at that," she said, extending her arm towards a massive archway through which a long, narrow stone bridge crossed dark waters. It wasn't the barrier she was pointing towards, but an enormous humanoid that made Orion look like a baby. Shadowy shapes shifted around the guardian.

"Do you think—"

A scrabbling horde of critters came flowing over the edge of the building. These weren't the transformed humans from before, but entirely horrific manifestations with too many arms or mouths, claws for hands, and other deformities.

Iona barely got a force wave off before she was overwhelmed, falling to teeth and fingernails—

§

She woke back in the portal room. Orion arrived a few seconds after.

To her surprise, the only other person in the room was Zuri and the air smelled like sorcery. The refrigerator was burned black with the door barely holding onto its hinges.

"What happened?" asked Iona.

Zuri glanced to the outer door.

"Blake threw a fit when you both didn't come back."

"We found a new route. I think we can get us to the next area. Isn't that right, Orion?"

The big man headed out of the room without answering. Iona threw up her arms in confusion.

"It's okay, I believe you," said Zuri.

"For a little bit there, I thought we might be connecting, but now I'm not so sure."

"Probably for the best that ended there," said Zuri, rubbing her temples. "I was getting a terrible headache from all that faez use."

Iona grabbed her backpack and met Zuri at the door. She had a pensive look.

"What's up?"

"Do you trust me?" asked Zuri.

"Of course."

"Even if I asked you to do something really stupid?"

Iona paused.

"Is this taking a bath with a school of piranhas or going to class without clothes on stupid?"

"A bit of both."

"What are you thinking?"

Zuri flattened her lips.

"How much do you hate Professor Cornwallis?"

SIXTEEN

The cubby near the professors' offices was abnormally cold. Zuri shivered as she waited for the others to arrive, fussing with the pack on her shoulder.

The scuff of a footstep startled Zuri. Iona appeared with her white hair pulled into a topknot and a blue tome under her arm.

"Any problems?"

Iona handed over the borrowed credit card.

"Didn't ask a single question."

"Good." Zuri peered down the hallway. "Where's Justine?"

"I told her the time."

She squeezed the pack to her chest, feeling the lumpy materials inside.

"Is it just me or has she gotten stranger?"

Iona shifted her mouth to the side.

"She was singing a song about 'how the guts fall out' when I found her. Other than that, seems perfectly normal."

A minute later, the diminutive wooden girl came ambling down the hallway. Her glass eyes had an intensity that bordered on manic.

"This is fun," she said gleefully.

"As long as we don't get caught," said Zuri.

"About that. How are we getting into her office? She has a soul lock on it."

Zuri lifted the pack.

"Follow me."

Their footsteps rang in the hallway. They didn't bother to sneak around, as word was that the professors were out of the Obelisk at a dinner with the acting Head Patron, Professor Sinclair.

When they reached the door, Zuri revealed the protective enchantments, which were overlapping fields of gray, a sickly green, and blotches of blue. She pulled brass buttons with sticky glue on the flat bottom side out of her pack and placed them around the outside of the frame and nowhere near the wards.

The matrix took Zuri a half hour to unravel, but the time last year working with the Kemetic circuits had taught her a lot about how wards influenced each other and created opportunities to break their protections.

"How's the lookout?" she asked Iona through the matched speaking stones. She was on lookout at the main cross hallway.

"All clear."

Zuri crouched down to see eye to eye with Justine. She'd done it so she didn't feel like she was speaking down to her, but regretted it right away as the strange puppet stared back with an odd smile on her wooden face.

"You ready for the next part?"

"I can't wait."

Zuri pulled the desiccated finger bone out of the pack. The professor's sister had died during the invasion and had been buried in a graveyard outside the city. Then she pulled out the nutcracker she'd gotten from the antique shop in the third ward.

"Forgive me, Janine," said Zuri before she placed the old bone between the two ends and squeezed until it cracked and turned to dust.

She swept up the bone dust and placed it in a jar, then added powdered amethyst and a few drops of mercury. The mixture sizzled when she added faez.

Justine stuck her little wooden fingers into the orange-brown paste and wiped it on her face like a child playing in the mud. Then she put some on her bare arms and legs.

"I hope this works," said Zuri.

While Zuri held her breath, the puppet leaned on her tippy-toes and turned the handle. The door swung open, revealing the professor's office. Justine waddled inside and toggled a switch which turned off the enchantments, after which Zuri removed all traces of the ward disabling from the walls and door.

Professor Cornwallis' office had a huge bookcase. Zuri searched the shelves for the diary, but it wasn't clear where it was.

"Can you help?" she asked Justine, who had been poking around the professor's desk.

After Zuri finished scouring the shelves, she slumped against the desk and crossed her arms.

"Where is that stupid diary?"

At that moment, Iona raced into the room, cheeks blotchy with concern.

"Is she back?" asked Zuri in alarm.

"No, but Professor Gideon is headed this way."

"Ravenscroft? Why is he in the Obelisk? Are you sure he's headed here?"

Iona lifted both shoulders.

"There's no other office down this way and his is on the opposite side."

"I've seen them whispering together," said Justine with a deranged grin.

"Great," said Zuri.

Stay or run. Stay or run. She sighed and locked the door, then activated the toggle that would turn the wards back on. She waited with her heart in her throat. If they were discovered, getting kicked out of Coterie would be the best-case scenario.

The sound of heavy footsteps was followed by arcane murmurings, then a rattle of the door handle.

"Annette? You there? I thought you were in the city with the others but my ring warmed. Did you sneak back because you wanted me to come by?"

The fact that the professor had a signal ring for Professor Cornwallis' office made it very clear that their relationship was more than professional.

The door rattled again.

"Annette? I can hear you. Is this another one of your games? I'll admit, I really enjoyed last time. I still have dreams about the wooden horse." A pause. "I'm coming in."

As Zuri heard more mutterings, she panicked and in her best posh English accent said, "Not now, darling."

"Annette? Are you sure? The others are gone. I would be your steed again. You can whip me all you'd like. Please."

Zuri gagged, but when the silence drew out, Iona punched her in the arm and swirled her finger rapidly.

"That's why you can't come in now, darling. You've been a bad steed. All bit, no buck. I'm going to have to whip you for your behavior."

"Oh, Annette. I'm ready."

The handle rattled again.

"Stop," said Zuri in a voice that was too much like her own. She mouthed a few curse words as the silence drew out.

"What I need you to do," she said, returning to the posh English accent, "is return to your quarters and ready yourself for me later. You've been a very bad steed, so I'm going to take my time. But if you're not ready when I get there, I'm going to be very, very angry. And I might have to show you a new trick or two."

Scratching, followed by a breathless request came through the closed door. "What is the new trick?"

Zuri searched for a reply, looking around the room for inspiration. She spotted a glass globe on the shelf.

"I'll squeeze your balls like glass," she said, cringing at her own words.

"Oh," came the moan, then more scratching as if he were hunched against the door. She tried not to imagine what was happening on the other side and continued the farce.

"Now hurry along," said Zuri. "I have many preparations for tonight. And remember, you can't say anything about our conversation. I want you to act like you didn't know I was going to show up."

No answer came. The three of them leaned towards the door. After a minute, Zuri undid the protections and checked outside to find it empty.

"Oh, seven hells. I can't believe I had to do that with Professor Ravenscroft. Now I'm not sure I think he's hot anymore."

Iona snorted.

"All bit, no buck? That sounded a little too real to have pulled that out of your ass."

"Oh, piss off."

"Nice accent though. Was very convincing."

Zuri rolled her eyes.

"I've spent a lot of time in London. I can't help it if I pick up on accents. Let's find that book and get the hell out of here before the real

Annette shows up."

"Found it!"

Justine had been digging around in the desk. She held out a worn brown diary.

"Alright. Let's copy this stupid thing."

First Zuri used the book that Murder had given her to copy the diary, and then Iona handed over the one she'd purchased that day. She shoved the two copies of the diary in her pack and prepared to head out.

"Wait," said Iona, hurrying to the desk. "We can't have Gideon waiting all night for her."

"No, no. She might figure it out. You don't know Professor Ravenscroft's handwriting."

Iona wagged her eyebrows, but continued writing on the pad of paper. Zuri leaned over the desk while Justine climbed up the chair to get a look.

On the center of the yellow pad of paper was a crude drawing of a horse with a stick figure behind it doing something near the tail. Iona made a few other doodles near the head that Zuri couldn't quite figure out.

"What are those?"

"No idea, but Annette should have fun trying to figure it out."

They closed up the office behind them, reapplying any wards that had been disabled, and headed back to their suites. Justine peeled off to head back to the third level, leaving her with Iona.

"What's the second copy for?"

Zuri didn't want to reveal all her plans, but she didn't want to lie to her teammate either.

"Insurance."

"Fair enough. Just be careful with whatever's in there."

Zuri saluted Iona.

"I won't get us in trouble."

SEVENTEEN

The table flipped, spilling drinks across the prep room, while Blake paced. No one spoke, but Iona could see how Zuri was seething inside, having to work with her best friend's killer on a regular basis.

It'd been fine at the beginning when Blake wasn't being a jerk, but now that they'd been stuck for three weeks and it was already December, tempers were flaring. He'd already destroyed two couches and one refrigerator. The only thing keeping him from worse was Scarlett's constant ego fluffing and the stoic presence of Orion Dreadmarsh. More than once, Blake looked ready to take it up another level until he realized who else was in the room.

"We'll find a way, babe. I know you can do it," said Scarlett.

"No thanks to these idiots," he said, throwing up his hands.

Zuri grunted and fled the room while Blake stared at the slammed door.

"What's she getting mad about?" he asked.

Scarlett rubbed his back.

"She's not a winner like you, babe. Can't take the heat."

Orion rose from the couch and disappeared out the door.

"Since we're not continuing," said Iona, shrugging her shoulders as she left.

Iona hurried to follow Orion, who had already reached the elevators with his long strides, but she went for the stairs instead, racing down them in leaps and jumps. Eighteen floors. She hit the street level and immediately looked for Orion, but didn't see him at first until she saw that he wasn't headed towards Coterie, but northeast into the first ward.

A buzz in her pocket had her pulling out her phone.

"You still there?" asked Zuri.

"No," she said as she hurried after Orion.

"I don't know if I can do this much longer," said Zuri.

"Have a better idea how to get to the fourth level?"

"What if I just kill Blake? Maybe that would let us get through."

"You'll probably have to kill Scarlett too. And maybe Orion and myself as well."

"Dammit, Iona."

A car honked as she ran across the intersection ahead of the light.

"Where are you?"

She wasn't sure she wanted to tell Zuri that she was following Orion. The rule had always been to let him be and not antagonize him. But her attempts to befriend him, except for a few moments during the games, had mostly fallen flat. She needed to learn more about him so she could find a way in. Especially with Blake growing more erratic. If he came to the same conclusion that Zuri did, then he might try to kill them and they'd need Orion on their side.

"On an errand. I'll tell you about it later," she said before hanging up.

Heading into the first ward hadn't surprised Iona, given his family's last name. She'd seen him go that way after other sessions, but this time she wanted to see his final destination.

Iona applied a Look Away enchantment and stayed at least a block behind him. Not that it was probably necessary. Orion marched straight forward without deviation while the oncoming sidewalk traffic bulged around him like a bubble.

The inner part of the first ward was filled with skyscrapers, the largest of which barely came up to the halfway point on the Spire. Given that it was the middle of the afternoon on a Tuesday, the sidewalks teemed with business people on their phones. Occasionally, she spotted hazy privacy shields, but most of the inhabitants of the area were non-mages.

There were fewer vendors and street shows in the first. No one had time to stop for frivolous enjoyment. The tourists tended to stick to the second and third for the most part.

As Orion reached the residential section of the first ward, she expected him to turn into a side street and disappear past the high wrought iron gates that populated the area, but he kept marching forward. Not only was she surprised that he hadn't gone into one of the big compounds, but it also confused her that he hadn't taken a taxi or the train.

They'd already traversed a couple of miles and were nearing the seventh ward. She hadn't seen him stop to add any enchantments, nor had he slowed his pace, which was considerable. Iona had applied her own enchantments to help with the long travel, but they weren't reducing the hunger in her belly that woke every time she passed a restaurant or caught an errant smell of food.

Traffic on the ring road that separated the inner and outer wards was heavy, but an arched pedestrian walkway made crossing easy. When she hit the sidewalk, she saw no sign of Orion.

Iona thought she'd lost him until she saw his enormous back heading north into the seventh. She hurried to catch up, eventually getting him back in view a few blocks in when he stopped to talk to a group of gang members loitering outside a group of apartment buildings called the Atlas Gardens.

"What are you doing?"

She watched from a distance, being careful to stay out of view. Orion looked to her surprise to be laughing with the gang members about something one of them said, and after sharing some fist bumps, he headed around the corner, presumably to enter one of the buildings.

As she crossed the street, heading towards the opposite corner to avoid the gang members, she pondered the meaning of this latest revelation. Had he come here to buy drugs or illicit magic items? Orion didn't seem like the type, but she couldn't figure out why else he would have come to this region of the city. Not that it was run down. The apartments looked fairly decent. Nothing like Zuri's place, but that kind of abode required a higher level of income.

Which was why his arrival didn't make sense. He was a Dreadmarsh, which came with all sorts of wealth and privilege. The name alone inspired fear and admiration.

That the gang members knew him was another wrinkle. This wasn't his first time in the area. She turned around, planning to see if she could find out which apartment he'd gone into, and ran right into Orion—

"Stop following me, or I'll kill you."

It was like she'd hit a brick wall. Iona stumbled backwards. His expression was pure anger, with nostrils flaring and fists at his side. She'd never seen him like this. He was normally so stoic.

"Orion, I'm sorry, I just wanted—"

"I don't care what you want, or what you think, or anything else. You shouldn't have followed me."

Iona opened her mouth to argue further but she saw a second emotion beneath the rage. Betrayal. She'd crossed an unspoken line without realizing it.

"I'm sorry. I'll leave now."

She turned and headed back the way she'd come. The gang members, who had ignored her previously, watched her like a pack of hyenas watching prey. Orion had told them to let her pass, she realized, which added a new twist to their teammate. Not only could he stop and joke with a group of criminals, they took direction too.

After checking for the nearest train station, Iona looked back to the Atlas Gardens apartment complex. It looked normal, no gang tags and the bushes looked well manicured, but she had a suspicion that something bad was going on inside.

The further away Iona got from the apartments, the less she thought about what was going on, and the more she felt a sinking feeling in her gut that whatever tenuous relationship she'd been building with Orion had been severed irrevocably. Which couldn't be worse timing with Blake's constant blowups.

Iona looked up Ilyana's information on her phone and let her thumb hover over the red phone icon for a few seconds before closing it back up. If they couldn't figure out the portal problem, or win the Second Year Games, then figuring out what she would do after Coterie was becoming a priority.

EIGHTEEN

The tooth had sharp, serrated edges and rattled around between her wooden hands as she shook it. Justine tossed the tooth on the stone, watching it tumble across the floor. She'd found it near the body on the first level a few months ago.

Justine retrieved the tooth and set it on the ledge next to her other trophies, including a tuft of hair from the warlock Fenris, a petrified beetle she'd found in another tomb, and chipped scales.

After changing into her explorer outfit, which she'd had Zuri buy for her in the city from the doll shop, Justine slipped into her pack and headed into the level. She hadn't seen the creature in a few days, but kept to the hidden paths to avoid getting caught.

Near the back of the pyramid level, Justine used a little crowbar to lift a stone block, revealing a passageway. A flashlight blew away the darkness and she headed down the sloping path until she reached a larger chamber.

The discovery had been made a few weeks ago when she'd found the loose stones. It'd taken her a few days to move them out of the way, revealing a passage only big enough for her.

The chamber was huge even by her standards. None of the buildings on the level had interiors remotely as large. Justine ambled to the archway on the far wall covered in Kemetic runes and pulled out her notebook. She'd been transcribing it for later to show the rest of her team, but they'd been so busy with the Second Year Games, they rarely returned to the Obelisk, except for meals and sleep.

Near the archway was a huge diagram that looked like a map of the subway system in New York or Tokyo, except it was inlaid with gold and a strange glistening black stone. Justine pulled out her notebook and checked the notes she'd transcribed a few days ago during a moment of inspiration. She reached out and touched an end circle, which caused it to light up, then moved to another section and touched a different circle, which made the first one go out. She repeated the ritual, except she picked a different second circle. On the fourth try, it lit up. She let out a giggle and examined the board for a third circle to touch, picking the one between the two, which set off a rumbling from another area.

Justine went in search of the noise. A new opening in the far side of the chamber led to a set of stone stairs. Footfalls sounded louder as she explored, following the stairs to a hallway which eventually turned to a dead end.

But this didn't dissuade Justine. After months of quiet exploration, she'd learned to identify certain markers. She pressed a section of stone, which made the wall shift to the side, but it ground to a stop before opening the entire way.

She giggled as she slipped through the gap. This wouldn't have been possible in her old flesh. Then again, she'd probably be at the Second Year Games if she hadn't been murdered by the warlock Fenris.

The new passage was dark, but her enchanted eyes cut through the dim. After a series of turns, she found what looked like low-ceiling maintenance tunnels. A series of pipes traveled along the ceiling. Justine put her ear to one but heard nothing.

She followed the pipes through a maze of new passages, exploring various dead ends before returning to a hole in the ceiling. Using the pipes, Justine scrambled upward, eventually finding a crack that led back into the main floor of the third level.

The passages had led further away than expected. She was standing near the area she knew the creature had made its lair. The old, weak parts of her tried to warn her that this region was dangerous and she should return to the chambers below, but the new part of her that had fused with Ludmilla bubbled with a strange desire.

It wasn't long before Justine found the first body part. A half-eaten hand. Probably fallen off as the corpse had been dragged this way. She'd heard from Zuri that a fourth person had been killed. Most of the Coterie students thought it was a pack of ravenous gloomrends, but Justine knew different.

The hand was at least a few days old, rotting and covered in gnats. Justine followed the drag trails through the buildings until she came upon what she could only describe as a nest.

A pile of cracked bones, bits of cloth, and other detritus formed a shallow bowl that was large enough for a creature the size of a large dog. The discovery filled Justine with bubbly excitement. Tufts of hair and a few bits of scale lay at her feet.

She threw herself into the pile, digging for trophies. She pulled out a tooth. A human tooth. Her wooden fingers were covered in old blood, which she wiped on her face like war paint. Justine examined the tooth, which still had the roots, which would make a good base for an enchantment she'd been reading about. The tooth disappeared into a hidden pocket and then she went searching for more.

Touching the bones and blood, Justine was reminded that she was no longer like them. No longer a meat puppet, controlled by the expectations of her father and society. No longer having to follow their rules, their shattered reasons for morality.

There was something intriguing about the creature. It was living on its own terms, taking what it wanted, living on the edges of society. Just like her. And maybe for the first time she started to understand her father. He'd always told her to take what she wanted. Take what she deserved. But she'd never really understood it. Afraid of it. What would someone think about her?

But now that she'd shed her mortal frame, those thoughts came to her less. Justine smiled as she rubbed the human tooth with her wooden fingers thinking about how she'd escaped and would never have to return. A part of her even wondered why she was bothering with Zuri and Iona, but she reminded herself that they'd helped her when no one else would.

But they only did that because they needed allies, not because they wanted you.

The voice was not her own, but she pushed it away. It'd been coming to her more frequently. Almost daily now.

"That's not me," she said aloud.

The scratching of claws alerted her to the return of the creature. She turned to leave, but found herself staring straight into its black eyes.

"We can share."

A rumbling noise formed in the back of the creature's throat. It was bigger than a dog now, long snout with too many teeth, bumpy skin, and clawed hands that sent shivers of excitement down her back.

Creature.

That word had less meaning to her now that she was looking into its hungry eyes. Not a beast either.

A monster.

It stomped towards her, each heavy step a warning, but she couldn't move. Didn't want to either. The excitement of the monster's approach left her dizzy.

"I'm like you."

A noise that sounded like a voice came out in guttural tones. This was new. The monster could talk, but she didn't know its language.

As the monster grew near, the long protruding snout reminded her of a crocodile, yet the hands were claws and the rounded backside seemed like an entirely different creature. Justine was certain that if she were made of flesh and blood that the monster would have snapped her head off already, but felt its confusion.

The monster bumped her chest with its nostrils, wetness dripping out as it sniffed. One or two bites would snap her in half.

"What's your name? I'm Lud...Justine."

A rumble of speech-noises followed. The monster placed its claws against her chest and pulled down, the sharp tips doing nothing to her enchanted darkwood body.

"I like your teeth."

Justine reached out and tapped her fingers against the long teeth in the monster's mouth. She wanted to climb inside and feel what it was like to be cradled by the monster just like a mother might pick up an unruly pup to be carried back to the nest.

The black eyes of the monster dialed onto her. She felt it weighing a decision.

Then a noise from somewhere else on the level made it snap its head to the side. A whoop of joy. Someone had entered the third level. Multiple someones.

The monster headed in the direction of the entrance portal while Justine followed. It turned its head in her direction a few times as if to warn her away from following, but she was transfixed by the possibility of what was to come.

"I'm ready," she whispered.

A trio of mage lights hovered around the portal entrance. First years. Justine recognized them from her forays around the Obelisk.

She'd lost track of the monster on the way to the portal. It'd gone a longer way around. Justine stayed in the shadows, the dual heart-seeds pounding in her chest.

A part of her wanted to warn the first years. This should be a moment of triumph. She shared their elation, having experienced it only the year before, but she feared discovery. If the professors knew what she'd done and where she was, they might kick her out of Coterie.

Besides, she wanted to see what the monster could do. She'd only seen the results of its hunts, not the act itself.

As the three first years cautiously explored the area around the portal, Justine watched with interest bordering on mania. Her entire wooden body vibrated with excitement.

"Go back to the second," she whispered.

The part of her that was still human didn't want it to happen. She started climbing on a stone block, preparing to make a sign when one of the first years stepped away from the light in the direction that the monster had been hunting.

Before she lost her nerve, Justine cupped her hands around her mouth and shouted, "Watch out!"

The first years startled. The boy who was starting to explore hurried back to the portal. The three nervously glanced between themselves before disappearing back to the second.

Justine hated herself. She'd *wanted* to see it hunt, to see it tear them apart, blood splattering everywhere, but she feared what that meant for her and who she was destined to be.

Once she realized what she'd done, Justine worried that the monster would not be happy. She hopped off the block and scurried across the stone floor, checking over her shoulder until she reached the mausoleum where she made her home.

The entire event seemed like a letdown until she remembered the human tooth in her pocket. After examining it carefully, then cleaning it off with an alchemical solution, Justine set it on her trophy wall.

NINETEEN

Zuri sat in a coffee shop in the third ward, enjoying a darkwisp chocolate espresso and staring at the huge snowflakes floating out of the sky. The city was awash in holiday decorations, and covered in a blanket of thick, wet snow. Cars sliced through the slush while their windshield wipers worked furiously.

The blue book that she'd copied from Professor Cornwallis sat on the table. Zuri tapped her onyx fingernails on the cover. She'd read it from cover to cover three times over. The information inside was explosive on so many levels and for so many people. How the professor had acquired such private and damaging information was a mystery, but it explained how the woman was at the top of high society. No one would dare to cross her with this kind of blackmail at hand.

Which left Zuri with a painful conundrum. So much was upsetting, secret information. Betrayals, extortion, murder, and worse. The father of a girl a few years her junior at St. Jude's spent his weekends hunting non-humans in the lesser parts of the city and had a hidden room where he kept trophies of horns and teeth. The matriarch of the DuPont family liked to bathe in demonic blood once a month, while a woman Zuri was vaguely aware of through her parents' connections had been sleeping with Deadra Billington all through high school.

She was staring at the gentle and heavy snow when she caught the glint of a mote zipping away from the corner of the window. It'd moved like an energetic hummingbird. A spy mote. She was sure of it. An uneasy chill went down the back of her spine. Someone was watching her, which didn't bode well.

Zuri quietly and quickly shoved her things into the backpack and slung it over her shoulder as she slipped out of the booth. She paused near the creamer station, staring at the front door as if it were trapped.

"Hey, Janis," she said to the barista behind the counter.

The twenty-something girl glanced up from her phone.

"Huh?"

"I just saw my ex on the street. He's waiting for me and I really don't want to run into him if you know what I mean."

"So don't talk to him."

Zuri forced a smile.

"Do you have a back way I could sneak out?"

The barista thumbed her phone while staring back ambivalently. Zuri sighed and reached into her wallet, finding a couple of bills to shove in the mostly empty tip jar.

"Mucho appreciated." The barista nodded towards the employee door. "Straight back. It'll lead you to the alleyway."

"Thanks," she said, hurrying through the door in case the spy mote was watching.

Except for the area around the back entrance, which had a five-gallon bucket filled with sand and bent cigarette butts that looked like misshapen worms climbing out, the alley was covered in pristine white snow. Zuri checked the air to see a glint of light high above the brick buildings.

Zuri quickly applied a speed enchantment and burst into motion, bouncing around the dumpsters and leaping over a stray cat that had wandered into her path. When she hit the street, she heard shouts as the fourth years headed her direction. Zuri kept going, straight through traffic and causing two trucks to lose traction and go sliding across the lanes.

The chaos gave her space, but they didn't appear to be giving up. Zuri reached into an inner pocket and pulled out a bracelet. She shoved it over her wrist, then activated the magic inside with the press of her thumb.

When she went around the corner of a laundromat filled with people staring into their phones while the machines worked, Zuri dropped to her knees, cleared a patch of snow with her hand, and slapped a ball of alchemical explosives onto the cold concrete. She whispered the command word and hurried away.

A heavy thump shattered windows when the fourth years turned the corner. She turned her head enough to see them lying in a pile, covered in sheet glass and trying to figure out what had happened.

Zuri cut through another side street, heading to the train station. She rarely ever used public transport, but the crowds and cameras were the safest place to escape her pursuers.

Once she was on a busy train, Zuri stood with her back against a side wall until she was certain they hadn't boarded. Adrenaline flooded her system, leaving her hands shaky. A girl wearing big headphones smiled up at Zuri, revealing teeth that glowed rainbow colors.

She couldn't keep doing this. It was bad enough having to group with Blake and Scarlett in the Second Year Games, but with the fourth years trying to kill them, they couldn't be in the city without constantly checking over their shoulders.

The phone appeared in her hand before she'd really decided what she was going to do. She typed out a message and hovered over the button before finally jabbing it.

ZURI: Hey, Ana. Just letting you know I found some information about the Siren Sisters' family business. It appears they're using some D'Agastine Industries trademarked elixirs for their clients. I'll be sending you some documents later on that prove the link. Hope it helps.

She thought for a moment before adding a second text.

ZURI: Also, I know you're doing business with the Townsend family. Would really appreciate if you could put in a good word, tell their son to lay off. Jack and his friends are making it hard to concentrate on Coterie business.

She hated making that request right after the good news, especially because she'd promised to help because of what had happened to Gemma, not as a trade in favors. A minute later, a thumbs-up icon was returned. Zuri shoved the phone into her pocket and leaned against the wall with her eyes closed as the train rumbled around the tracks.

"This had better work."

TWENTY

Iona stepped out of the black SUV, checking both directions before climbing onto the sidewalk. After Zuri had been attacked last week, they'd decided no one should be in the city without backup or a quick way to get the hell away.

"All clear. You can head out. I'll message you when I'm done," she told Gentry, tapping on the top of the black vehicle.

"I'll be waiting, Miss Storm."

The SUV cut through the wet slush as it returned to early evening traffic. Iona wondered how long she would have to wait when she heard a voice in her head.

Iona.

On the opposite side of the street, Ilyana watched in a stylish royal blue trench coat. She stepped off the sidewalk, right into traffic, but the vehicles slowed to a stop, forming a path across the street.

Iona checked to see if anyone else was noticing, but the people on the sidewalk were oblivious to Ilyana's display of power.

"You've been avoiding me."

The accusation brought a stab of cold fear into Iona's gut. Ilyana's blue eyes were like luminous orbs, seeing all.

"I'm trying not to get kicked out of Coterie."

Flat lips curled at the corners with a sinisterness that bordered on gleeful.

"You don't need that place, sister. You're better than them."

"It doesn't feel like it."

"They play with things they don't understand."

"Why did you want to see me?" asked Iona.

Ilyana hooked their arms and pulled her down the sidewalk.

"Come, sister. I have a treat for us. And some answers, if you're willing to play along."

Trepidation filled Iona's gut.

"Where are we going?"

"You'll see."

They'd met near the ring road in the tenth ward, but headed deeper in. A nose-wrinkling smell announced the presence of the Newtown Fishmarket in the next ward over, but Ilyana steered them in a different direction.

A group of hard looking, but well-dressed men and women stood outside a nondescript brick building. Iona's stomach did a little flip when they headed straight towards them.

"Ilyana, we're not—"

"Hush."

Iona ground her teeth. She hadn't expected a fight. Her heart climbed into her throat.

The guy in front wore a crimson vest over a white shirt with his black hair slicked back. Tattoos littered his forearms and neck. Iona didn't see a gun, but two long blades were strapped to his hips.

"The White Witch has returned."

"You're looking as handsome as ever, Tiago."

He gave a flourishing bow which gave Iona the impression of a matador before a bullfight.

"I aim to please." His hard eyes shifted over. "Is this the *muy vazny*?"

"It is."

Tiago grinned at Iona, revealing canines filed down to sharp points. He was trying to intimidate her, but she stared back.

"You know you still owe me a meeting with your boss," said Ilyana.

Tiago's gaze shifted away from Iona.

"Yeah, yeah. Maybe later. Adrian is busy with some new ventures."

"Problems?"

"Not at all. But the gangs from the Undercity are poking their heads into the light and we're having to be extra careful. But I hope they do. It'll give ol' Tiago a chance to show the big boss how valuable he is."

Iona sensed that Tiago wasn't pleased about guard duty, but he wasn't going to say more in front of his fellow gang members.

Ilyana put a hand on his arm.

"Later then."

"Enjoy."

The gang members formed a corridor which Ilyana strode through like an empress. Iona followed, feeling their eyes on her body, but not in a sexual way as she first had the impression. It wasn't until they'd reached the blank brick wall that she realized they were sizing her up. They clearly respected—no, feared—Ilyana, which by association had been transferred to her too.

Ilyana pressed a random trio of bricks while speaking in an ancient tongue. The wall shifted away like puzzle pieces, revealing a well-lit passage.

Once they were inside, the wall shifted back to its previous state, leaving Iona trapped for all intents and purposes. The hallway was filled with paintings of wild animals hunting prey, which included humans in some instances.

"What is this place?"

Ilyana turned her head slightly, showing the curve of her pale jaw. "Let's not spoil the surprise."

The door at the end of the hallway revealed a hostess station. The rich scent of uncooked meat caught in Iona's nostrils, waking the hunger and making her a little dizzy.

"Welcome back to the Vânatoare. Your usual spot, Miss Storm?"

"No, I'd like the Horned room tonight."

"Very well. It looks like it's open. Please follow me."

As they traveled through the maze-like hallways, Iona heard strange, wet noises from beyond the frosted doors. The deeper they went into the establishment, the more she feared the reason Ilyana had brought her.

The hostess opened the door, which led to a private room with a second door on the opposite side. The table was set immaculately beneath a miniature chandelier. Paintings of a horned god in various sexual positions with humans were displayed.

"Don't be nervous," said Ilyana from across the table. "We're sisters, remember."

Iona felt a little jump in her gut whenever Ilyana mentioned their relationship and couldn't help but see their strong resemblance, despite having different mothers.

A waiter entered the room wearing a thick leather apron over his white shirt and black pants.

"Welcome back, Miss Storm. How should we begin tonight's dining experience?"

Ilyana held up two fingers.

"The *sânge bogat.*"

The waiter stiffened.

"Two? Are you aware of the price?"

Ilyana snarled.

"Did I stutter?"

The waiter's face went pale.

"No, ma'am. My apologies. I'll bring that out right away."

When the door closed, Iona tried to smile, but her mouth wouldn't form the expression.

"Do you eat here often?"

"A few times since I've come to the City of Sorcery. I prefer less formal settings for most of my meals, but I wanted to show you something about yourself. I sense your hunger."

"I am, but—"

Ilyana wagged a finger.

"No buts. Today is on me," said Ilyana, staring intently.

The focus of her blue eyes made Iona fight not to squirm in her chair, so she examined the nearest painting on the wall, which showed a huge beastly man with antlers tearing the head off of a lion while having sex with two women and one man. Iona was formulating a question when Ilyana grabbed her wrist.

"Did you kill Fenris?"

The accusation left Iona reeling, the words having difficulty forming in her mouth. Iona felt her mind being probed. It was an oily feeling that made her want to spit. She concentrated on the feelings the painting had given her rather than let her mind wander back to the events of last year.

"I told you, I don't know where he is or what happened to him."

"I sense your lies."

"It's not a lie."

A knock on the door saved her from further questions. The waiter entered with two ornate glasses and a glass decanter made to look like a swan filled with a thick crimson liquid. As the waiter set the empty glasses before them, a white smoke flowed out from the bottom of the swan decanter, forming an obscuring mist across the table.

The hunger that had been lurking in her belly woke with terrible purpose as the waiter poured the thick crimson liquid into each glass. She fought against licking her lips and felt her breath coming in shallow.

"Bon appétit."

When the room was empty except for the two of them, Iona couldn't help but stare at the crimson-filled glass surrounded by pale mist.

"What is it?"

"A cure for your hunger. And answers."

"I don't like the look of—"

"Drink."

The word echoed in her head, snapping it back as if she'd been slapped with cold iron. A war between her stomach and mind was lost when she reached out and grabbed the warm glass. The crimson liquid was slipping past her lips before she could stop herself.

The world faded away. It felt like she was slipping into a warm bath. Sparks flashed against the inside of her eyelids. Iona was aware that she was making noises but she couldn't stop herself, nor did she want to.

Eyes flashed open at the sound of her name. Ilyana stared back with the eagerness of a huntress about to loose the arrow.

"Your eyes, they're so...blue."

It was like looking at the color of the sky from Everest. Or the calm blue seas in an island bay in Fiji. Neither places she'd ever been, but staring at Ilyana made her feel like she had.

Sounds came in waves. A noise that sounded like both ecstasy and pain was coming from a room nearby. She heard water flowing through the pipes in the walls and the laughter of an old man.

Ilyana's hair was like glossy pearl. Iona reached out to stroke it, finding it soft, silky hair rather than hard gemstone, then let her hand shift against the curve of her jaw.

"What. Is. This?"

Dizzy from staring at Ilyana up close, Iona turned away, but this barely helped as she examined the painting of the Horned God, except this time she saw things that she knew didn't exist earlier. Inside the snapped-off head of the lion was a human face and the body looked like a suit rather than real flesh, while the other three that the Horned God was having sex with looked less human and more animal. More feral.

A heat rose in her belly until she wanted to climb out of her skin. Everything, even her own body, was too much.

"I can't be in here anymore. It feels like my blood is boiling."

"Good," said Ilyana, grabbing her hand and gently pulling her towards the opposite door. "I have more wonders to show you."

The worst part was that Iona wanted to experience them. As overwhelming as her experience was, she didn't want it to stop.

The outside was cool against her face and the sun had set except for a hazy light in the west. The light of an early star sat above the jagged horizon of the city.

"Follow me."

Ilyana raced forward at great speed, but unlike during the battle with the fourth years, Iona could follow with her eyes. Her half-sister stopped at the base of an apartment building, waving her forward.

Running felt like flying. She was next to Ilyana before she realized she'd moved.

"Are you still hot?"

"It's a little better now, but I still feel like someone put a cauldron in my chest."

"A little further now. It'll take the worst of it away."

Iona hadn't realized it, but Ilyana had stripped off the royal blue trench coat, revealing a stark white dress that matched her pale skin. She put her hand on the brick wall, and in the matter of a few seconds, she'd climbed two stories to a short ledge.

"Come, sister."

Iona put her hands on the wall, feeling the rough stone against her fingernails. She squeezed. Despite her fears, Iona wanted to follow. She wanted to experience what Ilyana had to show her, so she climbed. And climbed.

By the time she caught Ilyana, they were on the rooftop. Iona peered over the edge to see that she'd just scurried up eight stories of the apartment building.

"Do you understand?"

"No. Yes. I don't know. What was it that I drank? Was it really that expensive?"

"Each one cost as much as a small car. A trifle really. But it was worth it to help you see what you can become."

"But what I drank...it was?"

"Iona, darling. You know. You don't need me to tell you."

She swallowed, feeling a little sick in her stomach.

"That's not—"

"Come, sister. I have more to show you. Look down there, where we entered. See Tiago and his friends."

The hard men and women were standing in a group outside the restaurant. Even though they were a couple hundred feet below, Iona could see as if she were standing right next to them.

Tiago smelled like menthol cigarettes. She could sense the pack in his inside pocket. And he had a chip in his hip bone from an old battle that made him favor his left with a nearly imperceptible limp.

"I can see everything."

"You can see more. Lean in. Feel it."

Iona stared more intently. She could hear the beating of his heart, the way the saliva squelched down his throat when he swallowed, the grinding of his back teeth. Tiago was left-handed and had a tumor in his guts that would probably grow to be a problem in a few years.

She told Ilyana as much.

"There is power in your blood. In all blood, but especially ours."

"I can feel it."

"Do you understand the nature of power, sister?"

Iona thought of Fenris, and the older Coterie mages. She thought of how Blake had escaped justice from Gemma's murder and how Professor Cornwallis had thwarted her attempts to find a mentor her first year.

"It's complicated."

"Not really," said Ilyana. "There are those that have power and those that don't. We have it. You just need to embrace it and the world will be open for you."

"How can that be? Isn't it finite?"

"There's more. Always more. The blood will teach you."

"How? How can I see more?"

"This time, look not with your eyes, but with your magic. Open up your conduit to faez and let it mix with your other senses. The combination will show you secrets that you never imagined possible."

The cold stab of magic at the base of her skull left her twitching. It was like having to hold an ice cube in her mouth while it melted.

Ilyana whispered in her ear, "Feel Tiago, look into his soul. Not with your eyes, but your magic."

Dizziness came in waves as she tried to do as Ilyana had asked. It felt like being asked to compose a symphony when you'd never heard music before.

She stared, and stared, and stared, and—

When the magic and her senses connected, she nearly fell over but Ilyana grabbed her.

Tiago was the same as before, but now she saw shifting shadows around him. Faint black shapes covered him like a cloak, even as he joked with his fellow gang members about the time he got a blow job from a nun.

"I can see it. What are they?"

"Concentrate on one."

It was hard to pick out a single shape from the dozen or so that surrounded him, but eventually she grabbed one and let her senses drill in.

Her mind flashed with an image: she stood in a dark place, a cavern with faint illumination, the sound of knives yanked from sheaths, then the quick, hot action of battle that moved in a blur, ending with an ache in her chest as Tiago stood over her.

Iona gasped.

It felt like her heart had been pierced.

"Not that deep, Iona."

A hand yanked her back from tumbling off the roof and turned her around, until she could only see Ilyana's comforting blue eyes. Her heels were on the edge of the roof with her back towards the yawning expanse. A chill wind picked up, throwing their white blonde hair around their faces. An odd smile had hooked itself to Ilyana's lips.

"See, sister. I told you there were mysteries to be unlocked."

"What happened? What did I see?"

"You tell me."

"Tiago killed someone, but I felt it from their perspective. We were in a dark place. Underground."

"The Undercity gangs have been warring for the last few years, though some say it's over now. You probably saw one of his most recent kills."

"His kills?"

"Yes, you have the ability to see into the Veil. Or really, the Veil that exists in our world. The people we kill surround us. The imprints of their final moments catch on our souls. There is so much we can learn."

A sudden, cold realization hit Iona between the eyes. Ilyana saw it as well. Her expression turned hard. The reason for the evening became abundantly and painfully clear.

"Now you understand why I know you're lying," said Ilyana.

"No, no. I told you. I didn't kill Fenris. I don't know where he is."

"Then why do I sense him surrounding you?"

"I—"

The words never made it out because Ilyana jammed her palm right in Iona's chest, flinging her backwards off the eight-story apartment building.

§

The world fell away from Iona as Ilyana watched from the edge.

It happened so quickly.

Windows rushed past, hair whipping her face.

A scream caught in her throat as the ground rushed towards her.

§

The world stopped suddenly.

Like a hand had reached down and grabbed her by the waist, halting her descent.

Teeth clacked together. Iona bit her tongue, tasting the warm coppery blood immediately.

She turned her head to see that she was suspended a few feet from the ground, then whatever was holding her let go and she crashed against the concrete.

The ecstasy and exhilaration were replaced with fear and dread.

Ilyana stood over her, white dress untouched by events.

To Iona's utter surprise, a hand reached out, pulling her upward.

"One last chance, sister. Tell me how you killed Fenris. No denials. No lies. I must know."

The truth lingered on her tongue, before she swallowed it.

"You must be mistaken."

"I am never mistaken."

Iona stared into Ilyana's blue eyes, which had turned icy. Despite the fear rising up from her gut, Iona reached for her magic, using it to see into her half-sister for a clue how to escape the trap.

She bored her senses into Ilyana, and after a few seconds, she feared that whatever she'd drank earlier had worn off, and she could no longer access that part of her, but then she realized there was another answer. Ilyana didn't know. If she really could see the souls surrounding her, she would already know that she'd killed Fenris. All this pomp and circumstance was to get her to admit what had happened, because she couldn't see it, even with her enhanced powers. Maybe their relationship was interfering, or something else she didn't understand.

But that still didn't help with the accusation. Iona reached for an answer from her memories, wanting it to hew as close to the truth as possible in case she did see some aspects of Fenris' last moments.

"There was a ritual we did, not long before he disappeared. He said it was dangerous and I asked him why he was doing it, but he said it was necessary. For him and me. It was preparation for something that was to come, involving my tattoos. I never understood it, but there was a time during the ritual that things didn't go well, when I let too much faez out of my tattoos. I was still learning how to control them. He said he died a little when it happened. I don't know if that's true or not, but maybe that's what you see? I really don't know, Ilyana. I swear on our shared blood that I did not kill Fenris."

For a few seconds, Iona was certain that Ilyana was going to kill her. There was nothing she could do to stop it. Ilyana had already proved she was far superior. The only question was how quick it would be. Iona worried that it would be slow, painfully slow. The reason for the noises from the other rooms in the Vânatoare became clearer in retrospect.

Ilyana's expression softened. The knot between her brows loosened.

"Maybe that's what I saw, sister. Maybe that's what I saw. After all, you're right about one thing. You're not strong enough to kill someone like Fenris. You're not even strong enough to kill me should it ever come to that."

Iona steeled herself from showing relief.

"Am glad you can see that now, sister."

Ilyana smiled at the familial title, the curve of her lips revealing her lingering suspicion.

"Come now, Iona. Let's return and partake of dessert. I can see that hunger in your eyes is not yet sated, and it would help take the sting off of that fall."

Iona swallowed the blood that had been in her mouth from biting her tongue.

"I'm not sure I could take any more. That was too much. If it's alright with you, I'd like to take my leave. We have a big day in the Second Year Games tomorrow."

"Very well, sister. Another time. I'm sure once you've had a moment to reflect, you'll have more questions and maybe a few requests."

"I might, sister. I might."

Ilyana kissed her on both cheeks, which Iona returned, and then her half-sister was striding back to the Vânatoare, disappearing through the hidden door.

Iona composed herself before she dared to walk past Tiago and the other gang members. The drink still lingered in her system and she could feel their questioning stares and a measure of reserved power.

Hating the feeling of powerlessness when Ilyana had shoved her off the roof, Iona forced herself to grin at the gang members, which caused them to recoil.

It wasn't until she was down the street that she remembered the blood in her mouth. Using her phone, she checked her teeth to find them covered in a sheen of blood. They wouldn't forget her by any means.

By the time she'd contacted Gentry and headed to the pickup location, her hands had stopped shaking. But as she waited for the private SUV, a thought worried at her like a grindstone wearing down steel. Whatever prevented Ilyana from sensing the truth of Fenris' killing would do nothing if her half-sister ever met Zuri. She could never let that happen, or Ilyana would know the truth.

TWENTY-ONE

The Wizard's Coffee was only a block away from the Obelisk. Zuri could see the top half glistening in the sunlight as she sipped her iced cappuccino and waited for Ana to arrive.

Across the booth, Iona stared intently at the foot traffic outside the window, tapping her fingernail on her mug. She looked ready to climb out of her skin.

"You don't have to worry," Zuri said. "Jack and his team have agreed to back off. Breaking into the professor's office and copying her diary paid dividends."

"I don't know if I can ever relax," said Iona, mouth twitching. "Nor do I think we should. It's not like they're our only concern."

"Iona. We're in public. Nothing's going to happen."

Her friend made a show of leaning back in the booth, but her heavy gaze never left the outside. The tension didn't match the situation, which meant something else was going on.

Hoping to soften her mood before Ana arrived, Zuri asked, "What are you doing for your hair? It's never looked so lustrous. Your fingernails too. Did you stop biting them?"

Iona stared at her fingers, mystified.

"Maybe the good food in Coterie is working. Real veggies and all that. Better than the microwave burritos and ham rollups that I ate in the old farmhouse."

"Maybe. Honestly, it looks like you're using some rejuvenating elixirs, but I haven't seen any D'Agastine products in your room."

"No idea," said Iona tersely.

Zuri sensed she was obfuscating, which didn't make sense. Why did she care about revealing how she was taking care of her hair and skin? She was about to challenge Iona on it when Ana arrived in a sleek black coat.

"This is my friend, Iona," said Zuri after greeting Ana.

"I've heard all about you, but my, my. Nobody told me that you were gorgeous," said Ana, laughing. "To think, I was led to believe you're some backwater cretin from the middle of nowhere. I was expecting buck teeth and stringy dirty blonde hair by the way society talks about you. You'll have to tell me about your skin care regimen. You're absolutely glowing."

Iona swallowed and looked away.

"Thanks?"

"Should I grab you a coffee?" asked Zuri.

"I can't stay long, luv. But I wanted to personally thank you for what you did with the Siren Sisters. Once we showed them the documents, they immediately backed off and we used that leverage to get a few of our clients that had jumped ship back."

She leaned forward on the table.

"How *did* you get that information?"

"A girl never reveals her secrets." Zuri flashed a smile at Iona. "Beauty or otherwise."

"Smart," said Ana. "But of course I already knew that. Gemma always went on about your brilliance."

"Not feeling too brilliant these days with our progress in the games."

Ana reached out and put her hand over Zuri's.

"Speaking of which, I have a little intel for you. Might help. Might not. But I know you'll put it to good use."

"Intel?" asked Iona, suddenly interested. "I didn't think that was possible with the charms."

"Anything's possible with enough time and money," said Ana, winking. "Money especially."

"What's the intel?" asked Zuri.

Ana looked like she was going to explode with excitement.

"I have no idea what this means but I figure you'll know better." She leaned in conspiratorially. "The dog has nine lives."

Zuri leaned back in the booth.

"The dog has nine lives?"

"That's all I've got."

"There aren't any—"

Her mouth stayed open as she fought to finish her thought, but the protective enchantments to keep people from talking about what was happening inside the games with outsiders had kicked in.

"See, it must be important if you can't talk about it," said Ana with unrepentant glee. She looked like she'd just handed over a gift of gold bars rather than a vague bit of intel that could mean nothing. "As much as I'd love to stay and catch up, I have to move. I have a brunch date."

A round of cheek kisses and hugs later, Zuri was left alone with Iona, who had a hunched forehead.

"The dog has nine lives. That sounds like nonsense. Are you going to tell the others?"

Zuri tapped on her chin.

"No. I don't think we should."

"Don't trust Blake not to find a way to use it against us?"

"Not Blake, but Scarlett. I think I've misjudged her."

"At least they've been behaving themselves. You doing okay? I don't know how you work with Gemma's killer day in and day out."

A knot that always lurked in Zuri's chest pulsed as if to remind her that she would never be free of that pain.

"Biding my time."

"Not like we're anywhere near the front of the pack in the Second Year Games. At this rate, we'll never make it to the fourth level and all five of us will get kicked out of Coterie."

"I can't think like that," said Zuri, firming her jaw. "We're going to win the Second Year Games and we're going to figure out how to get to the fourth level. Elixir or not. I haven't worked this hard all my life to have it all go away."

"You have some other plan in mind? You're not thinking about using the book again, are you?"

"Why not? It fixed this problem."

"Use it too much and eventually Professor Cornwallis will figure out that you're burning her blackmail. I'm sure she could figure out who did it with some investigative spells."

Zuri leaned forward.

"We have to use *everything* we can. I don't want to get kicked out because I held back."

Iona matched her intensity, rising up and resting her forearms on the table.

"You don't want to get kicked out because you pushed things too far. Let's not forget these are real people in that book. You can't just mess with people's lives and not expect to have blowback. There are a lot of ways using that information could go wrong."

"That's how things work in Coterie, and in the circle I run in."

"I? But I guess I should have understood that. You're grouped with me because you have to, not because you want to."

"That's not fair and you know it. And I didn't mean it that way. You're not in those circles, yet, but I don't see any reason why you shouldn't once you graduate from Coterie. They won't be able to say you didn't belong if you come out the other side, especially with the extra scrutiny that being who you are has come with."

"I don't know why I bother. They'll never accept me, even if I manage to pull off graduating," said Iona, staring wistfully out the window.

"Is that what this is about? Now that Fenris is dead you're having second thoughts? Or is this about Ilyana?"

"It's not that," said Iona, glaring back. "Trust me. And stay away from her. She's dangerous. Really dangerous."

Hating the tension between them, Zuri grabbed Iona's hands and pulled them closer.

"Iona. I don't care about Ilyana, or Ana, or the Coterie alum. I care about our team. You, me, and Justine. I promise you, if I use the book, I'll be careful, but we've got to use every tool available. No other solutions to our portal problem have presented themselves, which means we've got to win the Second Year Games. It's our only shot right now."

"Do we really have a shot?" asked Iona.

"Absolutely. I've never lost a challenge like this and I don't mean to start now. Our luck is going to change. I know it. We solved the problem with the fourth years and next we're going to figure out the Second Year Games. Trust me, Iona. I never lose."

TWENTY-TWO

The leg bone is connected to the tooth bone. The tooth bone is connected to the finger bone," sang Justine in her mausoleum hideaway as she touched each trophy that she'd acquired.

A bird trill alarm broke her out of song. She clicked the button on the side of the watch that she'd rescued from the body on the first floor a few months ago.

Justine slipped into the miniature backpack, grabbed the warding charm, and headed into the main level. It was easy to avoid the black pools and other traps after months of living on the level. The first years had begun to explore, but hadn't made it very far, so she didn't have to worry about avoiding them except whenever she was around the entrance.

A knotted rope helped her climb onto the stone building with the crenellated roof. The interior was pointless, except for a couple of deadly traps that protected nothing, but that's not why she'd come. Justine hummed under her breath while she waited.

"Toothy, Toothy, where are you?"

After two hours, she worried that either it wasn't coming out today, or had already left its nest and she'd missed it. She was deciding about heading back to study the tome she'd been reading in hopes of hardening her wooden skin, when she heard the scraping of claws on stone.

The monster ambled out of the shadows, trudging forward with the inevitability of death on all fours. Toothy turned its head slightly as if it suspected her observation, but continued on its heading.

Justine waited a thirty count before daring to follow. While she'd survived the day she'd encountered Toothy in the nest, it was probably the appearance of the first years on the level rather than her inedible body that had been her savior. She didn't want to chance getting torn in half by that jagged row of brutal teeth.

Toothy headed straight for the portal. It preferred its prey to be alone and unaware. The first years were too attuned to danger from the traps and puzzles to let their guard down on the third level.

After Toothy went through the portal, Justine followed, heading directly for the first level where the monster was likely to be hunting. She hurried through the hieroglyph tunnel, which was the place she was most likely to run into other students.

Soon after she hit the fifth floor of the first level, she heard voices. A group of first years heading to the portal, but she was able to hide behind a statue of Malden while they passed. Being a two-foot puppet had its advantages.

Figuring out where Toothy had gone took her another half hour. The monster liked to either stay near the portal, or head down to the second floor where the students had their lodgings. The nearness of safety made them more reckless.

Justine found Toothy near the Arlington suite, lurking beneath a deactivated arch that some said had been a portal in previous decades. She found it not by sight, but the presence of a cloud of impenetrable shadow that her magically aided sight could not penetrate. Mage lights or a darkvision enchantment weren't able to discern the difference. It'd taken Justine a few weeks to find a spell that allowed her to see the monster hiding in its cocoon of unique darkness.

It was fitting that a monster had gotten into Coterie. The other students thought they were monsters, but that conceit quickly fell away when the beast rushed out of the darkness with a mouth full of teeth. Their arrogance turned to wet realization as blood splashed upon the marble tiles, coating the walls with their last moments of existence.

Justine found herself rooting for the monster. The other Coterie students had never accepted her oddness. They'd treated her like a sideshow, and she'd never been able to reveal her true self. Not until she'd met Iona and Zuri.

Tucked into her hidey-hole, Justine fantasized about the members of her former group wandering into hallway, and Toothy snapping out like an African crocodile, snapping off limbs like twigs.

So when a scuff of shoes announced the approach of a student, Justine found herself anticipating the lunge and scream. Twin seed-hearts thundered in her chest as she leaned forward.

She recognized the student when they appeared. Daniel Yates. Old magic from St. Jude's. He was neither cruel nor kind. Mostly forgettable. Much like she'd been. The camouflage of banality. The armor of ordinariness.

A twinge of concern was quickly extinguished by anticipation. At least until Daniel stopped a dozen steps from Toothy's hiding spot, not far from the Arlington suite door.

Daniel reached into a pocket, pulling out an opaque gemstone that emanated a faint light blue glow. His gaze searched the shadows, looking for the source of the danger, lingering on the special hiding spot more than once, instinctually knowing that something horrible lurked there.

A mage light bloomed into existence, floating over the open area, but never fully penetrating the shadows. The light bent around the cocoon of unique darkness, creating a bubble that when Daniel noticed, forced him to step backwards.

Toothy shifted in his cave, claws scraping against the marble and alerting Daniel of the danger.

When the monster rose out of its darkness, Daniel gasped, the glowing gemstone tumbling out of his hand to bounce across the floor. The hard bounce was almost comical in contrast to the danger.

Transfixed like Daniel, she watched as the monster rose to two legs, black eyes over a long, bumpy snout boring down on its prey. She was as surprised by the switch to bipedal motion as she was at Daniel's delay.

He lurched into motion, quick fingers eliciting a swirling hammer of force that slammed into Toothy with the fury of a hurricane, but the impact of a whisper. The blast rolled off the monster's hard flesh, receiving a growl for the effort.

To Daniel's credit, he switched to flame, using it more as a barrier than a weapon. The spray spread wide, little flame spits bouncing across the marble, making the monster flinch, but then it roared out of its hiding spot.

Daniel knew he was outmatched and fled, but not returning the way he'd come, which was the longer route back to the eastern stairwell. Instead, he burst down the side hall, which was the most direct route.

Which brought him directly past Justine's hiding space.

She'd never intended to interfere. She'd meant to be like a wildlife observer, watching the kill from her blind out of supernatural curiosity rather than any malice.

But when he came streaking past, she thrust out her wooden leg, catching his left foot. It wasn't a lot. He outweighed her by several factors, but the deflection was enough to bring one shoe against the other and he was tumbling over, slamming into the wall and then the marble.

Toothy was on him in an instant. The first scream was the worst. Not because it frightened Justine, but because it didn't.

Justine couldn't really say what caused her to do it. Curiosity? The desire to watch Daniel's last moments, to see the light go out in his eyes? Or maybe it was simply to see the monster feed. She'd only stumbled upon his victims long after their thrashing ended, the mysteries of those final moments left to her active imagination.

In some ways, what Justine witnessed with her enchanted eyes wasn't as bad as the sounds of the gnashing and sloppy wet noises that followed the initial bite. Half the body was devoured before she realized that Daniel wasn't going to escape, and when the inevitable guilt didn't come, she worried even more.

It wasn't fear either. Halfway through the feast, the monster side-eyed her in the shadows, acknowledging her existence and her part in the killing.

When the monster slowed its eating, Justine emerged from the darkness and approached the body. Toothy was hunched over the upper half, a pool of blood covering the entire hallway. She splashed through the warm liquid until she was near Daniel's hip and the monster's toothy snout.

Toothy snorted, sending out wetness from between its teeth, while its black eyes regarded her.

"Are you a god or a monster?" she asked.

The monster grunted and kept eating.

The hem of her smock was covered in blood. She'd been meaning to change out of it but why did it matter what she looked like? Justine squatted and ran her fingers through the blood, then drew lines on her face.

"Both," she said.

She'd never been religious. Most mages weren't. Why believe in deities beyond the firmament when there were real gods and monsters wandering around their lands?

But it occurred to her that she was mistaken. Maybe not about most of it, except for the existence of hell. Rather than descend into the abyss, they climbed over the bodies of their fellows in the search for absolute power, knowing even a moment of inattention would end in tragedy.

This was the hell visited upon them by their parents.

To change them into gods and monsters. Or both.

Except now there was a real monster loose in the Obelisk. One that didn't care about their alliances and their gilded upbringing. This was the true power. It was both frightening and illuminating.

Justine leaned over the half-eaten body and touched the monster's snout. The creature snorted but kept eating, the pace slowing as it gorged, yet it kept its black eyes upon her the entire time.

Eventually, Justine retreated, heading wide around the carnage to collect the trinket that Daniel had dropped in fear. The bauble still glowed pale blue. She shoved it into her pack for later investigation.

The monster rose to its clawed feet, covered in blood and viscera, trudging slowly on four legs in the general direction of the portal. Justine watched for a few moments more before deciding it was no longer safe to be in the monster's presence.

TWENTY-THREE

Iona arrived at the meeting place before the appointed time. Now that Jake and the fourth years were no longer hunting them, staying together in the city wasn't a priority.

Across the street a group of students, Halls probably, headed into a trinket shop, laughing and filled with the comradery of shared purpose. She stared longer than she should have, then shoved her hands back in her jacket and decided the alleyway was more appropriate for her attention.

Iona stewed in her feelings. They needed a break. Progress in the Second Year Games was frighteningly slow. Despite their magical prowess, they were only in the middle of the pack for the contest. Zuri privately blamed Blake's leadership, but Iona thought it was more than that. The other groups could rely on different skill sets, while they, at first glance, knew only the same magics taught by Coterie.

But she knew better.

A squeak announced the appearance of a rat in search of food. He was chewing on an empty box of cookies that had fallen out of the dumpster.

"Rats are just like rabbits," she said as her stomach growled.

It wasn't just hunger that drove her. They needed new insights, or a way to figure out what "the dog has nine lives" meant. As much as Iona had been frightened of what Ilyana had shown her, she knew that it was something that could help too.

Iona blasted the rat with a force bolt, sending it spinning across the alleyway. She felt lucky that she didn't squash it completely, and retrieved it by the tail, holding it up for close examination.

If it'd been a rabbit back in Missouri, she'd hang it from a tree by its hind legs using a piece of wire, then after disemboweling the creature would carefully separate the fur from the meat using a blade. She only had a folding knife and no wire, but she didn't need to save the fur.

The raw flesh was chewier than expected and the blood squished through her teeth. She wished it was as simple as consuming raw meat from the supermarket but she wasn't that lucky. Iona couldn't get more than a few bites down before she tossed the body behind the dumpster and used a leftover napkin from the bakery to clean her hands and mouth.

After a clean belch, Iona stumbled out of the alleyway, nearly running into Zuri. Shame burned Iona's cheeks. She avoided Zuri's questioning gaze.

"What were you doing back there?"

Iona hid her hands behind her back, wiping the blood on her backpack.

"I heard a noise."

"A noise?"

"Never be too careful."

Zuri stared blankly before snapping out of her thoughts.

"Whatever. Let's go. I don't need new reasons to be annoyed."

Iona followed a step back while she reviewed herself for more blood. It was only a rat, she reminded herself. It wouldn't have lived long on the streets anyway.

The thrum of power wasn't as acute as when she'd been with Ilyana, but new aspects of the world drew in without even trying. Zuri's heart was thundering like a stampede and she seemed distracted, or in a hurry, nearly getting run over twice when crossing intersections before the lights turned.

Iona was tempted to check for Veil auras, but didn't know how much insight she could glean from one rat, and didn't want to use it up before they arrived at the Spire.

"You're late," said Blake.

He and Scarlett had been conversing in the corner while Orion sat on the end of the couch like a guy who really didn't want to be on a date.

"Can we get on with this?" asked Zuri.

The other three went straight through the portal. Iona moved to follow, but caught Orion staring with the weight of understanding.

"What?"

He brushed past and she was alone.

The others were on the balcony when they arrived in the Veil. Blake was explaining the plan, which really wasn't much different than they'd been doing. The details felt like accusations as they mostly related to areas where they'd died in the past.

Iona ignored the conversation and stared across the city, hoping for new insights. The stone gargoyles on the opposite building had sad, mournful eyes, and the air smelled dust dry despite looking like it should be damp. She could have used her sight to investigate Blake or Scarlett, but they were both known quantities, and confirming that he'd killed Gemma wasn't going to help them with the games.

The start of their attempt began like all the others. Once the magic flew, the residents in the city turned to screaming banshees, rushing towards them with all the subtlety of a burning arrow.

Iona had her part in the early battle down pat. A force bolt at the corner to knock the baker over. Spread ice over this alleyway to slow the workers from the store. Rush to the opposite corner and shoot a flaming dart into the haberdashery so the customers didn't arrive at the same time as the kids from the park.

Everything was going to plan. Until it wouldn't, once they neared the inner wall. They'd yet to get past the first gate and on most attempts couldn't even reach it without getting overwhelmed. Even the roof path had proved unreliable because it drew too much attention.

After Iona sent the flaming dart, she was about to rejoin the group when she caught a reflection in a storefront window on the opposite side of the street. It was showing her the side street where they hadn't been because Blake wanted to take the shortest path possible to their destination.

Checking behind to see the rest of her team in full battle with the Veil beings, Iona used a cloud jump to reach the first ledge, staying at the window level rather than the roof where she knew enemies lurked.

The customers from the haberdashery went screaming below, headed straight for the rest of the group. It was early in their attempt, so she wasn't worried that they couldn't handle it.

Edging along the narrow ledge, Iona scooted past windows. She was so busy checking over her shoulder she didn't notice that one of them was open. A woman in a peasant dress grabbed her around the throat and began choking her. Iona yanked her forward by the hair, using the momentum to keep herself from toppling after the woman, who landed hard on the cobblestones.

She reached the next corner, spotting the sign she'd seen in the reflection. None of the signs in the city of the dead had names. They were simple icons depicting the type of business in a way that anyone despite their native language would understand.

The sign she'd seen displayed a dog with wings. Upon closer inspection, she saw the dog had a cat-like tail.

"The dog has nine lives."

Iona scooted around the corner when a heavy thump startled her to spin around, ready to blast whatever had jumped onto the ledge.

"Merlin's tits, Orion. You scared the shit out of me. You're lucky I didn't put a force bolt through your skull."

The big man looked too big to stay on the ledge. He stared back with the ambivalence of a stone wall.

"Blake's going to be pissed," she said.

The non-answer was all she needed to know.

"Come on. I want to check out something."

With the cobblestone street clear, she jumped down, the impact jamming through her knees. Orion landed beside her.

"You know, for a big man, you're quite nimble on your feet," she quipped.

"I took ballet until I was thirteen."

Iona didn't know if he was joking and stared at him as such, but the fact that he'd spoken at all was meaningful, and she took it for truth.

"Alright."

A bell rang upon their entry to the dog heaven store. Iona put her hands up, preparing to defend herself when she found an old woman sitting in a rocking chair, knitting needles working furiously.

"Hello?"

The woman lifted her chin, eyes like chips of coal, steel gray hair wispy around her head. She wore a puffy black dress that looked like it was in fashion during the Black Plague. A plate of treats sat by the rocking chair. Hard candies wrapped in wax paper. A half-eaten cookie that looked like it'd been cooked on an oven stone.

In the other stores and buildings, the people lived as echoes of their former selves, going through the motions until they turned into killing screams. Up until now, there'd been no signs of the particulars of human consumption.

"Who are you?" she asked the woman.

"No one."

She went back to her knitting.

"Why aren't you attacking us like the others?"

"Would you like me to?" the woman responded, eyebrow arched with mischievousness. "Or have you tired of endlessly dying?"

Iona mused on the countless ways she'd been stabbed, choked, and trampled during their hundreds of attempts to reach the center of the city of dead.

"I'm tired of a lack of answers."

"Then maybe you should try asking some questions," said the old woman.

A ruckus formed behind Iona as Blake and the rest of the group pushed past Orion to enter the strange little store.

"What the fuck are you two doing? We nearly got overrun back there. Come on. If we hurry back, we can salvage this attempt."

"Hold up, babe," said Scarlett. "I think they might have found something interesting."

"Is she some sort of oracle?" asked Zuri. "Why isn't she attacking us?"

"That's what we were trying to find out," said Iona.

Blake marched forward with the subtlety of an avalanche, stopping at the old woman's feet. He reached down and snatched the half-eaten cookie from the tray.

"What's the deal?"

The woman looked old everywhere but her eyes, which held the defiance of youth.

"Death is the only sure deal in this life."

Iona was pondering the answer when a shout had them spinning around. The horde had found them. They put up a good fight, but the numbers were too many and they quickly found themselves back in the prep room.

Blake flew at Iona with fists at his side.

"You fucked us again, Pig Girl. What a wasted attempt, talking to a stupid old woman, and that cookie tasted like shit."

"The definition of insanity is doing the same thing over and over and expecting a different result," she responded.

He jabbed a finger in her chest.

"You think you're so fucking clever."

Scarlett pulled him back by the shoulder.

"Come on, babe. That old woman might be important."

"Why?" he asked.

Zuri barked from the side of the room.

"Because killing isn't always the answer."

Blake spun on Zuri, and for a few seconds, Iona thought it would turn to a sorcerous battle. While the tension grew she side-eyed Orion to see which side he might join should it happen, but then Scarlett stepped in Blake's way, tilting her head when he tried to look past her.

"Babe, come on. You're better than this. That old woman seemed important. We should go back and check it out."

Blake pushed past her, kicking over the table and storming out of the room. Scarlett put up a fake smile.

"I'll talk to him."

Zuri shook her head.

"I'm not putting up with this bullshit today."

In the span of a few seconds, Iona was alone with Orion, who once again looked like a third wheel on a date. Remembering the fading power in her veins, Iona tapped her magic to peer at him through the Veil lens.

A single black wispy shape shifted around his enormous frame like a cloak fluttering in the wind. The image of Orion leaning over her with hands on her throat, his cheeks red with anger and veins on his forehead threatening to explode, left her reeling.

Then he was gone, taking his visions with him.

Iona let herself ponder what she'd seen for a minute before rushing after. She caught up to him in the residential district of the first ward.

"I told you to stop following me!"

The shout blew hair around her face. The rage she'd seen in the vision was hinted in his demeanor.

"I'm not trying to follow. I wanted to talk."

"You don't know what you're messing with. It will change you."

"What are you talking about?" she asked even though she knew what he meant.

Black eyes searched her in the same frantic manner of someone who wanted to shut off an alarm but couldn't find the button. He held out a meaty fist, one finger held out accusingly.

"If you follow me again, I'll break every bone in your body."

"Then why'd you follow me in the game?"

Orion stuttered to a stop, head hanging.

"You shouldn't have left the group," he said softly.

"Left the group? I'm surprised you're even in *this* group. You spent our entire first year alone. What's the deal?"

A half turn.

"You shouldn't have stayed in Coterie."

"Then why have you?"

"I have to."

"Why?" she asked. "And why were you nice to me last year? You warned me of the gloomrend and told me not to antagonize Blake, which meant you said more words to me than the rest of your class."

"You shouldn't have been in Coterie."

Heat rose in her chest.

"So you're gonna be like them?" she spat.

When his expression turned to something that wasn't stoicism or rage, she almost didn't know how to interpret it.

"That's not what I meant."

"Then what did you mean? And not just that, but a little bit ago when you told me it would change me. What do you know? Do you know what I am? Because I don't know. And sometimes, I'm not sure I want to know."

For a few seconds, she thought he might answer, then he squared his shoulders to the street and marched forward with the inevitability of the tide.

Iona put her forehead in her hands, trying to make sense of Orion Dreadmarsh. One thing was for certain, all the stories about him traveling to other realms as a mercenary to kill wantonly weren't true. He'd only killed one person, which still was a lot in the big scheme of things, but compared to the mythology her fellow Coterie students had conjured of Orion, it was a letdown.

It wasn't just his anger that bothered her, but the way he'd looked at her as if he knew exactly what she'd done, and then the warning. Did he know who Ilyana was? Did he know about her family? Or Fenris? And who was that person he'd strangled? A rival? A girlfriend? Had it been murder or self-defense?

Orion Dreadmarsh was an enigma. The more she learned about him, the less she knew. Zuri had tasked her with getting him on their side, but the only thing she'd done so far was piss him off. If things came to blows with Blake and Scarlett, Iona was relatively sure he wouldn't intervene.

TWENTY-FOUR

Zuri was heading to class with Professor Ravenscroft for a lecture about the efficiency of runes when designing Kemetic circuits, when her warding bracelet buzzed. She quickly planned out her escape routes as she renewed her protections.

Battles in the classroom areas of the Obelisk were frowned upon, but not forbidden, and after the last few contentious sessions at the Second Year Games, she wouldn't be surprised if Blake and company tried to get rid of them.

When Candi and Coral, the Siren Sisters, came around the corner, she nearly let her guard down until she saw the murderous looks in their eyes.

"Stop."

The twins spoke in unison, their sorcerous voices worming into Zuri's head until her legs halted their attempt to escape. But she managed to reach into an inner pocket, pulling out a small vial, thumbing off the lid and downing the bitter liquid before the sisters reached her.

"You fucked us," said Candi, pulling out a blade that looked like wavy seaweed.

"I helped you," said Zuri, activating her bracelet, which put up a small shield.

The Siren Sisters bracketed Zuri in the short hallway.

"You gave us information we would have figured out eventually," said Coral.

"Then what's the deal?" she asked, even as she suspected the answer.

Candi tilted her head, which made her kelp-thin hair cascade against her shoulder. Despite being completely dry, they always looked damp as if they'd recently been swimming.

"We were preparing to devour the Bettencourt empire, but suddenly their lawyers presented us with a bit of information that turned the tides against us."

"What does that have to do with me?" asked Zuri.

"We know you were good friends with the family and had a meeting with Ana Bettencourt earlier this year and again a month ago."

"She's a friend. We both grieve for Gemma."

"Don't treat us like we're stupid. You should know that our family is known for birthing oracles. It's how we've been so successful all these years."

"Divination is not a sure thing. It's not a horoscope by any means, but it's not fact either."

"It is when we do it," said the sisters in unison.

"What's your point?" asked Zuri as she calculated whether or not she could battle past the Siren Sisters and make it to the safety of Ravenscroft's class.

"Blood is in the water," said Coral. "Your blood. And we mean to feed."

"Wait!" said Zuri. "What if I told you I could make this right?"

"Then you might be worth something to us alive," said Candi.

Zuri scoured her mind for a bit of information from the blue book that would help the Siren Sisters, but not impact her friend's family. Some of the blackmail was explosive and would have larger implications, which made it unsuitable to hand over to the Siren Sisters.

"You're running out of time," said Candi, stepping closer with the blade pointed at Zuri's gut. "And that shield won't help you. I trained with the Mer on Atlantis."

"What about...what about..."

Coral looked to her sister.

"She's stalling. I'll disable the shield. You kill her."

A section in the blue book popped into her head. Not the particulars, but the generalities of the blackmail.

"The Durge!"

The Siren Sisters appeared puzzled by the outburst.

"The Durge? As in the band?" asked Coral.

"Yes. Would you like to be their managers? They're going to be the next Garbage Kings. Everyone knows it."

The Sisters shared a glance.

"That might make up for the losses we've incurred with the Bettencourts," said Candi.

"If. If you can make this happen. If this is an attempt to delay us, know that we're not like Blake. If we want you dead, you won't be breathing past sunrise," said Coral.

"I swear to you. The current management company has been skimming from the top. The band isn't getting but a quarter of what's owed them, but they're too busy touring to notice. Let me go and as soon as I get back to my room, I'll send over the documents that prove their malfeasance. If you get the Durge in your pocket, that will not only make up for the other losses, but signal to the other big bands that you're a safe place for harbor. This could be a very valuable piece of information, but I have to be alive to give it to you."

"Where did you get this information?" asked Coral, scowling. "It's not like you were known for blackmail at St. Jude's."

"I've been holding my powder for when it mattered. It's not like I had a lot of other options once the Blake thing went south."

"Fine," said Candi, letting the blade drop to her side. "You can live. For now. But if we don't get that information by the end of the day, your blood will be in the water by tomorrow."

"And for the record, we don't believe a word of this bullshit about how you acquired the information. There are only so many players in that game, and you're not one of them, which means you stole it. At the moment, we don't care, but if events don't work out the way we expect, then we might have to whisper in some ears and see who perks up first."

"It's been lovely doing business with you," said Zuri, holding out her hand.

The Siren Sisters stared at the gesture as if it were a live eel and then turned heel and headed back where they'd come.

Zuri let out a huge sigh and leaned against the wall with her eyes closed. That'd been close. Too close. And they weren't wrong about their suspicions either, which made using the information even more perilous.

But despite nearly getting murdered on the way to class, a buzzy warmth filled her midsection. The power contained within that little blue book was palpable. Things were getting complicated, but also more exciting. She'd been so used to relying on her wits and magic, especially after the last two years, that she'd forgotten there were other ways to achieve power.

TWENTY-FIVE

The room smelled like sex and perfume. Scarlett sat naked against the wall, inhaling a jar of sweet smoke while Blake lay on his back, chest glistening with sweat and marked with red lines. Beads of blood dotted his hip where she'd broken flesh with her teeth.

"If you give me a minute or two," said Blake with a sleepy gaze, "I can return the favor."

Scarlett rubbed his leg.

"I'm sure you will, babe," she said.

He always said that and never did, but sexual release was something she could find in other ways.

Scarlett put her nose in the jar again, letting the smoke tickle her nostrils, refreshing her mind while a trickle of sweat traveled down the valley between her breasts.

"We really should kill them," said Blake with his eyes closed.

There was no need to explain who "them" was. Zuri and Iona were a constant topic of discussion. An obsession.

"We will, babe. But not yet. We need them for the Games."

"If we kill them, the portal might open for us."

"Or it might not, and then we're screwed."

Blake cracked his neck and put his hands between his legs, rubbing himself.

"I just want to see the look on her face when I put the blade in her neck. I want to watch as her eyes go blank, feel her life running out over my hands."

"You'll get to do that eventually, babe. You will. And if we can't figure out the Games, or someone else wins, then you can kill her. I'll even help."

He sat up straight, still holding himself between his legs.

"I get to do it. Me. Alone."

"Of course. She was your girlfriend after all and she hurt you. You should be the one to kill her. I'll take care of Pig Girl, and we'll finally rid Coterie of that uppity bitch. I still can't believe they let her stain our hallowed halls."

All the talk was getting Blake aroused again. She was enjoying her thoughts. Setting them aside to deal with it was only going to make her annoyed.

"Any luck with Orion? If we're gonna have to kill them, we need him on our side, or do it when he's not around. He's a wild card. He could do anything."

Blake wasn't wrong. The big Dreadmarsh was a mystery. He barely spoke during their attempts, but was an effective team member. More than effective. His brutality and mastery of destruction frightened her and she wasn't easily frightened. She often thought he was holding back, but wasn't going to challenge him on it.

"I checked with Victoria. She's friends of the family. Said that even the other Dreadmarshes are nervous around him."

"If just a quarter of the rumors are true then they're right to be worried."

Blake leaned over and grabbed a glass of amber liquid, throwing it back with a grimace.

"I would have liked to see him rip the Boyer kid in half."

"That's a dumb rumor," said Scarlett offhandedly. "He was killed in a car crash and it was an ugly one. That's why it was closed casket. Orion wasn't in the country at the time."

Blake's jaw rippled with anger.

"Babe—"

It was a warning. She put on a sweet smile and rubbed the inside of his thigh.

"Something I heard," said Scarlett as she ran her hand between her own legs, pumping her eyebrows as a come-hither offer. "But you really don't care that much."

The corners of his lips curled upward and then crashed to flatness.

"Of course I care. I don't like it when you think I'm wrong. I'm never wrong. You should remember that."

His gaze shifted towards the side table where she knew he kept the knife. He'd found it in the Obelisk. A nasty looking ritual knife with a lioness head pommel and a solar disc across the hilt. The blade had a channel down the center that was configured to collect the blood as it went into the flesh. He carried it everywhere, telling the rest of the team that he was going to use it to split Zuri.

"I didn't mean it like that, babe."

Blake reached into the drawer, producing the wicked blade. He held the tip against the flesh between her breasts.

"Don't call me babe. Babe."

"Blake..."

The anger in his eyes went beyond his normal capriciousness. The tip pierced her skin, producing a bead of blood. She didn't flinch, because that would only entice him to press further.

"Blake."

He kept putting more and more pressure on the knife. The heat of the pain made the muscles in her hand weak. The smoke jar slipped out of her fingers, tumbling onto the bed while she maintained eye contact. She did her best not to show fear, but he seemed to lose himself at times when he had the blade in his fist.

"Say it."

"Say what?"

"Don't mess with me. Babe."

Scarlett lifted her chin, the only defiance she was willing to show in the face of his threat.

"You're our leader. You're always right. I shouldn't have said what I said before."

"And?"

"I was wrong."

His eyes glinted before his jaw relaxed and he pulled the blade away from her chest. She didn't dare wipe the blood away, revealing that she'd been worried, so it ran down her smooth belly and between her legs. Blake watched it the entire time, a hunger in his gaze that was unnatural.

"Would you like to lick it?"

He nodded feverishly and leaned forward, pressing his face between her breasts, sucking at the wound. She put her hands gently on the back of his head and pulled, wondering if she could smother him.

Not now, but one day I might need to.

The thought brought heat to her cheeks and wetness between her legs. Blake was a coarse tool like using a hammer to cut a piece of cloth, but he was effective, and the other students were too afraid to challenge him.

In three and a half years, she wouldn't need him any longer and then she could decide how to get rid of him. But for now, he was exactly what she needed.

Scarlett leaned back her head and let those warm thoughts carry up from her midsection. She was so enthralled by her dreams that she didn't sense his shift until horrible pain startled her.

"Blake!"

She opened her eyes to find the ritual blade shoved into her shoulder about two inches deep. He was fixed upon the point that the dagger had entered her flesh as his eyes alighted like beacons.

"Don't fight it. Don't fight it."

"What are you doing?" she asked between heavy breaths.

The pain was worse than anything she'd ever experienced. He twisted the tip, causing crimson rivulets to spill from her flesh.

"Don't worry, babe. I'm not going to kill you. You're still useful to me. But if you start thinking too much for yourself, then I might have to. Now tell me you love me."

The deranged stare left her confused and worried.

"I love you, Blake. You're my everything."

"Good. I am your everything. Don't you forget it."

He yanked out the blade, and after a brief war of indecision, licked the length, which smeared blood across his jaw. Then he left her in the bed, bleeding profusely, and went into the bathroom fully erect. Moments later, she heard the shower running.

The wound wasn't so deep that a spell couldn't fix it, but it took three tries because Scarlett's hands were trembling. She'd thought Blake was in her control. A bit wild, but generally he followed her nudges and suggestions.

She knew what the problem was. The lack of progress in the Games, and having to work beside Zuri on the regular was making him irritated and unpredictable. If she couldn't channel his energies into other pursuits, then he was going to be a problem. As much as she hated it, they needed Zuri and Pig Girl. Killing them would only doom their prospects at Coterie, and Scarlett had no intention of failing.

After the wound was repaired, Scarlett ran her fingers over the bloody mess on her chest. Another time, she would have climbed into the shower with Blake and cleaned herself off, but today was not that day. She used the pillowcase to wipe off the worst of it and put her clothes back on, no longer interested in a day of leisure.

They needed a break in the Games, or he was going to take out his frustrations on her, which meant they needed to follow the lead that Iona had revealed a few weeks ago. Blake preferred fighting to discussion. Hell, he really preferred anything to talking, but that needed to change if they were going to get to the inner circle in the City of the Dead. She briefly thought of turning on Blake and siding with the other two women, but she couldn't stand the thought of allying with that yokel from the Midwest. She might graduate from Coterie, but no one would touch her because she'd be ruined by association.

Scarlett knocked on the bathroom door before entering. He looked like he'd just finished pleasuring himself, which was a bit of good luck for her. It made him drowsy and more pliable.

"Why'd you put your clothes on?"

She startled.

"I can take them back off."

"No. It's fine. I'm bored with you today. What did you want?"

"You really want to kill Zuri soon, right?"

"That's a stupid question, Scarlett."

He never used her name. It was always "babe" or some other pet name. Never Scarlett.

"But before you can do that, we need to win the Games and get the elixir."

He turned off the shower and grabbed the towel, which he used to dry his face.

"Start making sense, Scarlett."

"The faster we get through it, the faster we no longer have to stare at their stupid faces every day. But battling through the dead isn't working. Zuri and Pig Girl aren't good at that. They kinda suck overall, but we're stuck with them."

"And?"

Scarlett hesitated. The solution couldn't come from her, or the others on the team. Or could it?

"Remember when we went to that stupid dog shop?"

"Of course. I thought I was going to kill those bitches for dragging us away from my plan."

"You know that wasn't Pig Girl's discovery, right?"

"What do you mean?"

"She stole it from Orion. You know how he never talks. She took advantage of him. Stole his discovery and claimed it as her own."

"Did she now?"

"How else has she gotten this far? I've always suspected that scholarship video was faked. That she had someone else do it, or it was an illusion."

"That would make a lot of sense."

Scarlett didn't want to push the issue too much. He had the lead, now she had to let him find the path.

"Anyway, I've got to go. Shopping with Alicia this afternoon. We're going to be checking out some new purses from—"

Blake held up his hand, demanding silence, which made her smile inside. He hated shopping.

"Fine. Whatever. Go have fun. I'll be here, working on how to get through the Games. How to save us, like I always do."

"You're the best, babe."

Blake stared at the floor with the towel in his hand, still dripping wet, when she left. She closed the door softly and snuck down the hall before allowing herself to relax. Today had been a close one. She was certain that he could have murdered her in the bed and found a way to dispose of her body. She had to be more careful, watch what she had to say, and make sure Blake felt like he was in charge, or things were going to go south.

TWENTY-SIX

The mummy room didn't look the same as last year, Iona mused as she examined the faded section on the wall where the mirror had been before she shattered it. Surviving the trap had been a close one. Iona wondered how she would feel about getting coated in a rain shower of blood this year and her mouth opened as if she were catching snowflakes unconsciously.

"Stop that."

"Stop what?"

Iona spun around, throwing her back against the wall, expecting an attack until she realized it was the little puppet standing in the middle of the room in her dirty black smock.

"Justine. You scared the crap out of me. How did you get in without me hearing?"

The puppet tilted her head unnaturally.

"I entered two hours ago. I was in the corner thinking about death."

Iona took a deep breath to calm her beating heart. The inhale caught the scent of rot.

"Is that you?" she asked, sniffing the air.

It smelled like old meat. Justine held out her smock, which on closer inspection looked like it had been used as a rag to clean up a murder site.

"You really should change clothes now and then. I can run them through the laundry for you. Or better yet, when I'm in the city I'll buy you some new outfits from the toy maker."

"That would be nice. Thank you."

Iona crouched on her heels, getting to eye level with the puppet.

"I'm sorry we haven't been around much. We're finally starting to make progress in the Games again since Blake decided to listen to someone other than himself. Zuri still thinks we can win, but I'm not so sure. But if we, you know, don't make it to our third year and have to leave, you can stay with us."

The smile looked like it'd been painted on by a child.

"Everything is going to be fine."

The strange pronouncement made Iona uneasy, but she didn't know how to respond.

"Are you sure? What have you been doing?"

"Finding secrets."

"That's great, Justine. I'm sure we'll be able to use those. Is there anything you need? Besides the clothes? I hope you're not lonely," said Iona, thinking of her time in the farmhouse.

Even when Fenris had been there, she'd felt alone. Which made her think about Ilyana. They hadn't talked in a few weeks, except for a few messages. For once, her half-sister was busy with some personal project that didn't seem to include figuring out who had killed their father.

"Not alone. I have a friend."

Iona wasn't quite listening until the last part, then she perked up.

"A friend?"

"He's been showing me secrets on the third level. We found a hidden chamber beneath the mausoleum. It has new pictures and a secret path. He says one day we're going to go through it."

"Who is this friend? Another student?" Iona asked worriedly.

If someone else knew about Justine, that could be a problem.

"He's like me."

Iona relaxed, offering a reassuring smile.

"Of course he is."

Turning into a puppet had scrambled her mind. Iona had helped clear the room full of dolls so she knew all about Justine's "friends." But the meeting was a reminder that they really didn't understand Justine's transformation at all, and the longer it went on, the more odd she was becoming, which was why it wasn't the only appointment she had that day.

"I've got to go, Justine. I have a meeting with Professor Green. Same time next week, okay?"

"Yes."

Iona was going to offer a hug, but the puppet was rancid and she didn't look that interested anyway. Justine barely looked like she was paying attention.

"Make sure you clean up for next time. If you don't the other students are going to find you on smell alone."

Iona had an uneasy feeling about her teammate, but put those thoughts aside until she was back in a safer part of the Obelisk.

Once Iona reached the professors' level, she let herself relax a little. It was never prudent to let your guard down completely, but certain areas of the Obelisk were safer than others.

Cutting through a courtyard with a colorful garden was the fastest way to Professor Green's office, but she regretted it the moment she saw Professor Cornwallis sitting on a bench next to a rosebush, reading from an ancient tome made of black leather. The stern professor scowled in her direction.

A knock on the door received a warm welcome. Professor Horace Green was leaning back in his chair with a phone in his grip, happily thumbing through the screen with an air of delight.

"Miss Storm. So lovely to see you," he said, sitting up while swiping upward on his phone. "I'll never cease to wonder at the marvel of modern technology. Sometimes I find these phones more miraculous than the spells we cast. How can I help you?"

After the unusual meeting with Justine and passing the grumpy Cornwallis, Iona was pleased to find Professor Green in a good mood. The Obelisk could be so dark and unwelcoming, when there was a reason to smile it felt better than normal.

"These may sound like strange questions, but I was wondering about what happens to a soul when it enters a phylactery. Can a person exist in something other than their original body?"

The professor steepled his fingers as he leaned back in his chair.

"That is a strange question. But one I have heard before actually."

"Really?"

"Last year, around this time. A friend of yours actually."

"Justine talked to you?"

"She did."

The professor squinted as if he could see the truth written on her forehead.

"Justine was quite the student," said the professor. "She'd read many tomes on the subject of souls and their malleability."

"I didn't know."

"Are these questions in relation to what she was investigating last year? Or something else?"

"I...I'd prefer not to say, Professor. I hope that isn't rude."

"Prudence is never rude. It's downright required in Coterie. Though one must be careful who one is rude to."

"Justine was investigating these things before her death. I wanted to understand her better, to honor her memory. I haven't had many friends in Coterie, so I cherish the few that I have."

"Well said, Miss Storm," he said with a half-grin that suggested he knew more than he was letting on. "Let's just say that the topic of souls and phylacteries is rather unexplored. For good reason, since it's a one-way trip. A soul is both a hearty and fragile thing. It's resilient in ways that can make one marvel, but it needs all its parts to function correctly. And that's the thing. We don't know what makes up a soul, or how much is required for a person to be, well, a person. I suppose if you could take a soul, shave off one bit at a time, and examine the results, you might find your answer, but until someone performs that deed, it's a mystery."

"So theoretically, if one managed to get their entire soul into a phylactery, they might be relatively normal."

"Relatively," said the professor. "But a grapefruit is relatively like an orange, but I despise the taste and would never stoop to eat one."

"Can souls go rotten?"

"They do all the time. We only have to look to some of our students to know that truth," he said with a barely contained smirk.

Sensing that she'd have to give away more than she wanted to in order to find more answers, Iona bowed her head.

"Thank you, Professor. You've given me much to think about."

"Come back anytime if you want to discuss these topics more. I enjoy the scholarship. All theoretically, of course."

She hadn't really known what to think of Professor Green her first year, but she was growing to like him. He didn't seem like the others, who were sculpted from bitter grievances and a reverence of the past that bordered on fanatical. It probably helped that he wasn't an alumnus of

Coterie, but a friend of Malden. She had no idea what the Patron of Coterie was like, but she was inclined to favor him based on his invitation of Professor Green alone.

"I will, Professor. Thank you. I've enjoyed our discussion."

"I have as well." The clear pause made her hesitate before leaving. "A word of warning. I've been hearing rumors about your teammate and they're not favorable."

"That could mean a lot of things in Coterie."

He sighed heavily as he ran his hand across the edge of his desk.

"I might avoid Professor Cornwallis if at all possible."

The warning stiffened her spine. If the professor knew about the theft of the book, then Zuri, and by association, she, were screwed. More than screwed. Professor Cornwallis made Blake look like a petulant toddler in comparison.

"How thoroughly should she avoid Cornwallis?"

Professor Green mused on the question.

"You or your friend don't want to give the professor any reasons to be any more suspicious than she is already."

Iona bowed again, but deeper.

"Thank you for the warning. I will pass it along."

"Good luck, Miss Storm. And stay alive if you can. Coterie's a dangerous place, but it's much more interesting with you in it."

TWENTY-SEVEN

Zuri knew that Blake was in a good mood the moment she walked into the prep room, but she didn't know why. And that bothered her. A plate of sweet cakes sat on the central table. An offering.

"Elmira's Sweet Cakes," said Zuri. "How generous of you."

His grandmother had taken him to the shop when he was a young boy for winning the juvenile Thunderball league, and he'd never forgotten it. Zuri either, because it was the first time she'd really noticed Blake. At the time, she'd thought his rampage through the other competitors, bloodying noses and knocking skulls, had been a marker of his passion, rather than a sign of his sociopathy.

"Everyone grab a piece. You'll need your energy. We're going to do something different today," he said.

Zuri almost froze in surprise as her fingers brushed the flaky treat, but managed to complete the maneuver without giving away her emotion.

Iona scooped up a piece beside her, and then as she turned, gave a questioning look.

Even Orion grabbed a square, devouring it in one bite and going back for a second piece.

"Tell 'em the plan, babe," said Scarlett once everyone had eaten their fill.

Blake presented himself like a general before an army with his hands behind his back, chin lifted as he looked into the nonexistent distance.

"Today, we're going to go after a lead that Orion discovered a few weeks ago."

When Iona started to open her mouth, Zuri elbowed her in the ribs. She turned to glare, but then realization set in, resulting in a nod.

The big man, on the other hand, stared at Blake with the confusion of a dog listening to its owner talk about sports.

"I was thinking that maybe we could get to the shop with the weird old lady without fighting, then we might discover what's really going on in the Games. Let's go."

The others went through the portal quickly, a marker of the mood shift, since previous attempts were approached with a sense of apathy and doom.

Scarlett caught Zuri before she headed off the balcony and while Blake was out of hearing range.

"Don't ask questions. Just play along."

Zuri wanted to taunt the redhead with a biting quip, but the unease in her blue eyes signaled that she wasn't just saying this out of caution, but fear. Blake had put her in her place. Scarlett probably believed that she could handle him, which was how she'd thought in the months before Gemma's death. In hindsight, it'd been easy to see the danger signs.

"You know eventually he's going to tire of you. He might have already."

"That's not what this is about."

Zuri leaned in closer until she could smell the coffee on her breath.

"You think you can control him until it's too late. I know, I tried. Cut your losses while you can."

Scarlett snarled and pulled away.

"Don't project your inadequacies on me."

The redhead marched down the stairs, leaving Zuri alone. She hadn't expected to persuade Scarlett, but seeding doubt was worth the attempt.

"Alright, gang," said Blake as if he were speaking to a group of preteens at a dance. "Instead of the defensive spells we've been applying before each attempt, I want you to use Look Away enchantments. We're going to walk straight to the dog heaven shop. Slowly and without talking, so we don't spook the ghosts."

The preparation felt prudent, even if Zuri was mystified by Blake's thoughtful and calm demeanor. Either this was Scarlett's doing, or they'd managed to get intel from another group.

"What's going on?" whispered Iona in her ear.

"Play along."

Usually their attempts began with a blast of sorcerous magics which incited the mob to attack them. This time, they walked down the middle of the cobblestone street as if they were on a Sunday stroll.

Blake kept them to the middle, avoiding getting too near any of the dead that inhabited the area. If Zuri hadn't been battling them for months, she might not have known how murderous the apparitions were, because they went about their daily routines like busy automatons.

A couple of times, Blake stopped them unexpectedly in the middle of the street, or pulled them to one side. The sudden change was unexplained until a couple of kids burst from a doorway in one instance, and in another, a woman on a bike with a basket on the front peddled past, ringing her bell in greeting as if they were old friends.

When they entered the dog heaven shop, they found the old woman knitting. The amused curl to her lips faltered the moment Scarlett stepped forward. The redhead checked with Blake before speaking to the old woman.

"Where are your children?"

The question surprised Zuri until she saw the black-and-white picture of the old woman with two dirty boys standing before a hovel that looked like it'd been around during the Dust Bowl years.

"Playing a game of stick and ball with the other kids near the black gate."

"It's almost dinnertime. Do you want us to fetch them for you?"

The old woman cracked a smile. She reached into a front pocket, producing a coin.

"Show this to the gate guards. They'll let you through. My boys shouldn't be far."

Blake snatched the coin out of her grip, which caused a hardening of her gaze. He examined the prize and handed it over to Scarlett, which prompted the rest of the group to crowd around. The worn silver coin had a man's head on one side and a sprig of wheat on the opposite.

"What does it mean?" asked Iona.

All eyes fell upon Zuri.

"It's familiar but I can't place the meaning. Let me think about it while we head to the gate."

They headed out of the dog heaven shop using the same precautions as before. Blake seemed less sure of the route, hesitating at corners, or showing signs of minor panic when a resident would cross paths. Once, when an older gentleman using a cane and wearing tattered gray clothes grew near, his face spasmed with anger, but they shifted away and the crisis was averted.

Their luck held out until they reached the interior wall and a carriage from behind came upon them quickly. Zuri thought nothing of it until the coachman jumped off the bench and then they were in the middle of a pitched battle. Death came not long after as they weren't prepared with their normal suite of wards and protections.

"That was a good attempt," said Blake back in the prep room. "We just need to figure out the pattern to reach the black gate. I'm sure it won't be long with this group."

After the others left, Iona grabbed her arm.

"How did they know to do this?"

"They must have cashed in some favors, or traded information."

"I thought the Games were protected from schemes like that."

"There are always ways if you have enough power or money. Just like when Ana gave us the clue, it was worded in a way that didn't trigger the Games protections. Maybe Blake already had the information, but it didn't make sense until we found the old lady. Either way, we need to hurry and catch up. We want to get as far as we can while Blake's in a good mood. We don't know how long it will last."

The afternoon was spent getting incrementally further into the center of the city of the dead. Unlike the first part of the city, it wasn't a simple matter of avoiding the dead, but finding a way to distract them. They learned as much with the carriage that always came through the street at the moment they had no way to avoid it.

It wasn't until Orion spotted a loose cobblestone in the wheel ruts that they were able to pass the carriage problem. He leveraged the stone out of the hole, which created a wheel-snapping pothole. On that attempt, the wagon had to stop to fix the wheel which let them move deeper into the city.

At the end of the day when their nerves—and particularly Blake's—were starting to fray, the group was stymied by a set of guards that blocked the inner gate. It wasn't the Black Gate, where they would find a use for their little silver coin, but the one that divided the main city in half. The guards allowed them to talk, but quickly turned to violence when they didn't have the proper paperwork.

"I don't understand," said Blake back in the prep room. "They're not supposed to block us. We should be able to reach the next area without this, this bullshit."

"I'm sure you'll figure it out, babe," said Scarlett.

"Shut your stupid mouth. You're getting on my last nerve."

The rebuke made her stiffen like a board. Blake charged through the portal leaving Scarlett with her head down. Zuri motioned to Iona, who was already heading after him with Orion.

"Don't," said Scarlett when it was the two of them.

"Don't what? Tell you to watch out? Because I don't have to. You already know how this ends. You just have to be willing to make the choice."

Before Scarlett could answer, she left the prep room. There was no point in poking the sore spot longer. The wound was festering. Let time and Blake's natural inclinations take shape.

A half hour later, they reached the guard gate, staying out of range of interaction. Blake paced across the cobblestones, mumbling to himself while the rest stood back. Zuri had the sense that he'd traded something valuable in exchange for this information. Either he'd remembered something wrong, or the other party had purposely left something out.

Scarlett was watching him warily, the earlier conversation clearly on her mind.

Zuri checked behind them, spying a vendor stall that sat against the high stone wall. Given a little teamwork, they could make it over using spells and Orion's unnatural strength.

"Scarlett," she whispered low enough that Blake wouldn't hear over his own talking.

The redhead wrinkled her nose, but after a second time, came wandering over.

"Don't bother if this is the same old shit."

"See that stall back there?"

Scarlett's eyes followed hers.

"What of it?"

Zuri let her gaze climb up the wall, which after a second, caused the light of understanding to form in her eyes.

"Worth a shot, right?"

"Why are you telling me?"

"He's not going to listen to anything I have to say."

Zuri could see the internal response. *He's not going to listen to me either.* But Scarlett couldn't say that now. Not after the earlier denials. She had to act like nothing was wrong.

The hesitation in Scarlett's step was worth a thousand verbal lashes.

"Hey, babe?" asked Scarlett timidly.

She looked ready to jump back should he bite. Blake simmered as he decided if he wanted to answer.

Scarlett tried a second time, which prompted a curt response.

"What?"

"What if we don't go through the gate? What if we go over?"

"That's the stupidest thing I've ever heard. It's too high."

"What about that vendor stall back there?"

His eyes traveled back along the cobblestones until they came upon the stall.

"Never gonna fucking work. Now shut up and let me think. At least those other idiots know when to keep their mouths closed."

Scarlett sheepishly returned to the group. Zuri tried to offer support, but the redhead turned her back. Cracks were forming. Zuri only had to sit back and occasionally poke them until they were wide enough to walk through. It wouldn't help them with the Games, but eventually, if they managed to win, they'd have to get through the portal to make it to their third year. Blake and his friends would have every advantage because they would know they had to go through it. They only had to sit and wait for them to try. Seeding doubt in his group was the only way they were going to have a chance against such odds. Zuri had never been more proud of herself.

TWENTY-EIGHT

The late February afternoon showered warmth upon Iona's back as she headed into the third for a pedicure with Zuri. The bags in her left hand contained custom clothes she'd ordered for Justine from the doll shop.

The city was filled with tourists and drunk college students because of the Comóir Sidhe Parade which had been winding through the second ward all afternoon, and now the participants were streaming into the other wards. She passed a group of women with fairy wings and tiaras, laughing with illusionary sparklers and colorful drinks in their hands.

The event celebrated the city's links to the Fae realms—though Iona was pretty sure the actual Fae would want no part of it—by holding a drunken parade filled with half-naked out-of-state college students and tourists who had no business bringing their children out.

Iona had been curious. She'd never been to any of the events that seemed to occur every other week, celebrating a new facet of magic, or some non-human group that made its home in the city. But the promise of a relaxing afternoon getting her feet washed and massaged after weeks of tedious repetition in the Second Year Games was more enticing.

Half a block ahead, a bus deposited a group of drunks on the sidewalk, right in her path. Iona took one look at them and darted into an alleyway, which would take her around the drunks and cut off half a block of walking.

The damp spaces between the apartment buildings smelled like old trash and leaky natural gas. Iona kept a good pace, keeping her chin up as not to notice if there were any rats about.

At the other end of the alleyway with the street in sight, a guy wearing a festival sweatshirt stepped out from behind the dumpster as he urinated on the asphalt. Iona thought he was alone, and went wide around, only to find a larger group leaning against the wall waiting for their friend to finish peeing.

"Hey, sweetness," said one of the guys, wearing fairy wings and smoking a cigar. He surged off the wall and blocked her path to the sidewalk. "Need someone to give you a hand?"

He tried to grab a bag, but she yanked it away.

"Step off, or it's going to go very wrong for you and your friends."

Fairy Cigar blew smoke in her face, which made her choke.

"Hey guys, someone thinks she's hot shit. You're not the only one."

He held out his hand, which burst into flame for a few seconds before he shook it out. The glint of his black eyes suggested malice.

These weren't ordinary visitors to the city. Darkness clung to them like cobwebs. A rowdy group of supernaturals using the parade as an excuse to cause trouble.

"I'm a Coterie mage," she said defiantly.

"We know, sweetness. We know."

A cold pit formed in her gut. This interaction wasn't an accident.

They'd been waiting for her.

Six against one. Fairy Cigar was right in her face. He looked the most human of the group, but as she side-eyed the others, she saw thicker foreheads, long yellow fingernails, and a few snaggle teeth.

Iona thought about running, but she didn't know their capabilities and that might only incite them to further violence. And that would take her away from the sidewalk, where they would find it easier to do what they wanted.

Fairy Cigar leaned forward and sniffed her as if she were a bouquet of flowers. His nostrils flared at an unexpected scent as if he were seeing her for the first time, doubt creeping in like a thief and stealing his excitement.

The others weren't so attuned. They rallied around their leader like a pack of hyenas ready to tear into a wounded lioness.

"Who sent you? Was it Ilyana?"

"I don't know that name, sweetness."

He was telling the truth. Which meant it was someone else. Blake and Scarlett? Another group in the Obelisk? Maybe Jack Townsend had decided to enact his revenge at a moment of his choosing, long after everyone had thought their conflict over?

"I'm not really interested in a fight today," she said.

"Who said we're going to fight? We just wanted to help a beautiful young woman safely reach her destination. Carry her bags like gentlemen. Is that so terrible a thing? Or is chivalry dead?"

He smiled, revealing long canines. She saw through the glamour to the beast beneath, which sparked her resolve. They had the advantage of numbers. Seizing the initiative would give her a chance.

Fairy Cigar realized what was happening a moment too late. Fingers worked the force blast at waist height, keeping the spell hidden until she was ready to unleash it into his gut.

Battle rage filled her vision as she exploded elemental magics in their midst, sending them splashing against the brick wall or into the metal dumpster like bowling pins. The particulars of the fight were lost beneath the fury that consumed her like flames.

They were no match. Half the group fled after the first volley. Fairy Cigar, with his cheap plastic wings crumpled on his back, tried to make a go of it, but she threw him into the alley and pounced on his fallen form with unexpected strength. The scream of a snapped bone fueled her excitement.

Iona raked her fingernails across his face, which left four jagged lines in his cheek. Beads of blood brought the hunger, and Iona found herself salivating. A slice of his artery would create a gusher. She only needed something sharp enough to break through his thick skin.

A woman's scream startled her out of a trance. A mother pushing a stroller had passed the alley, forcing Iona to confront the scene she'd created. Two men lay unconscious and bleeding while she crouched over the third.

Iona burst to her feet. The nature of her attackers faded behind human guises, no longer shaded with darkness, or fitted with yellowed claws. They were supernatural no longer. In their place, she saw a group of drunken college guys in the wrong place.

Was this a new glamour? Or her hunger?

She stumbled away as Fairy Cigar mewled on the concrete, holding his broken arm that was bent in an awkward position. A sick feeling filled her gut.

Iona ran the opposite direction to get away from the scene before others arrived. As her feet pounded beneath, she tried to make sense of what she'd seen both before and after the fight. Had they revealed their true selves at the beginning, or had she deluded herself? Was this some trick of Ilyana's? Or one of her Coterie rivals?

The one thing she was certain of was that they'd been waiting for her in the alley, which meant whoever had put them in her path knew her final destination. She had to warn Zuri. Iona dialed her number, willing her to pick up. When the call went to voice mail, she screamed into the receiver and took off running.

TWENTY-NINE

The soothing mask made of éliata leaves harvested from the realm of Harmony was like being bathed in mint and having the tension drained away with a syringe. The foreign leaf was a narcotic, but nonaddictive and more expensive than a night out at a three-star restaurant. Adding to the relaxation was the misting of alchemical smoke drifting past her nostrils and the firm massaging of her sore feet. The only thing keeping Zuri from falling into a slumber was that Iona was late. Part of the enjoyment was going to be seeing her uncultured friend drowning in delirious pleasure. Getting an appointment at the Longing had required multiple favors.

Zuri was considering checking her phone to see if Iona had messaged when she realized that no one was working her feet and the relaxing sounds of otherworldly jungles was no longer playing.

The cold metal on her neck had Zuri surging into a sitting position, ripping the éliata mask from her face. Coral stood at her feet while Candi was behind with the blade to her neck.

"I could have gotten you an appointment," said Zuri as her heart beat furiously in her chest. "No need for drastic measures."

Coral tossed a bloody object in Zuri's lap. A pinky finger. She sat up straight and checked the visible Siren Sister for all her digits.

"Don't worry. We have our fingers. If we didn't then you wouldn't have woken up from your slumber. Ever."

"Then…?"

"The unfortunate manager that we tasked with bringing the Durge over to our company. He was told in no uncertain terms that this will be the last warning. You didn't tell us they were being managed by a fucking criminal gang."

"I...I didn't know."

"I actually believe you, because we know you're using someone else's blackmail."

"I told you before that it's mine."

"Bullshit," said Coral, leaning into her vision.

Dead black eyes regarded her like a shark readying to tear into a leg.

"You know this discussion would be easier without a knife to my throat."

"And our lives would be easier if your throat had a big gaping hole in it," whispered Candi as the blade was pressed against her flesh.

"Wait. I can fix it."

"Is it too late for that, sister?" asked Candi.

The other Siren Sister looked like an emperor presiding over gladiatorial games, deciding whether the thumb should go up or down.

"She still might have use to us alive. Though dead would feel *very* comforting. Especially if it keeps Blake and Scarlett from passing their second year."

An invisible belt tightened around Zuri's midsection as she tried to keep her face from reacting.

"You don't have to hide anything, dear Zuri. We already know. It's not like it isn't common knowledge because the rest of Blake's team told us. I think they'd be happier if the five of you didn't pass. Think of how much easier our remaining three years would be without you, Blake, Scarlett, and Orion."

"What about Iona?"

Coral rolled her eyes.

"She doesn't count. She should have never been here in the first place."

The fact that the Sisters hadn't killed her yet was a sign that there was a way out.

"What do you want?"

"We want what's owed us," growled Candi in her ear.

"I'll fix it. I'll get you the Durge. Or something equivalent."

"No. You'll get us the Durge. Period. No substitutions. No replacements. You were right before. The Durge is perfect for us. Once we get them, we'll have dozens of other big acts to choose from," said Coral.

"Okay. The Durge it is. Let me go and I'll start working on this right away," she said as she considered multiple avenues of blackmail.

Zuri started to sit up, but Candi pulled her back into the chair.

"We're not done with you yet. You don't seem to understand the gravity of your situation. So we want to make it crystal clear where your priorities lie."

"I'm one hundred percent on board. You don't have to threaten me twice."

Candi grabbed her by the throat.

"This *is* twice, you stupid bitch."

Zuri fought for air, but Candi was stronger than she expected. It was like being held down by metal clamps. After a few moments of quiet choking, Candi released her. Zuri rubbed her neck as she caught her breath again.

"What do you want?" asked Zuri, sensing things were worse than she'd first thought.

Coral unfolded her hand, revealing an eyeball. The size and shape suggested that it wasn't human, but she didn't know how to identify it.

"Am I supposed to know what that is?"

"It's from a thoratic fox. It cost a pretty penny to acquire."

The nature of the eyeball became clear. The eyes were a potent reagent for curses, because they could "see" the subject, and an eyeball from a psychic creature was worse.

"You want to curse me."

"We want you to *accept* the curse," said Coral as the corners of her lips curled.

Accepting the curse would make it nearly impossible to get rid of. She'd be dooming herself with whatever condition they wanted to impose.

"What's the deal?"

"One. You have to fix the Durge problem within a month or the curse will trigger. Two. If you try to mess with us by using any of the information in that stolen book of yours, the curse will trigger."

"The curse?"

"Professor Cornwallis will be notified of your transgression and your location."

Professor Cornwallis. It would be an unavoidable death sentence. If she fought back and managed to kill the professor, it would only draw the other professors down on her head once they discovered the truth. It was the perfect curse. It kept their hands clean and would eliminate her and the rest of her Second Year Games team. Zuri wondered if the Siren Sisters even wanted her to succeed, but the prize of the Durge was probably greater than the elimination of their rivals.

Certain death now, or the chance to avoid it later. There really wasn't a choice, unless she wanted a pyrrhic victory by forcing them to kill her now. It would doom the rest of her team, except for Iona, who would probably find a new life after Coterie much easier than the others. There was a certain poetry to the outcome, except that it meant she'd no longer be living.

"Fine. I accept."

The curse was simple. The Siren Sisters provided the scaffolding and the noose, while Zuri only had to put her neck through the hole and tighten the rope. The worst part wasn't even slipping the slimy fox eyeball past her lips, but the knowledge that her avenues of escape were narrowing down to nothing. When they finished the spell, Zuri felt a cold hand clench around her heart. There was no avoiding it now.

Zuri was alone, sitting in the pedicure chair and staring at the wall when Iona showed up, out of breath and looking like she'd had her own battle.

"What happened?"

The explanation was almost worse than the experience because she had to clarify the points that Iona didn't understand, which forced Zuri to illuminate every dark corner of the curse she'd willingly swallowed.

"There's a way out of it, right? Someone else to blackmail from the book? Or a counterspell that can unravel the curse?" asked Iona.

Zuri feigned musing the subject because she already knew the answer. There was no escape from the noose that she'd put around her own neck. The only thing she could control was whether or not she regretted stealing the book in the first place.

She refused to do that.

No. The problem wasn't that she'd decided to use the book to blackmail the Siren Sisters, the problem was that she hadn't been ruthless enough.

THIRTY

Three weeks. It'd taken them three weeks to get past the guards and through the middle city to the Black Gate. It was already the middle of March and the constant rain showers made coming to the Spire every day a chore as the city streets were choked with backed-up vehicles and puddles covered the sidewalks like miniature lakes.

Iona noticed Zuri standing apart with her head down while the others were discussing the problem they'd been presented by the gatekeeper that blocked their path. He stood at the head of a narrow bridge that crossed a wine-dark river.

"Thinking about the Siren Sisters?"

Zuri pinched her lips back. She looked like she'd eaten a lemon.

"Not them."

"Need help with the gang?"

"No. I don't want to get you involved."

"I don't think it's wise if you go alone," said Iona.

"This isn't a problem I can fix with a fight. If it comes to that, I'm already six feet under."

"If you want to call this off, we can tell the others we can't continue today. We finally made it to the Black Gate after all."

"No," said Zuri sternly. "I can't fix the gang problem today anyway and you need this."

"You need this too, Zuri. Don't turn into a martyr on me," said Iona.

Zuri refused to meet her gaze and surged forward to join the others, which left Iona with an achy heart. She'd only known her a little over a year, but she thought of her as a friend. *My only friend really.* It was hard to count Justine, given her oddness and the lack of interaction. They often went weeks without seeing the diminutive puppet.

"What's the deal?" Zuri asked, receiving a flat look from Blake.

"It's some sort of dumb puzzle," said Blake. "My *girlfriend* reminded me that you're good at those, so why don't you get fixing?"

Scarlett offered a sheepish smile. "You know she's good at this, babe. It's the right choice letting her take the lead."

The others turned towards the gatekeeper, but Iona didn't miss the hateful glare directed at Scarlett's back when she turned around. The last three weeks, she'd taken a more assertive role, which had made Blake more mercurial than normal.

The only one that hadn't changed was Orion, who was his regular stoic self, standing to the side and watching passively, but following their directions when given. He looked like a lump of clay until he started to move and then it was obvious how physically talented he was.

When Iona had first seen the gate guardian from the building tops, she'd thought him enormous and grotesque. Up close, he was still large, towering over Orion, who had to be at least six foot six now, but it was his demeanor that was more curious. Part of his bulk and size came from multiple layers of clothing that appeared to be made of old skin, and his face, while horrific, contained the countenance of intelligence with bright eyes peeking from a hunched forehead.

"How do we cross the bridge, Gatekeeper?" asked Zuri.

"The way to your destination is burdened with past deeds. To reach the Palace of the Dead, you must cross the Bridge of Souls carrying the lantern so you do not lose your way. The number of petitioners entering the palace must always be redundant while returning must always be complete."

"And what about this?" she asked, holding out the silver coin that the old woman had given them.

"That is the price to attempt to cross."

"This is stupid," said Blake with his mouth screwed up. "We should just kill the Gatekeeper."

"If it doesn't work, we can try that, babe," said Scarlett, patting his arm like a toddler.

"This should be simple," said Zuri. "It's a classic river problem like the one with the cannibals and missionaries. There might be a few wrinkles, but I'm certain I can figure it out."

The glint of anger in Blake's gaze worried Iona, but for once he kept his mouth shut.

"Okay," said Zuri, turning towards the bridge. "I think it works like this. The gatekeeper is Charon and this is the River Styx. The clue is in the silver coin, which is called an obol, which was the price that had to be paid to cross the river to gain access to the land of the dead. Knowing that helped me understand the complete and redundant terms, which were used by the ancient Greeks when talking about even and odd numbers. We'll have to cross in odd numbers and return in even numbers."

"See, babe, this should be easy," said Scarlett, playfully elbowing Blake, who didn't look amused.

"It might not be that easy. This lantern." Zuri gestured to the object on the pole which had a handle on either side. "He said we must cross the bridge holding the lantern, which only has two handles. That's our maximum number of crossers, but unfortunately we can't cross as even numbers."

"More than one hand can grab a handle," said Orion.

"That's true," said Zuri. "The bridge is only wide enough for two, but maybe we can try that. Do you think you could carry someone? We could fit Iona or Scarlett on your back. Three go over, two come back, until the end and then the last three go together."

"Seems simple," said Scarlett brightly.

"Puzzles are that way once you figure them out. Not that I'm not convinced that this is the answer. It does seem more simple than expected, but I guess if you don't know the history of Greek mathematics it may appear more difficult."

Zuri directed the group for the first crossing. Orion, Iona, and Scarlett.

When they approached the end of the bridge, Iona looked to Scarlett. "Which one of us rides the big man's back?"

Scarlett looked like she'd been asked to French kiss a cobra.

"It's all yours."

"How do you want…?"

She hadn't finished getting the words out when Orion scooped her up like a child, balancing her on his thick upper arm. She felt like she was sitting in a tree. To steady herself, Iona placed her hand against the back of his neck. She was surprised to learn that his heart was beating rather quickly despite standing around for the last ten minutes.

If it'd just been her and Orion, she would have asked if he was nervous about the bridge, but she didn't want to embarrass him. The fact that he'd spoken a short time ago was positive enough. She didn't want to push him any further.

With the lantern between them and three sets of hands on the handles, they stepped onto the bridge. Iona relaxed slightly when they made it a few feet onto the narrow length without penalty.

The journey took longer than expected and not just because Orion and Scarlett had to match pace. A cruel wind whipped across the surface, bringing howling voices that circled around them like the dead. Iona heard whispers and cold fingers brush against her skin.

By the time they reached the other side, Iona wanted to take a long shower.

"That was awful," she said as Orion let her down gently.

"Really?" asked Scarlett. "I didn't think it was that bad."

"Orion?"

He stared back passively, dousing her hopes that he trusted her.

"Let's go," she said to Orion, holding out her hand for the opposite half of the lantern.

As Iona had a moment alone with Orion on the journey across, she said, "I hope you don't mind me saying this, but I'm glad you got stuck with us in this group. I couldn't imagine going through this without you."

Orion bunched up his lips and she was sure it was going to be another one of those times he never said what he was thinking, but then he quietly spoke.

"I'd really hate for you to die alone. Again."

Iona smiled at the big man, who briefly met her gaze before turning away.

"You okay?" asked Zuri when they returned to the other side.

"Better than okay," Iona replied.

"I'm going this time," said Blake, yanking the lantern out of Orion's hand.

"I'll ride with you, Orion," said Zuri.

Iona was alone while the three of them crossed the bridge without incident. It wasn't until Orion and Zuri stepped onto the cobblestones for the return trip that it all went wrong. As soon as they moved onto the bridge, the lantern winked out and the entire group was standing on her side looking bewildered by the sudden dislocation.

"See. I knew you didn't know what the fuck you were talking about. You assholes think that being smart is the only thing that matters but that proves it. Again," said Blake.

"Why didn't that work?" Iona asked.

Zuri cupped her chin in her hand as she regarded the bridge, clearly trying to ignore Blake's outburst. Iona could see the way she purposely turned away from him.

"I don't know. It worked on the way over but not on the way back, which is strange. Let's try other variations so we can learn something."

This time Orion carried Zuri while Scarlett walked with the opposite side of the lantern, but they didn't make it more than two steps onto the cobblestones before getting transported back to their location.

"I don't get it," said Scarlett. "We're an odd number."

"Let's try something. This time just Orion and me will go."

The two of them crossed without incident, but when Zuri tried to bring the lantern back they both appeared next to them.

"Again, but this time Orion will come back."

To everyone's surprise, it worked the other way. Zuri came back to them by stepping onto the bridge.

"So Orion is even and I'm odd. But why?" asked Zuri.

No one had an answer. They stood around staring at their feet or looking into the distance. Iona had been quietly observing, but the comment sparked a thought.

She called Zuri over to the side.

"Did you think of something?"

"An idea, yeah, but I need something from you," said Iona. "But not in front of the others."

"Anything."

"I need your blood."

Zuri reacted as if she'd been slapped.

"You need what?"

"Blood. It's why I'm always craving red meat."

Iona told her friend the details from the trip with Ilyana. At first the looks she received were painful and made her feel like the girl who'd come into Coterie that first day when they called her Pig Girl. Then as she continued, Zuri seemed to understand without the judgement of the beginning and it was when she spoke that Iona knew why.

"You can see the people we've killed. Wish I'd had you during the trial. But why does that matter for this?" asked Zuri, staring at Blake.

"The first part of the gatekeeper's riddle. *The way to your destination is burdened with past deeds.* I think I counted as even because of Fenris."

"I had a part in killing him too," said Zuri.

"You helped set up the circuit, but I was the one that made the final connection. That makes me an even. Iona plus a single soul."

"And I'm an odd since I've never killed anyone."

"So you'll do it?"

"I really don't want you drinking my blood," said Zuri apprehensively.

"It's not really happening, remember? We're in the Games."

Zuri cursed under her breath. "How much do you need?"

"Not a lot. I don't think."

Shielding their bodies from the others, Zuri sliced a section of her forearm and Iona sucked away a mouthful before pulling away. The initial taste had been revolting, but then her body attuned to the metallic flavor which made her want more.

A low thrum filled her body as she stood tall, letting the blood work its magic. When she opened her eyes, it was as if she was seeing the world for the first time. At the corner of her vision, the city was hazy and incomplete as if it didn't quite exist except when she looked at it. Or that she could see the truth of the world beneath the one they were seeing.

A black mist rose from the river and the featureless gray sky had more definition than she first thought. Black shapes winged through the air, staying beneath the clouds, but outside the city walls, which upon closer inspection were made of bones rather than stone. It was as if the city had put on a more pleasing visage than its normal necropolis self.

Iona wondered if she went back to the area with the "city folk" if she'd see them as the creatures that attacked them rather than regular people. When her eyes came upon Charon, the gatekeeper, she saw a man—no, not a man—that was more defined and real than anything else around them. He burned like a miniature sun, but not in light, but power. He was frightening.

"What do you see?" asked Zuri.

Iona wasn't sure how long she'd been staring at the world, but her friend's comment snapped her back to reality. She focused her attention on the other three members of the team.

Orion was unsurprising, since she'd already seem him in this Veil light, so she quickly shifted to Scarlett. To Iona's surprise, the redhead had no Veil spirits around her while Blake had three separate shapes. She didn't need to peer further to know that one of them was Gemma, while the other two had less defined shapes. Iona leaned into the vision, sensing one of them was smaller, a boy he'd killed when he was much younger, maybe in elementary school, while the other she recognized as a second year named Oliver Bellamy who had mysteriously died last year.

"Me, Blake, and Orion are evens while you and Scarlett are odd. Does that help?"

Zuri nodded, but the tightness around her eyes told the tale of her thoughts.

"You can ask me details later if you want," said Iona. "But I think we should focus on getting over the bridge."

"Fair."

They returned to the group and Zuri explained the plan on how they would cross the bridge. Like their first attempt, Iona rode on Orion's shoulder, but this time she had Zuri's blood rushing through her head. Iona hadn't meant to, but she peered further into the black shape that shifted around Orion like a cloak. The vision of Orion leaning over her with hands around her throat came quick as she tried to escape the memory, but it held her fast, and she watched as veins popped out on his forehead. He spoke words in the throes of the struggle, which didn't reach her mind until they'd made it to the other side and he let her down, staring suspiciously.

"Why are you looking at me like that?" he asked with his jaw pulsing.

"Tired, I guess," she lied. "Time to go back."

As she made the solemn procession across the bridge holding one half of the lantern of souls, Iona couldn't help but review the vision from Orion's Veil spirit and hear the words he'd spoken as he choked the person to death.

"I hate you, Father."

THIRTY-ONE

Justine was lying on a bed of plushies in her mausoleum reading a secret history of Napoleon's wars and how he'd used mages to win the battle of Austerlitz. Later, he'd mistreated them, ignoring their contributions to his victories and they abandoned him to lose at Waterloo. There'd been a whole section of dusty histories that she'd rescued from the Coterie library, and she'd been working through them for the last three days.

The writing was dry, but the sections talking about how the mages had to hide their abilities and had been designated as "logistics" for Napoleon's army had been fascinating, especially when they ran into actual logistics members who expected them to understand their insular lingo.

Justine found the idea of living in plain sight to be fascinating, which had kept her turning the pages, so much that she hadn't heard the noises outside until they were loud enough she couldn't ignore them.

"Ak'hal tal nom'adi fo."

The rumbling voice drew her towards the crack, until she was peering out into the third level which remained in dim shadow.

Justine almost didn't recognize the monster because he was standing on two feet and wearing robes which displayed embroidered runes across silk banners that cascaded down the front hems.

The monster spoke in his strange language again. It sounded like a version of Kemetic, but it was far enough to the edges she had difficulty understanding. Then the monster turned its back and headed towards the back of the level. He stopped momentarily, checking behind to see if she was following.

Excitement. Trepidation. They flooded her body in ways that almost made her feel human again.

Little legs took longer to catch up, but she was a few steps behind him before he passed the pyramid. The monster was much different than the last time she'd seen him feeding on the first year in the lower levels.

Who are you? Or what are you?

The answer came in the form of a name that best fit, because she didn't want to keep calling him "the monster." He was clearly more than that.

Ammit.

The name came from the ancient Egyptian god in charge of judging the souls of the dead and it felt close enough that she decided that's what she'd call him.

Ammit traveled past the black pools and across the circuits with little concern. Occasionally when the tarry, living substance in the pools started to bubble up, Ammit would speak roughly in its direction and the surface would fall back flat.

They reached a wall with no decoration or modifications. Ammit gestured in a way that suggested magic, which woke hidden runes on the sandstone. He touched them in a specific order and a door appeared and shifted to the side, revealing a dark passage.

Justine hesitated. Ammit had shown no ill intent towards her but that didn't mean he didn't have plans. If she'd been in her human body, there'd be no way she would have followed Ammit, but this sorcery-aided wooden body gave her freedom from mortal worries, providing an opportunity she wouldn't have otherwise. She went in.

A ramp led down to a wide chamber that she hadn't seen before. The walls were covered in Egyptian murals with oversized hieroglyphs. At the center a ritual circle had been carved into the stone.

"Help me. I don't want to die."

She hadn't seen the person strapped to the stone at the center of the ritual circle until he'd spoken. The mysteries of the room had kept her distracted.

The prisoner was splayed with his arms and legs wide, held by leather straps that came out of the stone. He looked like he was dressed to attend a fashionable party, wearing a tan silk shirt that had helped him blend into the stone. She didn't recognize him, which meant he'd probably come from one of the new magic prep schools.

Justine checked back to Ammit, who watched her like a father checking to make sure his brood didn't get too far away. The beat of her double hearts made her giddy and a little sad.

As she moved around to his head, he recoiled.

"What in Merlin's name are you?" he asked, voice cracking.

His eyes were blotchy and red from crying.

"What's your name?" she asked.

It'd been a long time since she'd spoken to someone other than Zuri or Iona.

"I...I'm Drake, Drake Porter. What is this place? Are we still in the Obelisk?"

The fear in his eyes was palpable. He looked like a sudden movement could make him pass out. She didn't want to torment him. Not with so little time left.

"Yes. This is the Obelisk."

Seeing his reaction to her voice reminded her that it was high and tinny, a function of her miniature voice box.

"Am I going to die?"

"I don't know," she lied.

His voice dropped to a whisper.

"Please. Get me out of here."

Their conversation was interrupted when Ammit approached and spoke in his language. She caught the intent, which was to say that it was time for the ceremony.

Justine reached out and squeezed his hand, which confused Drake as he watched Ammit's approach.

She left Drake's side, taking position ninety degrees from Ammit's location at his feet. Ammit began speaking again, the melodic flow of the ritual coaxing warm light from the runes around the outside of the circle. She sensed the power right away. This was not the parlor tricks of battle spells like making sparks with two rocks, but not understanding why. Ammit had complete command of his power, the words shaping and distorting the magic flowing from his limbs.

When he'd been a four-legged beast, snapping off limbs and devouring his unfortunate victims, Ammit had been frightening in the way monsters in the dark consumed the childish mind. But as a two-legged humanoid displaying a mastery of ritual magic, Justine found herself breathless with excitement.

Transfixed by the rough words coming from his long, jagged snout, Justine watched as the ritual came to fruition. When the runes glowed brightest and Drake squirmed in the center like a pig on a spit, Ammit slapped his hands together, creating a thunderclap.

Ammit turned to her, producing a ritual blade that had been hidden in his robes. The moment he offered it, she knew why she'd been invited.

Justine didn't know what would happen if she refused the deed. Would he snap her wooden body in two, or let her leave the chamber without consequence? Trapped by the indecision, she didn't immediately move to take the blade.

Ammit gestured with his clawed hand towards the blade and then towards the exit. A choice. Her choice.

The desire to grip the blade and plunge it into Drake's heart made her feel light-headed.

She glanced around the room. The ritual. The runes. This was real power. Not the awkward spells that her classmates deigned to cast.

Ammit shook the blade and spoke in his language. His toothy grin was filled with promise. Justine sensed that if she went through with the ritual, the direction of her life would veer from the bargain she'd made with her teammates, to one with possibilities untold.

"What happens if I do this?" she asked.

Ammit tapped on his chest twice. Then he made a fist and lifted it into the air, opening it at the apex.

The exact meaning of his gestures was hard to fathom, but she understood the suggestion of improvement and being lifted up. Ammit offered a bargain. Kill the first year in exchange for unknown power.

But if she went through with it, what would that mean for her? The part of her that she liked to think of as Ludmilla would do it in an instant. But Justine? She was still weak from her flesh-life. Too scared to do what was necessary like when she'd refused to kill Limon and was kicked out of her group. Why was this any different?

But she was less Justine and more Ludmilla these days. Living away from the other students had let her find her true self. But this wasn't just about who she was. It was a question of power and allies.

The fact that her current fate was tied to Zuri and Iona wasn't lost on her. If they failed at the Second Year Games, or stumbled during any of the following years, she would be trapped in the Obelisk without help. Existing outside Coterie without help would be dangerous. She was too small and physically weak to be able to protect herself cleanly. While she knew magic and could perform it adequately, she knew she was outmatched against most competent mages, who would probably see her as a thing to be destroyed.

Ammit repeated the chest tapping, rising fist gesture, then shook the blade.

She checked to the center of the circle. Drake was unconscious. The ritual had knocked him out. She wasn't sure she could do it otherwise.

Justine took the ritual dagger.

She approached the unconscious first year.

When she checked back to Ammit, the monster gestured for her to continue.

Justine closed her eyes as she gathered the blade between her two wooden hands. She raised it high overhead, checking back once more to see Ammit grinning his wide grin. She hesitated, knowing there was no turning back once she did the deed.

Drake's brown eyes flashed open, full of fear.

Justine slammed the blade into his chest.

THIRTY-TWO

Zuri had never been interested in the lives of the city's gangs until the Siren Sisters had gotten ahold of her. Before that, the gangs were like rats in the alleyways, an unfortunate fact of the city, but one she didn't stoop to understand.

She had a month to deal with the gangs before the curse kicked in, which gave her time to study. She needed to know what she was walking into, and how she might bend them to her will.

There were two main groups of gangs. The ones that lived in the Undercity and those that operated on the streets of Invictus. The Undercity gang was called the Alliance and had become a monstrosity of size and influence. A number of gangs, or clans as they liked to call themselves—as if that would change the nature of what they did—had been consolidated under one banner and were led by a mysterious maetrie figure that she'd heard had legitimate business contacts in the city.

But thankfully, the Alliance wasn't her concern.

Zuri was relieved to learn that it was a smaller gang called the Dark Nine that made its home in the second ward where it had moved from a primarily drug-based income to weaseling into the entertainment business amongst a few other ventures. They'd moved from sponsoring a few minor bands to grabbing the biggest up-and-coming group on the market with The Durge, turning the Dark Nine legitimate in the eyes of the world.

They were formidable with around sixty members, and a handful had faez crystals, which meant she wouldn't be able to easily intimidate them with her magic. In fact, she realized that trying to go head-on would only result in a quick death.

Knowing that force wasn't going to get the job done, she'd need to be more subtle.

More ruthless.

Had the Dark Nine been a part of regular society, the blue book might have had blackmail she could use, but until recently, they'd been operating on the fringes, so she was essentially working from scratch.

The building looked like any other business in the back of the second ward: brick front, huge glass window with a stencil that read Dark Nine Entertainment Inc., and a tricolor awning that blocked the sun when it was high in the sky. The only difference was the two guys smoking cigarettes and watching the sidewalk with the eyes of a hawk.

Zuri wore her best black pantsuit with gold edging that made her skin glow. She'd loaded up with elixirs and wards in the SUV then had Gentry drop her off outside the business where the guards stared at her suspiciously.

She strode to the front, pausing to glare at the nearest until he opened the door.

The interior was cheap carpet and garage sale furniture. A woman sitting behind a desk was playing a game on her phone that made dinging noises every time she touched it with her long fingernail. She did a double take before speaking in a whiny voice while still playing the game.

"How can I help you?"

Zuri opened a clutch purse, pulling out a business card which she handed over to the woman. She studied it briefly before an exclamation slipped out of her lips.

"Oh."

"I'd like to speak to Adrian Constantin."

The desk attendant let her tongue rest on her lower teeth.

"He ain't here right now. You'll have to come back later."

Zuri snatched the woman's phone out of her hands, and when she protested, a quick spell knocked her into the seat as eyes rolled into the back of her head.

After searching through her contacts, Zuri pulled up Adrian's information, then found the schedule, which had him at a nearby dining establishment. Before she left, Zuri slipped the girl an elixir that would make the last fifteen minutes of memory fuzzy. If anyone asked, she wouldn't be able to tell anything other than she'd been visited.

"To the French Constable," she told Gentry when she was in the back of the SUV.

The first part had gone off without a problem, but now was the hard part. If Adrian Constantin didn't believe her then this would be a very short and painful visit.

The French Constable was closer to the Spire in the second, which was where the legitimate entertainment businesses usually operated.

"I need you to take me to Adrian Constantin," she told the hostess.

"I can't do that," said the woman with a trembling voice.

Zuri grabbed the book off the hostess stand and when the woman tried to grab it back, she let a miniature flame tornado dance around her palm while she found the correct location.

"Is this a private booth or an open table?"

"Open table, but it's..."

Zuri left the woman, using the hostess map to navigate the restaurant. The interior was dim with lots of white marble and vivid paintings, some of which would have gone nicely on a wall in the Obelisk.

The hostess trailed behind, trying to tell her that she couldn't just barge in, but Zuri ignored her. She spotted Adrian in back, seated with two nervous looking guys half his age.

Adrian himself was quite handsome—a fifty-something distinguished gentleman in a tailored suit. His guests, on the other hand, looked like they were more comfortable snorting powders off the bathroom sink in a dive bar.

When she reached his section of the restaurant, two hard-looking men from another table stood up and put a hand on their jackets where Zuri could see a bulge. Knowing they wouldn't start firing in the restaurant, Zuri walked right past them, grabbed an empty chair from a nearby table, and dragged it across the marble. It made an awful squeaking noise until she set it down at the empty spot.

The half-smile was welcoming, but the glint in his brown eyes was not.

"Who the fuck are you?"

"I'm sorry, Mr. Constantin. She barged right past me," said the hostess.

Zuri maintained eye contact as she slid her business card across the tablecloth. He stopped it with one finger and read it without lifting the paper. The anger softened as he turned his head towards his two guests.

"Nathan. Lionel. It seems I have some business I need to attend to, but we'll continue our conversation later. You're going to be big stars."

The two guys looked relieved as they followed the hostess out of the main area.

"I was wondering when your boss might send someone along. I would have preferred to know you were coming, Miss Santos."

"And I prefer to live a long life," said Zuri.

He clucked his tongue.

"You look rather young for your line of business."

"Not only is speculating about a woman's age rude, but in this age of sorcery, it's unwise too."

He nodded.

"What does the Alliance want?"

"We're interested in getting into the entertainment business."

Adrian tried to hide his distaste, but his jowls pulsed in silent anger. While he was the head of a small criminal gang, he was in some ways like any other business that had a larger competitor planning to move into their realm. Adrian had clearly been expecting this, which made her job even easier. She hoped.

"I'm not interested."

"But the Alliance is. You would be well compensated, of course, and the option for further cooperation would be opened. My boss likes to keep things civil when possible."

"I've heard that," said Adrian. "He runs quite the operation in the Undercity. But isn't that a lot to handle? Maybe it'd be best if we kept our two worlds apart. There's been a lot of talk up here."

"Talk is good. We like talk. We had a lot of great conversations with the Black Crows a few years ago."

"I thought that was the RZR?"

Zuri smiled. There were too many gangs and alliances for her to really know what was going on. Better to stay vague.

"It's all the same now, isn't it?"

Adrian stared back with the menace of a silverback gorilla.

"I suppose it is." He took a drink from his whiskey. "I'm listening."

Zuri reached into her jacket, which caused a little ruckus from his guards until he waved them off. She pulled out a small ring case and slid it across the table.

"What is this?" he asked with his fingers on the velvet case.

"A gift."

His eyebrows arched when he peeked inside. Acquiring the faez crystal had cost her most of her current funds, and the trust that supplied her regular allowance wouldn't refill it until the end of the school year. She didn't really know what the faez crystal did, but that didn't matter as long as Adrian understood.

"It's not a gift."

"That's true."

"What do you want?"

"The Durge."

It was as if a gunshot had gone off. He pounded his fist on the table, rattling glasses and drawing attention to their conversation.

"I expected a polite request, something small and almost acceptable. Boil the frog kind of request, but this," he said in a hushed but angry tone, "this is outright theft. No stupid jewel, not even this"—he put his hand over the velvet case—"can make up for what you're asking. I've already had to deal with greedy outsiders once."

"That's the thing, Adrian. This isn't just about the Alliance, or my boss. You see, he has certain designs on the city, which require making deals with the assholes who run things."

Realization smoothed his brow as he leaned back, the fury in his chest contained for the moment, but she could see how easily he might blow.

"You're not doing this for you, you're doing this for those damn freaks."

"The Thalassa family is well respected in many circles. Including places like this." Zuri gestured around. "I wouldn't say that too loud unless you're prepared to back up your words. Need I remind you that they're powerful sirens as well as Coterie mages with connections that include the Dreadmarshes."

Adrian's nostrils flared as he considered her words. He took a long draw from his whiskey, slamming the glass onto the table and staring into the distance. They weren't connected to the Dreadmarshes, but she assumed he wouldn't know the inner workings of the elite just as she didn't understand the criminal underworld.

"Adrian. I know this is hard, but think of what you're gaining. You think like my boss. The other stuff we do. It's effective, but it comes with risks. But these families like the Thalassas and the Dreadmarshes, they get to pillage this world not as criminals, but people to be celebrated. They're honored at charity balls, or in the newspapers and magazines with big puff pieces talking about their cars and houses. But they're still criminals. They just do it with an air of legitimacy. You want that just like my boss does. Like my boss is going to get."

"What if I just kill you?"

His right hand was beneath the table. Even a year ago, she wasn't sure how she would have reacted, but after facing down certain death in the Obelisk from traps and her fellow classmates, the simple threat of being shot in the middle of a restaurant seemed laughable.

"It won't stop anything. I will admit I would be rather disappointed if the unlikely event happened."

Zuri snapped her fingers, which activated the spell. Her fingernails glowed a hazy crimson.

"What's that supposed to do?" he asked.

She nodded towards the business card, which showed the same hazy crimson. His gaze followed the other blotches of sorcerous light, which included the edge of his whiskey glass.

"What did you do to me?"

"Nothing as long as I walk out of here alive. I never go anywhere without precautions. You never know when someone is willing to burn it all down for spite."

The crimson haze was harmless. A trick from prep school to find out who had been kissing who at sleepovers, but Adrian wouldn't know that since he wasn't a mage, nor did he employ one in his retinue.

"This can be a very profitable relationship, Adrian. My boss has big plans. Why not get in on the ground floor early? What you make managing the Durge is peanuts compared to the real prize. Wouldn't you like to own parts of the alchemy industry in the city? Or own more than a dime store business front and a few dozen goons to do your bidding? Come on, Adrian. You want more than the occasional meal at the French Constable. Wouldn't you like to go to the places that you can't get into without knowing the right people? This gift is only the opening move. There's more to come. Much more."

"I'll consider it."

Zuri put her hand over his, which was still resting on the velvet case as she leaned forward. The spell she'd used had the side effect of making her flesh cold, which made him flinch.

"Notify the Durge that they will be managed by the Thalassa family, or my boss will send an army of his warriors into the city. By the time he's done, no one will ever utter the name the Dark Nine, even in memory or jest, for fear of his retribution."

She stared into his eyes, maintaining eye contact until he finally looked away while yanking his hand back.

"It'll be done."

"Thank you." She pushed back from the table, rising like a cobra above him. "I look forward to our continued business relationship. Feel free to contact me if you have requests. I'm sure I can open a lot of doors that are currently closed."

Zuri strode out of the restaurant high on adrenaline and hubris. By the time she slid into the back of the SUV, her hands were shaking and her mind was racing with excitement. She let out a whoop as the SUV surged into traffic.

"Seven hells, that was amazing."

Her pucker had been at DEFCON nine going in, but now that it was over—and she'd pulled it off—she felt like the day she knew she was going to be a mage. Zuri had always focused on scholarship and wit, thinking that those would carry her through the years at Coterie. She'd thought that those that relied on blackmail and other coarse tactics had to because they didn't have the skills to do what she did.

But now she understood the thrill of the hunt. And victory.

"I fucking killed it."

Zuri pounded a fist into an open hand. Her body raced with exhilaration. She leaned back into the seat, smoothing the fabric of her pant leg.

There was more to do. It wasn't like Adrian would sit back forever. He was probably screaming at his subordinates about how she'd just walked in and threatened him. Poisoned him too. Eventually, the scheme would unravel. She knew that. She couldn't pretend to be the Alliance's mage conciliator without consequence, but getting out from under the curse was her first priority. Professor Cornwallis was a death sentence hanging over her head. She'd rather face the entirety of the Dark Nine than the professor that had earned her reputation in the shadows of the Obelisk.

"Back to the Obelisk?" asked Gentry, peering through the rearview mirror.

"No," she said, humming with energy. "No. Take me to the Amber & Smoke. I need to celebrate."

THIRTY-THREE

The last two weeks, the group had worked together like a well-oiled machine in the Second Year Games. Iona couldn't believe it. Even Zuri had lost the scowl she wore whenever Blake was giving directions. Maybe it was the nearness to their goal that brought the cooperation, knowing that they'd only have to tolerate each other for a little bit longer, or that the inner city was one big brawl, which appealed to Blake's animal spirits. It helped that they were one of the few groups to make it to the Palace of the Dead. Victory was in sight. They only had to extend their grasp a little further.

Iona leaned against the stone gargoyle at the bottom of the grand stairs that climbed towards a decadent portico. The covered roof was the last major obstacle before they entered the palace and a perfect resting spot before they had to rejoin the battle. Blake had given them ten minutes to rest and renew their wards.

She reread the handwritten letter from Ilyana for a third time since she'd received it that morning. The paper was exquisite, the kind of chunky thick stuff that could only be found at specialty shops, and the penmanship immaculate, which told Iona how important the message was.

Dearest Iona,

I know you're buried with your university studies, but I assure you, these trials are meaningless compared to what I can show you. Our father gifted us with great power, it only needs to be unlocked. I think you know deep in your heart what that means.

Join me at Vânatoare in two days. I've requested the chef's special for two. I think you'll find this meal more illuminating than any of the dusty tomes you must suffer through in your place of schooling. If you join me, I'll tell you everything you want to know about our family and our heritage. Don't disappoint me.

Your loving sister,
Ilyana Storm

Iona tucked the paper into an inner pocket and stared back at the city they'd already traversed.

"Must be important to read it that many times."

To her surprise, Orion was sitting on the steps, hands clasped in front. He matched the size and the stoney gaze of the gargoyles.

"It's from my sister. Half-sister," she added, rolling her eyes.

"Family can be confusing."

Iona wanted to say something comforting, but she feared it would reveal her knowledge that Orion had killed his father.

"Very."

The final phrase "don't disappoint me" was loaded with threat. Join me at the Vânatoare, or I'll track you down and kill you. Iona had no doubt that Ilyana was more powerful than her and Zuri combined. Or even a dozen Coterie students. Which made trying to fight back a pointless endeavor. A death sentence for everyone involved.

"You look like you're weighing a decision," said Orion.

Iona let a smile ghost her lips before faltering to emptiness.

"I don't even know if it's a decision."

"They feel like that, don't they?"

Orion rose from the stairs. He was a giant of a man, but he moved like velvet across silk.

"Hey, Orion."

He paused, checking over his shoulder.

"Are we friends? I want to believe we're friends, but I don't know."

She watched him return to the others, pondering the meaning of both his final statement and his lack of response to her question. If anyone would understand powerful, but flawed and dangerous family, it would be Orion Dreadmarsh. Had he guessed her dilemma? Or was his comment about himself?

"You okay?" asked Zuri upon approach.

"I should ask you that. How does it feel to know one way or another that we won't have to see Blake and Scarlett much longer?"

"I'll feel better once I know that the elixir can provide the answer to our portal problem. Until then, everything's in limbo."

"At least you don't have a Siren Sister problem anymore," said Iona.

Zuri grinned wide, the light in her eyes shining like a beacon.

"It was like solving a puzzle without touching any of the pieces. It was thrilling. I don't know why I've never done that before."

"Careful. It almost looks like you're enjoying the game."

"Only for as long as necessary. I'm still boring ol' Zuri Musa. How's Ilyana? Any problems I need to worry about?"

The glance at her chest where the letter was hidden suggested she'd guessed the nature of the message.

"No problems. Just, you know, family."

Zuri checked over her shoulder to where Blake had broken from his conversation with Scarlett.

"Looks like we're back on soon. Better get ready."

Everyone started refreshing their wards and protections while Iona, for the umpteenth time, contemplated her decision with Ilyana. On one hand, her half-sister promised great power, and Iona's dabbling with blood magic had proved how much could be gained from that route. On the other, Iona didn't like the implications of where Ilyana was getting her power. It was one thing to cull a street rat, but Iona was sure that the restaurant served less available meats. Additionally, Iona didn't want to abandon Zuri, which would doom her chances in the Obelisk. But what choice did she have? Defying Ilyana was certain death, so wouldn't it be easier to let her half-sister show her the way? At least she would get to learn more about her family and herself.

I'm a monster, after all, why fight it?

"Alright, kiddies, it's time to get down," said Blake, bouncing around like a jock getting ready for the big game. "We're almost to the prize. Let's show these muthas how Coterie gets it done."

"Hells yeah, babe," said Scarlett, clapping her hands like a cheerleader.

For once, Blake didn't angrily glare at her, which had been a frequent response to recent comments. Maybe they'd made up, or maybe Blake was too focused on winning to be mad. Iona had been privately hoping the pair would break up during the endless and frustrating games, making the return to the Obelisk easier, but it appeared they had no such luck.

The five of them stepped to the top of the stairs, battle on their minds. After many months and thousands of hours of magical fighting in the City of the Dead, their tactics looked nothing like when they'd first entered the Second Year Games.

Orion took point, loading up on damaging buffs to help keep the mobs focused on him, while Scarlett used her illusions to confuse when the numbers grew too large. Zuri's main task was refreshing the spell that shared damage with the rest of the team while Iona used her charged-up tattoos to heal Orion. This left Blake free to unload elemental damage across the battlefield to annihilate their foes whenever they grouped up to attack Orion.

The moment they entered the portico, crawly things came pouring out of the side passages, like humanoid spiders with backward facing knees and elbows. At first the numbers were manageable, but then they kept growing, faster than Blake's flame waves could eliminate, which forced Iona to switch to offense, adding her magic to the fight.

Progress was slow. It was like trying to wade against the tide while carrying a hundred-pound pack. Every time Iona thought they might get a break, a new wave of crawlies emerged, until finally, when they stepped on a stone seal, their attackers faded away leaving them to contemplate the next obstacle.

At the end of the portico was a huge stone door covered in murals revealing an ancient battlefield. Standing guard and blocking their path to the inner palace was a pair of huge death giants that made Orion look like a child. They wore all black with skulls as their sigils and each carried a massive blade that could cut a car in half.

"Man they have some big balls underneath those loincloths," laughed Blake, expecting others to join him.

When it was no one but Scarlett, he frowned and gestured towards Orion.

"Same as before. Grab that agro right away. I don't think we can take any hits from those big boys."

Orion didn't acknowledge the request. He never did. He only stared back with the ambivalence of a lump of stone.

Then without comment or fanfare, Orion stepped forward, smashed his fists together, and unleashed twin shadow whips that slashed the chests of the death giants.

The two massive humanoids bellowed with rage, thundering forward and shaking the ground. The first brought his massive blade high overhead, while the second thrust his forward in a quick attack.

Iona saw that Orion had adjusted to the first, but the second attack was going to reach him earlier, so she let her bolstering ward drop and blasted the blade with a force bolt. The dislocating energy bounced off the heavy weapon, barely deflecting it from its trajectory.

At the last second, Orion managed to get his shield into place, but the majority of the momentum crashed into his chest, throwing him into the group. The others scattered like wind-blown leaves, their carefully constructed magical wedge broken apart by the brutal attack.

"Over here, you big-balled pussies!"

The two death giants gave her little attention, looking like they'd prefer to smash her fallen companions.

Knowing that her force bolts wouldn't be strong enough, Iona funneled faez from her tattoos into the blast, hitting the first giant hard enough across the jaw to snap his head back. The roar and subsequent rage made her wonder if she'd made a mistake.

Iona scurried behind the stone column, which was torn in half by the swinging blade, sending stone dust into a cloud. She ran to the next, but the giant's long strides made it hard to outrun.

A second column was demolished. Shards of stone slammed her in the back, sending her spinning against the wall near the huge doors. She thought she was dead until Orion appeared, blocking the swinging blade with his shield.

The battle turned to chaos. The other three were barely staying ahead of the death giant, while Orion was defending her from annihilation. She tried a few errant shots of magic, but the crackling energy did little to hurt their opponent. The death giants seemed impervious to magic from a distance. The only thing that was working was the heavy blows from Orion, but he was too busy playing defense to provide much damage.

A stupid idea popped into her head.

"Distract him on the count of three," she called to Orion.

Not knowing if he had heard, she prepared her spell, running towards the death giant as she was calling out her count. If he didn't confuse their opponent, she was going to be paste.

"Three!"

The moment she yelled the final number, Iona cast cloud jump, using the little fluffy pads as stairs to run right up to the giant's groin. She was vaguely aware that Orion had somehow grabbed the big sword and was fighting the death giant for control, when she slipped under the loincloth, held her hands out, and from near point blank unleashed the rest of her stored magic from the tattoo into a force blast directly into the death giant's cloth-wrapped balls.

The scream was followed by the death giant tipping backwards, holding onto its injured groin, leaving Orion full control of the massive weapon. By the time the giant hit the ground, Orion had flipped the hilt around and with the comically overlarge blade, decapitated the death giant.

Once the death giant was dead, the second was easy to topple, given their five-on-one advantage. In a matter of a few minutes of battle, the two death giants were dead and the way to the inner palace was open.

"Rest, recharge, and re-ward," said Blake. "We're almost there."

Iona caught up with Orion, who was breathing heavily for once.

"Thanks for the assist. It's kinda fun working with you like that," she said, offering a coy smile.

With a flat stare, he responded, "It's a ball."

The joke—and gods above and below she hoped it was a joke—made her snort with laughter. The corner of his wide mouth curled up momentarily before his eyes shifted towards Blake and his chin fell.

"I'm ready to be done with this too, buddy," she said, hoping the familial term wasn't overstepping her bounds.

Orion bobbed his head with a weak smile as he continued refreshing his wards.

Blake stood before the twin stone doors, rubbing his hands and grinning with glee.

"No one else is this far. We're going to finish this damn thing and then I don't have to see you people like this ever again."

Iona almost got the impression he was talking to himself. Or maybe he just didn't care.

When Blake pushed the enormous doors wide, Iona had a sense of impending doom. The challenges of the game had gotten successively harder and now that they were at the Palace of the Dead, they should expect brutally difficult obstacles.

The interior was much like the outside. Lots of plain stone sometimes shaded with corrosion, high arching ceilings, and gray marble floors.

"That can't be," muttered Zuri.

Across from the five of them, standing in a line at the same intervals, stood familiar figures. If the towering figure of Orion wasn't clear enough, Iona gasped when she saw the pale, white-haired version of herself standing with the other shadows.

"I guess if anyone's capable of beating me, it would be me," said Blake, shooting them a cocky grin.

Iona wasn't so sure of herself. She didn't like the idea of fighting a mirror Iona.

"I don't want to kill myself," said Scarlett grimly.

Blake snorted.

"Don't worry, babe. I'll happily kill you. Just don't let me die."

The comment made Scarlett's head snap up. Normally, she would smile back at Blake as if it were an inside joke, but she stared longer than normal.

"What's the plan?" asked Zuri.

"Don't die, you assholes," said Blake.

The five mirror versions of themselves watched passively as they approached. Iona was contemplating what kind of tactics might work when their five opposites broke into a sprint as if a silent gun had fired.

Iona waited until the last moment to blast mirror-Iona with a force bolt, but her other half leapt over the streaking magic. She caught a fist across the jaw, followed by the rake of fingernails, leaving blood trails on her face.

In a matter of seconds, Iona was fighting for her life. The mirror-Iona was stronger, faster, and more determined. She took blows across the head and chest, the relentless attacks curling Iona into a ball.

Hoping that her friends were faring better, she snuck a glance at the other battles to see similar fates. Orion was being choked out by the other version of him, while Scarlett was getting attacked by illusionary Scarletts from all directions. Only Blake seemed to be holding his own, fighting back with dagger and flame.

She never saw Zuri, because the mirror-Iona stopped pummeling her and opened her mouth wide enough to swallow a basketball. Then shadows rushed out of the horrific cavern, collapsing around her, pulling Iona into the marble floor.

THIRTY-FOUR

The air had an autumnal chill as the wind rustled the leaves like rattles. Zuri pulled her arms around her chest to protect against the cold as a sliver of a moon cast silver shadows across the forest.

"Burn, baby, burn!"

Blake stood over the pile of wood, sending flame into the kindling until it crackled to life, sparks jumping into the air and rising between the gap in the trees.

"I brought fire starters, babe. You didn't have to do that."

He looked over his shoulder, grinning with delight.

"I didn't *have* to, but I *wanted* to."

"We only have a few more years until we can get into the Halls. Don't go mad before we get there," said Zuri as she rubbed her hands together.

"You should be thanking me, not giving me a lecture."

"Sorry, babe. You're right. Thank you for the warm fire. I love the warmth of its heat and my faez-mad boyfriend," she said, rolling her eyes.

The crunching of leaves had her spinning around to see Gemma coming out of the darkness of the woods. Auburn hair with little braids framed her cherubic face which was pink from the cool air. She wore a cutoff Garbage Kings T-shirt that showed off the sleeve of tattoos on her left arm.

"Oh Merlin, I feel better. I had to piss like a racehorse on steroids," she said, climbing onto the log and holding her hands out towards the fire.

Zuri hadn't really questioned where she was until her dead friend had come walking out of the woods.

Gemma turned her head and, in true Gemma fashion, pursed her lips while raising an inquisitive eyebrow.

"Is there a big, fat, juicy spider on my face or something? Let me know where, because it sounds like a tasty snack."

Zuri swallowed as she tried to find the words.

"I...I miss you."

Gemma leaned away.

"I wasn't gone that long. It was a massive piss, but nothing record breaking. If it'd been a dump, I would understand. I could have named it Blake."

"Fuck off, Gemma."

He smiled, but it didn't extend to the eyes. She wasn't sure why she hadn't seen it before. Blake hated Gemma. Then she realized what day it was and panic set in.

"Hey, you two. I'm not feeling good. Can we go home?"

"No way, you big pussy," said Gemma, laughing as she punched her in the arm. "I have a bet to win."

The bet.

An invisible guillotine hanging over her friend's head.

"My guts are churning. Can't we do this another time?" asked Zuri, holding her midsection.

"No way," said Blake. "Miss Big Mouth isn't getting out of our bet that easily. Just as soon as she's ready. I brought everything she needs."

Memories that she'd pushed away for years came flooding back. Zuri couldn't breathe. She wanted out of this vision.

"No really. I need to go. Right now."

She got up to leave, but neither Blake nor Gemma made a move to follow. So she grabbed Gemma's arm, but she yanked it away.

"What's your problem? I swear. You get weirder every year," said Gemma. "Which frankly is a good thing. If you don't pull that stick out of your ass soon, it's going to turn to mulch."

"She's just fine as she is, Gemma. Stop fucking with her head," said Blake as he angrily poked the fire.

"Come on, you two. Please. Can we leave? I don't want to do this. Not tonight."

Not ever.

"What? You afraid someone's going to die or something tonight?" asked Blake, dead-eyed.

There it was. She saw right through him.

"I need to go. Come on, Gemma. Let's get out of here."

"And lose the bet? No way. I'm sick of hearing Blake's bullshit. I'm going to summon that imp and prove to him once and for all that he's a blowhard and I'm the Queen of All Things. Your basic bad bitch. So let's go. I left the summoning stuff in the pavilion."

A blink and she was standing in the pavilion with her arms clutched to her chest, while Gemma was carefully laying out the salt in a perfect circle. Blake sat on the picnic bench, watching like a vulture waiting for a rabbit to die.

"No, no, no. We're not doing this. Please."

"What's your problem?" asked Blake.

"I don't care what you have to say. If she does this, she dies. You messed with the salt or something."

It didn't get the reaction she expected. Blake smiled sweetly and patted the spot next to him.

"You're paranoid, babe. Why don't you sit by me? I'll keep you warm. Or better yet, we can sneak back to the fire while she finishes up. We'll knock a quick one out and then we can watch the festivities."

"I'm gonna do this," said Gemma, over her shoulder.

In a panic, Zuri ran forward and kicked the salt circle. The white powder exploded across the concrete floor, then reversed course and returned to the line.

"No..."

Zuri did it again. And again. And again. Each time the salt reformed.

"You've gone mad as my uncle," said Blake. "Babe. Sit down. Now. Before you hurt yourself, or Gemma. Don't you want her to succeed?"

Zuri didn't remember moving, but then she was sitting next to Blake while he had his arm around her shoulders. She tried to get up but her feet were anchored to the spot.

"No. Help," she whispered.

The ritual began despite Zuri's best attempts to stop it. She watched as Gemma performed the ritual movements perfectly, the Old English words sounding sinister in the cool autumn air. Zuri tried to rise from her spot, but her legs felt like lead and her arms wouldn't move as if she'd fallen asleep on them.

"No, please..."

As the ritual drew to completion, the wind picked up, whirling around the pavilion but touching nothing inside. For a few seconds, tiny frogs rained down on the tin roof and into the wet leaves.

Zuri couldn't breathe. She remembered this moment as if it'd been etched into her skin. Gemma would complete the ritual with a triumphant raising of her arms, ushering the slimy, squelching creature into the circle. And then. And then...

The small demon splashed onto the concrete covered in bloody goop. It looked like a terrier with a humanoid face and long claws.

Zuri was frozen as the demon sniffed at the circle and finding it lacking, burst through it, leaping onto Gemma's chest. The screams were echoed by her own.

The day that it'd actually happened, Zuri had tried to blast the demon off. The attempt had hit the glistening creature cleanly, but it'd been too late. A claw had gone right through Gemma's throat, leaving her bleeding out onto the concrete.

It was only after she'd died that Blake had jumped into action, banishing the demon in a few heartbeats, the complex spell leaping to his lips without thought or interruption. Only later in the depths of her grief when her mind forced her to relive the moment over and over did she see how Blake's actions stuck out from what she would have expected.

When the ritual circle failed, Blake stayed on the picnic table, rather than leaping to action as he normally would. Then the alacrity of his banishing spell, which he'd never really been interested in learning, but later claimed during the trial was a secret passion of his. The judge praised his quick action. She'd known then that he'd never be convicted.

But this wasn't that time.

Zuri was frozen on the table, locked into place by spell or curse, she didn't know, as her friend Gemma stumbled backwards with a gash in her throat spilling crimson blood over her chest and onto the concrete.

As the last light faded from Gemma's eyes, she reached out—

Zuri found herself back on the log, pulling her arms around her chest to protect against the cold.

"Burn, baby, burn!"

Blake stood over the pile of wood, letting the flame from his hands eat the logs.

"No, no, no," she said, aloud.

"What's wrong, babe? Worried about me catching faez madness?"

"No."

Zuri turned on the log to see Gemma tramping through the leaves, humming to herself, oblivious to what was to come...

§

The table was set exquisitely and the chandelier tinkled as if brushed by a ghost. Iona stared at the painting of the horned god fornicating with his charges, their eyes highlighting the surprise and betrayal of the meeting.

"Is something wrong?"

Iona's head snapped center.

Ilyana sat across the table wearing a white jacket over a white dress, matching her pale hair. Rich, red blood dripped from her mouth onto her chest, splattering her pristine clothes.

Between them sat two plates, the first, in front of Ilyana, contained a pool of blood that filled the white china, while the second, in front of her, held a human heart, the blood and ventricles so dark that she was sure it'd been harvested only moments before it'd been served.

"No," said Iona, blinking.

This scene was familiar. She'd been here before, except the previous two times she'd refused to eat the heart and Ilyana had snapped her neck. The feeling of her bones breaking, the way the world dialed down to a pin as she faded from consciousness was like a weight against her chest.

This isn't real, this isn't real, this isn't real.

"Of course this is real, dear sister. Did you think you could escape me forever? Did you think you could kill our father and get away with it?"

A memory crept through the pain and fear. She'd been in the Palace of the Dead, battling a mirror version of herself. Not only wasn't this real, but it was a game. Yet, it was more than a game.

Somehow, they'd mined her memories for a pivotal future moment of her life.

"Iona? Are you not hungry?"

She stared into the bloodred human heart, almost expecting it to beat.

"What is this? How do I get out?" she whispered to herself.

A memory of the first day of the games, when Head Patron Pythia spoke to the auditorium, came back to her.

The contest is about discovering the best, or worst, version of yourself.

Iona only had to look across the table to see what that meant. Ilyana was an older, more powerful version of herself. But clearly, denying herself the heart wasn't going to save her from the fate that her half-sister suggested.

"Iona."

The name was spoken as a threat. Ilyana's dark eyes were like shadowy pits. Places where bodies and secrets were buried. Where soon, she'd be entombed.

Iona put both hands around the heart. The gooey organ was warm and slightly pulsing. She lifted it to her mouth and sunk her teeth into the flesh. It was tough like chewing through leather. The first bite required ripping away the chunk and swallowing it whole before her mind allowed her to think about what it was she was eating. Swallowing was a battle for survival, but after she pounded on her chest, the piece slipped past her throat and sunk to her belly.

The moment it hit her stomach she felt like a goddess. Heat rose up from her belly until she felt like she was holding a furnace in her chest. Iona went back for a second bite, tearing into the human heart while Ilyana watched with great interest. The second bite was easier to swallow than the first. And the third even easier. By the fifth bite, she was devouring it like a wolf after its kill.

When she finished, Iona felt like the sun. She expected rays of power to come flowing out of her skin.

"See, sister. I told you."

But the vision persisted.

Iona knew what she needed to do.

"You're right, sister. You're right. And now it's time to die."

Iona flew across the table with her claws out.

§

Iona woke on the marble floor, staring at the high arching stone ceiling, trying to hold onto the feeling of absolute power she'd experienced in the vision.

She looked to her left when she heard laughing to find Blake bent over slapping his knees and talking to himself. The moment they met gazes she felt his anger more keenly than ever before.

"I should have known you'd be the only one to get out. I kinda thought Orion would find it easy, but I guess he's not the badass I thought he was."

Iona wasn't quite sure what he was talking about until she saw the three shadow seeds between them. The pulsing balls of darkness shifted and writhed like spider cocoons about to hatch.

"What do we do?" she asked.

Blake kicked the Scarlett ball with the toe of his boot.

"She's so stupid. Sometimes I wonder..."

Iona crawled over to the other two shadow seeds. They rocked and stretched. She could sense which one was Orion and which was Zuri without touching.

"Should we help them?" asked Iona.

"They're not going to get out without us. You know, I never understood why they let you into Coterie, but after these many months together, I think I finally understand. You're a real killer. Not like these chumps. Shame you were born from pig farmers or you might have done well in

Coterie."

She didn't know what to say, and then Blake shoved his arm into the shadow seed, pulling himself into it and then he was gone.

Which should she help first? It was bound to be a moment of intense emotion if her vision was any guide. Iona had a good idea of what she'd find in Zuri's vision, but Orion? Maybe it was best to leave him alone, but she was curious, and Zuri had tasked her with getting Orion on their side. Their time, one way or another, was coming to an end in the games. This was her best, and last, chance to understand the big man.

"Let's do this."

Iona shoved her arm into the Orion shadow seed. It felt like reaching into a vat of oil, and as she pushed herself into it, the seed pulled her deeper until she was falling through empty space.

§

The cottage looked like it was something out of the 1980s with a shelf of colorful ceramic figurines across the mantle. Upon closer examination, Iona found them to be collectable versions of the Hall Patrons. She picked out Celesse D'Agastine and Head Patron Invictus, but the others were less recognizable.

This wasn't the place she'd expected to enter. The furniture was the kind of cheap stuff they'd had in the farmhouse in Missouri. Iona could feel the way the springs pushed unevenly against the back of her thighs.

A couple of pictures on the wall showed a smiling family. A mother and father, a grandmother, and a young boy that looked big for his age. He had the same dimples as Orion, but this wasn't the home of a Dreadmarsh. Not as she'd been led to believe.

The second picture just showed the father and grandmother with the young Orion. They didn't look as happy as the first. Had his mother died?

A crash had her running into another part of the house, looking for others. She burst into the high-fenced backyard when she saw movement.

The grandmother was sitting on a lawn chair with blankets pulled over her head and body, creating a huge lump, while Orion's father was screaming at her. He was yelling something about being cursed, but she couldn't pay attention because she'd met gazes with Orion, the Orion from her time, with dread as his expression.

"You shouldn't be here."

"I didn't know. I came to help."

Orion scowled at his father.

"You can't help."

"You don't know that. Blake and I got out of our memories. When I didn't see you—"

"Please, go. I don't want you to see me here."

Iona tried to offer a reassuring smile, but it fell flat.

"This isn't anything I haven't seen before. I grew up in a place like this. I won't tell anyone. They don't deserve to know."

"Not that," said Orion, glancing at his father.

At that precise moment, Orion's father slapped the old woman in the chair. The weight of blankets cushioned the worst of the blow, but it was still surprising.

"You cursed us. You cursed your daughter, and my son. I never should have married you fucking demon-loving Dreadmarshes. I should kill the lot of you, put you out of your misery like a mangy dog," he screamed, spittle flying from his lips.

"Iona. Go. Please."

"What is it you need to do here?"

But she knew the answer. She'd seen it in the Veil vision.

"I can't. I can't do it again."

"Let me do it for you."

His mouth wrinkled in pain. While he shook his head, the words never formed on his lips.

As Orion's father lifted his arm to hit the grandmother again, Iona blasted him with a force bolt, then she was on him in an instant with her hands around his throat. He tried to fight back, but he wasn't strong enough. Unlike his son, he had no infernal heritage and no supernatural strength, and she had regained the power from her previous vision when she'd eaten the heart.

A hand tried limply to pull her back. Orion was standing behind, watching her choke his father like one of the rabbits she'd caught in a snare.

"I don't want you to do this."

"Orion. We have to. This is part of the game. If you can't get out, you'll be stuck here and we'll lose. I'm sorry."

The act of choking this man she didn't know to death was harder than the fight with Ilyana, but it was also strangely easier than she wanted it to be.

Orion intervened no longer, and a minute later, after his father's eyes went blank, they found themselves back in the Palace of the Dead. Orion was seated nearby, head between his knees, sobbing quietly, while Iona felt like the worst person in the world.

THIRTY-FIVE

"Burn, baby, burn!"

Blake cackled over the fire, coaxing it to rise like the gates of hell. A hell she was trapped in. Zuri numbly watched Gemma stumble out of the forest and exchange seemingly innocent banter before they appeared in the pavilion where she would fail her summoning and bleed out on the concrete with a gash through her throat.

She wasn't sure how many times she'd experienced the vision. Nor did she know what to do to escape. The times she'd attacked him, he'd killed her easily and Gemma died anyway. And any attempt to stop the ritual was thwarted by the rules of the vision. As far as she could tell, there wasn't any way to escape. She was trapped.

"Why didn't I see it before?" she muttered.

She knew the answer. Blake was handsome, funny, and really popular. He could even be kind when he wanted something. It'd always been a transactional relationship, but she hadn't seen it until it was too late.

It wasn't like she hadn't gotten something out of the relationship too. Before dating him, she was considered the "smart girl" by the rest of her class at St. Jude's. On the surface, it was a label that hadn't bothered her, but she always felt excluded from the big events, which usually came with excuses about how they thought she was at an arcane bowl, or some other magical quiz event.

When the Invasion happened and her sister, Nandi, became the hero of St. Jude's, that wasn't the boost to her reputation that she'd wanted. Her classmates made fun of her sister for working with the Silverthorne sisters and when Pythia was named Head Patron, instead of one of the original Patrons like Malden, they thought it was a betrayal.

Dating Blake had quenched those lines of attack. She went from the goodie-goodie girl to the Queen of Popularity. It'd been a stark turnaround from never getting an invite to have too many to choose from. An embarrassment of riches.

"Burn, baby, burn!"

Zuri stared at Blake trying to remember how she'd convinced herself to date him. Like everything else she'd done up until that point, it was a calculation to improve her standing at St. Jude's and ultimately Coterie of Mages.

Part of her wanted to blame her parents. After all, they pushed her to be the best at everything. It wasn't enough that she was tops in scholarship and magical aptitude—they expected popularity and status, too. It hadn't helped that in the middle of her formative years, when she was only thirteen, her older sister became the darling of the elite world.

They might as well have put a noose around her neck.

"No," Zuri spat out, catching questioning glances from Blake and Gemma.

After so many rounds of ignoring them, the vision versions of her former boyfriend and best friend had stopped trying to interact with her.

"I put the noose around my own neck."

Gemma laughed. "Is this a choking fetish?"

"She's a loonie. Not sure why I ever dated her."

The comment surprised Zuri, because it broke from the pattern of the vision.

"Why *did* you date me?"

"For the same reasons you dated me. It was a bargain. You helped me with my reputation and I helped you with yours. There was only a small price to pay."

They both looked to Gemma, who stared back incredulously.

"What?"

"I'm sorry, Gemma," she said.

"Why?"

"Because shortly, you're going to summon an infernal imp for a bet, and because Blake messed with the salt, the wards will fail and you'll die with a gash in your neck."

"Whoa, that's so blade. Are we doing a Halloween thing early?"

"I knew he wasn't good for me. Or you. He tried to sleep with you and you told me, but I refused to listen, saying that he couldn't possibly have done that."

"You were kinda a bitch about it."

"I was," said Zuri. "I'm sorry."

"What about me?" asked Blake aggressively. "Aren't you going to apologize for trying to ruin my life?"

She stared back into his brown eyes, so full of hate and himself.

"I'm sorry, Blake. I'm sorry that I dragged you through that trial."

"About time—"

"But not because you're not guilty. You killed Gemma. You deserve your punishment. But I'm sorry that I foolishly indulged my sense of personal morality, thinking that I would be made the hero for taking you down. I was a child then. A child who thought that right and wrong mattered and that if I spoke up, that you would be rightly punished.

"But I should have known better. I *do* know better. That's not how the world works. Sure, there's a shine of goodness slopped over the ugliness beneath, but it's thin. And the rot is deep."

Gemma stared back as if she was finally realizing how she'd been betrayed.

"And you, Gemma. My best friend. Not only did I not listen to you when you warned me he was bad, but instead of getting my revenge quietly and cleanly, I dragged it in front of the world to see. I was so very honest, but so very stupid. I expected justice to be fair and for those that deserved it, they would get their comeuppance, but I was blind. You always told me how rotten our system was, and I thought it was a posture, a personality that you were trying on to be discarded later when you grew up. And maybe you would have. But you were right at the time."

An ache in her stomach made her clutch her chest. Bile rose into her throat at the thought of how completely wrong she'd been about everything.

"I should have killed you, Blake Lockwood. When I found you after we killed Fenris, I should have ended you then. Maybe we wouldn't be in this mess, I don't know, but that's not what matters. I should have killed you so you didn't hurt anyone else. I tried to be fair, but all I did was embolden you to do more damage. When you came out of the trial, clean as a whistle, it told everyone around us that you were untouchable. That you were special. You'd been unsufferable before, but after that not guilty verdict, you became a god."

His smile could have cut glass.

"I thought killing Gemma was the best thing that ever happened to me. Until your stupid trial. After that, not only did everyone know that I did it, but they knew I got away with it too."

Zuri rose from the log and put her hands on Gemma's shoulders. She stared back with the eyes of a lost puppy.

"I'm sorry, Gemma. I failed you. I failed me too. And the rest of St. Jude's and Coterie. I created a monster when I should have put a silver bullet in his head. I won't make that mistake again."

She wanted to hug Gemma tight to her chest, but a mist rose up from the wet leaves, swirling around them until Zuri could only see Gemma and then she faded away, and Zuri returned to the Palace of the Dead.

THIRTY-SIX

A heaviness hung in the air after the battle with the shadow seeds. Iona wondered if each one of them was still contemplating the vision, or if something had changed within the dynamic of the group. As they explored deeper into the Palace of the Dead, she saw Zuri covertly glancing in Blake's direction. Questions about her vision had remained unanswered, but Iona had a pretty good idea of what had happened. Blake did too, which made their forward progress fraught with peril. The sooner they completed the Second Year Games, the sooner they could all go back to being mortal enemies.

"Where are the crawly things?" asked Scarlett, glancing into the rafters. "It's weirding me out that we're not fighting right now."

"I think we're done with the easy fights," said Zuri.

Iona moved closer to Orion to ask him how he was doing, but he shifted away.

Great, I've killed both my father and his.

Iona wondered if he'd ever be able to look her in the eye. Not only had she not bonded with him over the vision, she'd made it worse. If things came to a head, and it was certain they would once the contest was over and they were back in Coterie, Orion wouldn't be on their side. Her only solace was it was doubtful that he'd side with Blake either, but that wouldn't mean much in the darkness of the Obelisk.

"Now that's a fucking door."

At the end of the grand hallway stood double doors made of onyx and gold. They opened wide upon approach, revealing a dais with a grand throne made of smaller objects.

A girl sat on the throne wearing jeans and a cutoff black T-shirt, which made Zuri hiss with surprise.

"What?"

"Never mind."

The girl had silky black hair and held a scepter on her crossed legs as she watched their approach. She looked like a punk-rock girl who'd wandered in from a nearby concert looking for drugs. The throne was made of junk from their visions: bundles of wood, collector figurines, bloody china, and other things.

"Have you no respect for your queen?" asked the girl in a mix of haughty arrogance and playful ribbing.

Iona genuflected with the rest of her group—minus Blake, who stayed standing.

"You're not what I expected," said Blake with his arms crossed.

"I change with the times. You should try it. Then you might not be such an insufferable ass."

Zuri burst out laughing, which only made Blake's cheeks turn crimson.

"*You're* the Queen of the Veil?" asked Orion sternly as if he was insulted by her appearance.

"The one and only."

"Did we win?" asked Blake, checking around them.

"Not quite." She held out her forefinger and thumb with a small gap between. "Just one more tiny task left."

"Let's get this over with. I'm tired of being here," said Blake.

"As you wish," said the queen, amusement perched on her lips. "Your last task is a simple question. A trifle really. Only one of you need answer it for the group to pass and for you to claim victory in the Second Year Games. However, if you get it wrong, you have to fight through all of that to try again."

Orion's shoulders slumped as he stared back blankly. Scarlett didn't look that enthused either, but then again, both she and Orion had needed to be rescued from their visions.

"Fine. Whatever. We can do it again. It was easy. Ask your question," said Blake.

"I hear a but," said Zuri.

The queen gave a lopsided grin.

"You are quite perceptive. Each time you try again, it will be successively harder. *All* of it. Or you can ask again, but should you get it wrong, you must wait two weeks. Get it wrong again, double that time."

"We can't do that," said Zuri. "We need the time to get to the next level in the Obelisk. There's not enough calendar left in the school year."

"Maybe for you," said Blake, smirking

While they'd been battling the undead, his group was working their way through the fourth level.

"What's the question?" asked Iona.

The queen leaned back in her unusual throne and pointed the jeweled scepter at them, bouncing it upon the completion of each word.

"What is your nature?"

The question seemed both frighteningly easy and devilishly complex.

Iona was parsing the possibilities when Blake stepped forward.

"This one is easy. I'll answer."

"Go ahead, Blake Lockwood."

Blake lifted his chin with an air of supremacy on his face.

"I want to rule."

The answer hung in the air like a guillotine. A slow smile rose to the queen's lips before she held out a fist and turned her thumb down.

"Incorrect."

A gasp of dismay from Scarlett had Blake glaring angrily in her direction.

"Get yourself together, babe."

"I'm sorry, Blake," she said, pleading with her eyes.

"It's okay. We'll just do it again."

"But what if we can't get back here?" said Scarlett. "Or what if..."

She gestured back the way they'd come. Everyone knew what she meant. The shadow seeds. The mirror versions of themselves. Whatever had happened in her vision had left her shaken. Worse than Orion, if that could be believed.

"It's okay. I'll save you. Again."

The queen tsked.

"I won't allow that a second time. You'll have to get through your visions entirely on your own."

Scarlett whimpered and stepped forward. Her lips were wrinkling as if she were holding back a mouthful of worms.

"Can I answer then?"

"Scarlett. If you get this wrong, you're going to mess everything up. We'll be locked out for two weeks and someone else will probably get it. Let's go back and fight. I'm not scared."

"Blake. Babe. Please."

He crossed his arms, so Scarlett turned towards the rest of the group.

"I know the answer. I swear."

Zuri looked ready to disagree, but Iona spoke up.

"I'm good with it."

"I am too," said Orion right away.

"Three to one," said Scarlett sheepishly.

"Four to one," said Zuri.

Blake stared back angrily. He looked ready to snap her in half. "Don't fuck us."

"Your answer?" asked the queen.

Scarlett held trembling hands before her. She spoke in a whisper that was barely audible.

"I want control."

The queen's crestfallen reaction was their answer.

"I'm sorry. That is incorrect."

"You dumb bitch. I had a plan and now you ruined it. Ruined everything."

"What do we do?" asked Zuri. "We're locked out for two weeks. Someone could pass us and win the game. On the other hand, they might not."

Orion wasn't responding. He was staring at the floor. If they had to go through this again, he'd have to kill his father himself. Scarlett would have to relive her nightmare too. Whatever it was, it wasn't good. The trauma knotted up in her forehead looked ready to turn her to stone.

"I'll answer," said Iona, stepping forward.

"What? No. No way. If you screw this up, we're all done. No more Games, no more Halls, no more Coterie," said Blake.

"Iona, are you sure?" asked Zuri.

"I am."

"I'm okay with it."

"Orion?"

He stared back at her with what she could only interpret as relief. His mouth silently worked before he gave up and nodded.

"Scarlett?"

"Please..."

Blake put his hands over his face.

"Why am I cursed with such idiots? You're going to screw me. Everything I've done, for nothing, because I got stuck with a bunch of morons in the Second Year Games."

"Babe?"

He turned on her, violence in his eyes.

"Yeah. I mean you. I thought I could trust you, but clearly I can't."

Iona took another step forward.

"What is your answer, Iona Storm?"

Iona took a deep breath.

"I am a killer."

The flat stare from the queen had Iona's stomach doing backflips. She wanted to crawl out of her skin, or scream. Maybe both.

While she'd joined Coterie to get away from Fenris, she hated the idea of not getting to continue. There was so much to learn. She still had time to figure out who she was.

The slow smile on the queen's lips gave no indication of which direction their fate lay. A fist was raised and held sideways. The thumb flicked out and for a moment, Iona thought the fist was being turned towards the dais.

Then the queen triumphantly spun her hand towards the ceiling.

"You are correct."

The tension in her knees gave out and she sunk towards the floor in relief, stopping only when Zuri grabbed her in celebration.

"We did it. You did it. Seven hells. I thought I was going to have a heart attack."

"Me too," said Iona, holding her chest.

She turned towards Blake and the others to congratulate them, but he was staring back without a trace of emotion.

"Congratulations."

"You too," she said.

"Where's our prize? Or is this another game?" asked Blake.

The Queen of the Veil gestured forward and a swirling black-and-purple portal of unknown energies formed between them.

"Good luck," said the queen.

Iona knew the whole thing was a fabrication, an illusion on a grand scale, but she found herself wishing she could have spent more time with the queen. She seemed...interesting.

The five of them popped through the portal, landing in a simple room with five pedestals in a row, each one displaying an elixir under a glass case.

Before anyone could move, an illusionary, see-through version of Head Patron Pythia appeared in their midst. She was wearing the same outfit she'd been in the first day of the Second Year Games.

"Congratulations. You are officially the winners of the Second Year Games, which entitles you to the prize, five Elixirs of Foresight. While the potions will provide you with answers you desperately seek, don't forget the lessons that you learned in your journey across the City of the Dead."

The illusion winked out and Iona turned to congratulate Orion, but he grabbed his elixir from beneath the glass and marched out of the room before she could muster a single word.

"Thank you."

Iona thought the comment was for someone else until she saw that Scarlett was facing her and that Zuri was standing before one of the pedestals, staring at the elixir beneath the glass.

"What?"

"For getting that last question correct. I don't know if I could have gone through that again."

"I'm pretty sick of the City of the Dead myself. Ready to get back to the Obelisk, if that can be believed."

"Yeah," said Scarlett with a pained expression. "I guess we'll go back to being enemies."

There was a longing in her voice, a thread of regret that Iona wanted to explore, but she couldn't with Blake in the room. Whatever had happened in her shadow seed, especially from Blake's rescue, had really affected the redhead.

Iona leaned closer and spoke under her breath. "We don't have to be enemies."

The redhead's green eyes flashed with surprise. She opened her mouth.

"That would—"

The sudden flinch had Iona confused. Scarlett had looked ready to spill a deep desire, but then she let the words falter on her lips.

"Scarlett?"

Understanding came when blood pooled in Scarlett's bottom lip then spilled across her chin.

A second, more violent flinch was followed by Scarlett bending backwards as the silvery tip of a blade came jutting from her chest.

"Oh—"

The shock preceded the slow slumping away of Scarlett Calloway until she landed on the floor with a thump, revealing Blake with a blade in his fist and a fiery light in his eyes. She quickly noticed that the last pedestal was bare except for an empty vial.

"Zuri!"

Iona barely got the words out before Blake's sorcerous blast nearly took her friend's head off. The glancing blow spun Zuri into the wall, knocking over the pedestal.

"She always thought she was so smart. Look how smart she is now," said Blake, kicking the warm body.

Iona had never really thought of Blake as a skilled caster, but the Elixir of Foresight that he'd consumed seemed to have given him that ability. She barely got up a shield before he sent waves of flame roiling over her position.

Even though it was two against one, Iona and Zuri could barely beat back his attacks. It was as if he knew exactly what they were going to do before they did it.

"The door!"

Iona blasted it open and threw herself through with Zuri landing moments later.

She didn't understand where she was until she remembered that they were in the Spire and in a different location than their prep room.

"The elixirs!"

Iona started to rush back in, but Zuri grabbed her arm, yanking her back. A millisecond after, the open door exploded in pulsing, dark energies that looked powerful enough to have obliterated her cleanly.

"What the hell was that?"

"We have to go. We can't beat him now," said Zuri.

Together they raced towards the door at the end of the hall. To her surprise, they burst outside, stumbling into the light of the late afternoon. When the door closed, it was no longer visible, leaving them beside the massive tower that stretched to the sky.

"What do we do?" asked Iona. "He's got the elixirs."

"I should have never trusted him," said Zuri. "But I didn't think he'd attack us then. I thought he'd wait until the Obelisk. And I especially didn't think he'd kill Scarlett."

Realization dawned on Iona's brow. "He knew she would betray him eventually. The Games had proved to her how unreliable and dangerous he was. But she thought she could control him."

"I made that mistake too."

"We need to catch up with Orion. He has the only elixir not in Blake's hands. Maybe he'll share the knowledge of how to get through the portal with us. Let's beat him back to the Obelisk if we can."

"No," said Iona, thinking about the vision. "He won't be headed there."

"What? Why not?"

"He's going to the seventh."

"Are you sure?" asked Zuri.

"Entirely? No, but I'd bet it more than the Obelisk."

"Let's go then."

They burst into a run, heading towards the street where Iona hoped they could find a quick taxi. It was likely they'd be able to find him walking along the road since he preferred that mode of transportation over anything public.

Iona spotted a taxi and started frantically waving. She was so focused on the incoming yellow vehicle she missed the three black SUVs with tinted windows screeching towards them at high speed until it was too late.

Five men with automatic weapons leapt out of the vehicles, training the barrels on them.

"What is this?" she asked Zuri, but her friend's crestfallen expression was damning enough.

They were ushered into the back of an SUV, where they were sat side by side. A hard looking guy with neck tattoos bound their hands, then he pulled out a small, unusual looking gun.

"Adrian Constantin can't wait to see you again."

Zuri leaned forward. “Tell him—”

The henchman pulled the trigger twice, sending darts into each of them. Everything suddenly became infinitely heavy and the world faded from view.

THIRTY-SEVEN

Her head felt like it was being run over by a dozen limousines. The world was hazy and her eyes wouldn't focus. Zuri looked to her left to see Iona with her head slumped over, pale blonde hair cascading into her face.

Zuri examined herself to find that she was bound to a chair with leather bindings. She tried to move her fingers, but they'd been cinched with mage clamps that would keep her from casting spells.

For the next few minutes, Zuri tried to wiggle free of the bindings but they were too tight and too well constructed. There was no escaping her fate.

A low moan announced Iona's waking. She groaned for a bit before her head came up.

"What did they do to us?"

"It's the knockout drug."

"Did an elephant sit on my head? This sucks," said Iona. "Where are we?"

"No idea, but I'm sure we're being kept until Adrian Constantin arrives. I'm sorry, Iona. I got you all mixed up in this."

"You were doing what you had to do. You're trying to survive." She looked over her shoulder. "What's wrong with my fingers?"

"They want to make sure we can't use any spells."

"That's a bummer."

Zuri sighed. "The best I can do is try to bribe Adrian. My parents will pay a lot for our freedom."

"Your parents will pay a lot for *your* freedom."

Zuri grimaced.

"I hate that you're probably right."

"Just cold calculation." Iona turned her head towards the door. "How long do you think we have?"

"No idea. I don't know how long we've been out." Zuri sighed. "At least we don't have to worry about beating Blake back to the Obelisk."

"That was messed up back there. Killing Scarlett."

"You're probably right what you said earlier. He knew she'd betrayed him once he drank the elixir. He's bad enough being the sociopath that he is. Now with the smarts to go with that, I worry what he's going to do next."

"A problem we're not going to have to worry about unless we can get out of here," said Iona and then she started scooting her chair over.

"What are you doing?"

Iona offered a sheepish smile.

"Do you trust me?"

"Of course."

"I mean, really trust me."

A tightening of her gut had Zuri trying to smile but it came out awkward.

"Just tell me."

"Can I bite you?"

"What?" asked Zuri, recoiling. "I thought the blood only helped you see Veil spirits that someone had killed."

"That's not the only thing. It makes me stronger too. Maybe I can get out of these bindings."

Zuri was revolted and not just because it was her blood. The idea that someone was feeding on her as if she had no other meaning than as a blood bag bothered her.

"Is it going to hurt?"

"Most definitely. But probably a lot less than whatever Adrian is going to do to us."

Zuri swallowed.

"Okay. Just make it quick."

"Yeah, that's the problem." She hopped her chair over until they were side by side. "I can't reach you from here."

"We have to knock ourselves over," said Zuri.

She started violently rocking in her chair, hoping they weren't making too much noise. When she tipped backwards, the impact rattled her head and made her teeth clack together. Iona fell onto her sideways right after, lodging the corner of the chair into her side.

The next few seconds of reorientation resulted in Iona's chair bouncing off her face twice. Then they were sideways on the ground, facing each other with Iona's mouth near her arm.

"I've never done this before so..."

The first bite made Zuri scream silently in her own head. Iona's teeth weren't sharp enough, which created more pressure than serration. Tears rolled down her face as the gnawing continued.

Then she felt Iona sucking on her arm.

"Are you done?" Zuri whimpered.

"Don't move. I'll have to go back for more if it's not enough."

Iona strained against the straps, her neck tendons standing out as she tried to break the bindings. Veins on her forehead looked ready to explode.

"It's not enough."

"Go for it."

The second gnawing nearly made Zuri pass out as she could feel every gnash and bite of her teeth. When the agony was over, she heaved with breath as Iona thrashed, trying to break the bindings or the chair. The pounding was loud. Zuri hoped she would get free before someone came to check on them.

When the door rattled from a key, Zuri said, "Hurry."

Two big men in black turtlenecks entered. They looked like they could break a two-by-four over their knee without breaking a sweat.

"What do we have here? A couple of squirmy women trying to escape. How cute, don't you think, Bravos?"

"Iona?" she whispered but her friend shook her head.

It hadn't been enough blood. When she looked down, she only saw a few beads on her arm. Nothing like the cut she'd given herself in the Games. Iona would need a mouthful at least, maybe more.

The second guy grunted as he bent over Zuri to grab the chair, which gave her an idea. She spat in his face.

He chuckled and wiped it off with the back of his hand.

"Little girl is feisty."

"And big man is a coward. Tying up two girls. What kind of man does that?"

He picked her and the chair up easily, setting her down on the ground.

"You're not girls, you're mages. We're not so stupid. Adrian will be here soon and then you'll regret ever messing with the Dark Nine."

"Dark Nine?" she laughed. "I've never heard of such a weak-ass name. Did you have a ten-year-old boy name your gang? Or did you get it off the back of a cereal box?"

Iona hunched her forehead and mouthed, "What are you doing?"

Zuri ignored her and continued.

"Whoa, look at the little dick on this one. I've seen bigger cocks on a baby."

"Shut the fuck up," he said menacingly.

"What? You can't make me. You know why? Because I know your type. I've seen it before. You were a weak little bitch growing up, afraid of women, afraid of yourself, so you started licking the ass of the nearest thug until he gave you a job, but that doesn't change the fact that you're never going to amount to anything."

The fist that slammed into her jaw nearly knocked her out. It was like getting hit with a sledgehammer. She felt lucky her jaw hadn't been broken. The world was fuzzy, but when she checked her mouth, it still wasn't bloody.

"That's all you got?" she asked, looking up into his shocked face. "That was like a kiss on the cheek, you oversized child."

The second punch sent her head reeling. It'd been right in front of her mouth. Zuri spat out a tooth and shoved her tongue into the hole, feeling the gush of warm blood.

When she smiled at Iona, squeezing the crimson liquid through her teeth, she finally understood. In two great hops, Iona landed next to Zuri before the thugs understood what was going on. She leaned over and pressed her lips against Iona's and like a mother bird feeding her infant, spit out a mouthful of blood.

"What the fuck?" exclaimed the first guy, recoiling. "Why did you just do that?"

Iona shuddered and then opened her eyes. They burned with intensity.

"Let's gag these crazy-ass bitches," said the second thug right as Iona flexed backwards, snapping her legs upright and exploding the chair from her body.

The first thug reached for his gun, but Iona broke a hand free and jacked him across the jaw. He spun into the wall with his eyes rolled into the back of his head as Iona shook her hand from the impact.

"Iona!"

Before the second thug could grab her, she snatched a piece of lumber from the broken chair and brought it up between his legs. He crumpled to the ground and then she broke it across his forehead and he was out cold.

The ease with which she snapped the bindings and freed Zuri was a little scary. Once she was free, Zuri grabbed a gun even though she'd never fired one before.

"Do you know how to use this?"

"No."

Zuri tossed it away.

"Magic it is then."

They crept down the hallway, hearing a TV from the end room. There was no other way out. They would have to go through it.

"Go in blasting," said Zuri. "No mercy."

Five heads turned towards them when the door opened. Zuri didn't want to kill them, but she didn't want to die either. The force wave blasted them off their chairs, smashing the television screen and any glassware on the table. She worried it wasn't enough when she saw a couple of them reaching for their weapons, but then Iona, who had kept the chair leg, moved around the room at great speed, knocking them out with quick jabs to the head.

She thought they were home free until a new gang member stepped into the room. He looked different than the others. Zuri didn't understand until he blurred after Iona, slamming her against the wall.

He had faez crystals. Or at least one. It was enough to make their fight even.

Iona was fighting for her life as the thug produced a knife and prepared to jam it through her neck.

The force blast went into the side of his head, snapping his neck, killing him instantly. He flopped over like a rag doll, the knife clattering to the floor amid the carnage.

"Thanks."

They burst into the waiting room where the receptionist she'd spoken to last month was sitting with her hands up and shaking uncontrollably.

"Please don't hurt me."

"Do you have a car?" asked Iona.

"What?"

"If I have to check your purse to find a pair of keys, I'm going to be very unhappy."

The woman reached into a drawer and threw a pair of keys.

"Silver one across the street."

It was night in the city. The Spire was lit up like a giant candle with spotlights, and further into the second ward, an illusionary battle between two airborne dragons was playing for the crowds.

After dodging through traffic, Zuri climbed into the driver's seat and checked back to the Dark Nine building to make sure no one was following.

Iona wiped her mouth, smearing blood across her cheek.

"Thanks for the blood."

Zuri put her finger into the missing spot where a tooth had been. Blood was leaking onto her tongue from the gap.

"Let's never do that again," Iona said.

"Agreed."

"What now? Get your tooth fixed?"

Zuri put the car in gear.

"No time. We have to get back to the Obelisk."

"What about Orion?"

"We're never going to find him now. The thing I hope is that this little diversion messed up what Blake was expecting us to do. No way Mr. Smarty-pants could have anticipated Adrian Constantin's thugs, which might give us a slight advantage. Maybe we can sneak back in and get up to the third level."

"Why? We can't get through," said Iona.

"Not unless Blake solved the problem. If it worked for him, it should work for us. Plus, with Scarlett dead, we should test it anyway."

"Should we wait? Maybe he'll let his guard down later."

"I don't think it'll matter," said Zuri. "Better to do it now before he can get the rest of his group. For all we know, they might be on the fourth level and he'll have no way to reach them. There's a chance we could surprise him."

"Or we could die."

Zuri pulled into traffic.

"Always a possibility."

THIRTY-EIGHT

The Obelisk stretched into the sky like a black finger, its glossy surface absorbing random lights shone upon its surface. Iona breathed the cool night air as she checked back to the Spire, the aftereffects of the blood rage finally leaving her veins, letting her think more clearly.

"It's almost like Malden was competing with Invictus."

Zuri followed her gaze.

"Not much of a competition. You ready to go in?"

"Not really. Blake's going to have every advantage," said Iona. "I'm not sure we should even go into the Obelisk after he drank the Elixir of Foresight."

"The one chance we have is that the rest of his team is probably on the fourth level. It's unlikely that they would have known that we would win the contest today. Which means there's another good side to him killing Scarlett. It evens the odds."

"If she hadn't tried to kill me in the past, I might have felt bad for her."

For the past months while they'd been working the Games, the Obelisk had felt like home base since they weren't venturing into the dangerous areas, but now they were returning to complete the third level, the structure felt like a tomb rather than a place of rest.

Not far inside near the Cthulhu Jelly pool that led up to the first staircase, they ran into Charlotte Bellamy wearing a royal blue silk tracksuit with her hair in a high ponytail. She was seated on a bench thumbing through her phone. The moment she saw them a smile bloomed to her lips.

"Hey, you bitch. Congratulations. I heard a little bit ago about the Games. What a bloody triumph for Coterie," she said, rising and trading air kisses with Zuri. The side-eye that followed was warning enough for Iona not to bother.

"We didn't have any Brits on our team, or we might have tried to colonize the games instead of winning them," said Zuri.

"You guileless prat."

"Hey Charlotte," said Iona, receiving a withering stare. "Have you seen Blake?"

"Weren't invited to the celebration party at Amber & Smoke? Everyone who isn't on the higher levels is going."

"What about his team?" asked Zuri.

"I saw them leave with him a half hour ago." Charlotte's glance over at Iona could have started a small fire. "What a surprise you're not welcome. Or maybe they were concerned you wouldn't know how to act around your betters. But I'm sure they could find a trough for you."

"Only if I'm going to drown you in it," said Iona, getting into Charlotte's face.

"Whoa, back off, Pig Girl," said Charlotte, stepping away. "Seven hells, Zuri, I don't know why you hang around her. *She's* bringing my IQ down from proximity alone."

"I think that's all the nail polish you sniff," said Iona.

Charlotte marched away making tiny stomps.

"Do you get the feeling that this party is a feint?" asked Iona.

"One hundred percent. No way he'd leave the third level unguarded," said Zuri, shaking her head. "Unless drinking the elixir revealed another path, or some unexpected problem we haven't anticipated."

"It's got to be a trap somehow. Do we want to walk into it?" asked Iona.

"We'll have no better chance to get past the level while his entire team is out of the Obelisk."

"If they really are. Do you really trust Charlotte?"

"No, but Blake knows how much we don't trust him and he knows we know he drank the Elixir of Foresight," said Zuri.

"You're the puzzle master. I'm going to trust you on this one."

After applying wards and other protections, they made their way up to the first-level portal. Iona was certain that Blake and his crew were going to jump out at every corner, which made her twitchier than normal. It didn't help that the lingering effects of drinking blood made her want to get into a fight. Smashing in the heads of those gang members had felt better than just the thrill of escape. If Zuri hadn't been there, she would have probably kept hitting them with the chair leg until they were bloody pulp.

And then...

Iona didn't even want to think about what she might have done next.

"You okay?" asked Zuri, eyes wide with alarm.

"What?"

"You were mumbling or growling under your breath. Or maybe both."

"Thinking about earlier."

"Iona. You saved us. That's all that matters. We can figure out what that means for you later."

It felt good to see the Anubis portal again. It'd been months since they'd bothered. Iona hoped Justine wasn't too mad that they hadn't been around.

"Ready? Remember, they can't attack us near the portal. If they've set a trap, come back right away and then we can figure out what to do next," said Zuri.

Iona reached out to touch the portal as she thought about the level she wanted to land in. The experience of getting thrown across space to land in another location always left Iona dizzy upon arrival. She put her hands up, expecting a fight, but there was no one else near the portal.

"I'd forgotten how creepy this level was," said Iona, peering into the strange, dim light.

The distant outline of the pyramid brought back memories of the traps and puzzles they had to pass.

"I'm really not looking forward to doing this again," said Iona.

"I don't get it," said Zuri. "Why is the pyramid in that form?"

Cold realization hit Iona in the chest, making her stiffen.

"You're right. I thought some of the first years had made it this far."

"I'd heard that too. None of them have made it to the fourth, but at least one group made it to the pyramid. It should be unfolded. Which means Blake hasn't tried to go through. Or that we're missing something really obvious. What if we can travel to the fourth already and we just don't know it?" asked Iona.

"Let's try."

Iona placed her hand on the chunk of obsidian and thought about the next level up as she activated it with faez, but the trick didn't work.

"Maybe not."

Zuri stiffened.

"Someone's coming."

Iona crouched by the portal, readying herself to flee as she peered into the dimness. A shape was moving towards them through the buildings on the left side. It was low to the ground, approaching at a slow pace.

When the two-foot-tall puppet appeared in the gap between buildings, Iona allowed herself to relax.

"Justine, you scared us."

The puppet said nothing, continuing forward with a dead expression to her glass eyes.

"Justine?" asked Iona.

"Yes?"

"You were scaring us."

"But why? Everything is as it should be."

Iona shared a glance with Zuri, who looked equally perplexed.

"What do you mean?"

"Secrets. I've found so many secrets. Things no one else has ever seen before."

A pit of suspicion opened up in Iona's gut.

"Like what?"

"Come," said Justine, holding out her tiny wooden hands. "I'll show you."

"What are you wearing?" asked Zuri.

It wasn't until the question was posed that Iona realized Justine wasn't wearing the same dirty smock that she'd been in the last time they'd seen her. Her outfit looked like robes the color of sandstone with runes embroidered into the hem.

"It was a gift."

"A gift?" asked Zuri. "From who?"

"Come," said Justine, grabbing their hands and tugging them forward. "I have so many secrets to show you."

The puppet's surprisingly warm wooden hand wrapped around her fingers, squeezing reassuringly. Iona shrugged at Zuri and let herself be led forward.

"Wait," said Zuri, slowing them. "What about Blake? Have you seen him?"

"Blake's not here. He left an hour ago."

"So he was here?" asked Zuri.

"He was."

"Did he go near the pyramid?"

"No. He stayed near the portal and then left. I was watching."

The path Justine took them wasn't what she'd expected, nor did the puppet worry about the traps that normally would have plagued them. Once they even drew near a black pool, but the surface stayed flat and calm.

She led them to the far side of the level to an unexciting corner where she touched the stone in three places, which revealed faint Kemetic runes, and then a doorway opened. Justine tried to tug them into the darkness, but Iona stayed put.

"Don't worry. Everything will be okay soon," said Justine with an odd smile.

"I don't like this," said Zuri with lips pinched. "Do we really need to know these secrets right now?"

"We can't wait any longer."

A part of Iona didn't like Justine's use of the word "we." It sounded like she was talking about someone other than them, but she knew it was probably paranoia after the rough day at the end of the contest and then at the hands of Adrian Constantin's men.

"No one else is here. Let's just find out what she wants to show us and then we can tackle the pyramid."

Zuri held out her hand, which Justine took.

"Let's make this quick."

It took a moment for her eyes to adjust to the darkness as they were led down the long ramp. As they broke into a new area, Iona wondered why Justine hadn't asked about the contest or why they weren't at the Games like she had previous times. A sudden foreboding rose up, but then she was transfixed by the new sights.

They'd entered a wide chamber with walls covered in Egyptian murals and oversized hieroglyphs. On the far side was a blank sandstone wall beneath a portal archway, but it was unlike any of the structures they used for travel around the Obelisk. It looked like an older design.

But her eyes quickly shifted to the ritual circle at the center of the room, which had impressions for two people. One of them was currently filled.

"Orion!"

She started to move towards the circle to free the big man when a shape shifted out of the darkness—a long, jagged snout, textured robes lined with Kemetic runes, powerful clawed fists, and the hum of gathered power.

It was staring at her with great anticipation, and it didn't take her long to figure out why. This was the monster that had been in Fenris when he died, the one that had been eating the other students, and the one that she'd been destined to bond with until they'd killed Fenris.

"Zuri, run!"

Before she could take a single step, the monster raised its clawed fist and black eldritch energies snapped out like a whip, slamming into Iona and draining away her consciousness.

THIRTY-NINE

A terrible headache combined with her arms and legs being stretched in painful ways had Zuri waking with a sense of dread. Her chest heaved with coughing, which only made the pain worse as her limbs couldn't move as they were bound so tightly that it felt like they were about to come out of the sockets.

Zuri lifted her head to see that she was bound inside the ritual circle opposite Orion. Craning her neck, she quickly found Iona, who was suspended from chains on a pillar along the wall with her chin dipped towards her chest. Then she searched for the monster, finding him standing near the portal quietly watching with Justine at his side.

Upon first glance, she'd been frightened by his horrific appearance, thinking him primarily a beast of destruction, but watching him from her prone position revealed a quiet intensity that reminded her of the powerful mages she'd met in her time.

"Justine. What are you doing? Why are you with the monster?"

"All will be explained as soon as Iona wakes."

Zuri tugged on her bindings, but quickly realized they were too strong for her to escape and with Iona away from the circle, there was no way they could pull the same trick they had with Adrian's men. Not that she thought Iona could break rune-reinforced steel chains.

Lifting her head to review the area around her, she saw old blood, which told her how today's events were likely to end. Was this why Blake hadn't entered the third level? Had he come through the portal intending to set a trap, but with the Elixir of Foresight coursing through his veins he sensed that he wouldn't have to?

"Orion. What are you doing here?"

"I came to help."

"With this? Or Blake?"

"Blake."

"I'm sorry." Then she lifted her chin again. "Do you have your elixir?"

"No."

"Damn," she said, letting her head rest against the stone. "That might have helped."

"Don't you have yours?"

Zuri gave him a quick rundown of what had happened after he left the contest chamber.

"That is troubling."

"Do you have any idea of what's going to happen here?"

"We're going to die."

The matter-of-fact manner in which he replied told her that he was probably right.

A round of coughing announced Iona's waking and then she struggled against her bindings for a few seconds before realizing there was no escape. Then she reviewed the room, her eyes widening at the sight of the monster and the puppet at his side.

"Justine. What are you doing? Free us."

The puppet looked like a tiny priest in her robes. She stared ahead without acknowledging Iona's request, matching the quiet intensity of the beast.

"I think he's captured her somehow," said Zuri.

Iona rattled the chains again, trying to free herself before giving up with a heavy sigh.

"Why am I here, and you two are there?"

"I suspect we'll find out shortly, though I don't think any of us are going to like the answer," said Zuri.

The monster stepped forward, speaking in a rough voice before pausing and looking down at Justine.

"Am'attillazzi requests your silence as he explains today's ritual. He wants you to understand the value of your sacrifice. He promises to make your end as quick and painless as possible."

The announcement was like a punch to the gut.

"Why is he doing this?" asked Iona.

The creature spoke again, which was quickly translated.

"Please be silent. He is not finished with his explanation."

The robed figure continued, this time for much longer than the first time. Justine nodded at the end.

"The two of you in the circle will be killed. He requires your life energy, the conduit of faez you hold, to help him open a portal to his home, which he has been apart from for millennia. He apologizes for the necessity of your sacrifice, but promises you he will raise a shrine in your honor."

"I would like to forgo that honor if possible," said Zuri.

"What about me?" asked Iona, rattling her chains.

The creature looked to her and another long speech followed.

"Am'attillazzi intends to take you to his homeland. He wishes to study how the treacherous mage managed to steal his life force away, keeping him subjugated for these long millennia. You will be treated as an honored guest, not a slave, unless you cause him trouble."

"Seven hells, I don't want to go," said Iona.

"At least one of us will escape," said Zuri.

"Two, I think, if he takes Justine as well. Unless you can escape those bonds, Orion. Are you holding back?"

The big man strained against the bindings for a few seconds, the veins on his forehead bulging before he relaxed.

"I cannot."

"Am'attillazzi will begin the ritual in a few moments, unless you wish to speak. He will honor any last words."

"Nothing from me," said Zuri, squeezing her eyes shut.

Orion shook his head, but Iona strained against her chains.

"I'm sorry. I feel like this is my fault. I never intended any of this when I came to Coterie. I was just trying to escape my fate, not transfer it to someone else. This...this sucks."

"You don't have to apologize," said Zuri. "It's not like Coterie was very welcoming to you. I would prefer this was Blake and Scarlett in our place, but you can't win them all. I'm sorry for you, Orion. You weren't meant to get mixed up in this."

"I have no regrets," he said.

When no one had the urge to speak again, Am'attillazzi stepped to the edge of the circle and began the incantation. It was a form of Kemetic, but older and less easily understood. The runes warmed with a faint shine, gradually glowing brighter the longer he spoke.

The air pressure in the circle thickened, which made breathing like sucking oxygen through a straw. The hairs on Zuri's skin stood tall as electricity bounced from their bodies, crackling like a burgeoning storm.

Zuri wasn't sure if she wanted the ritual to go on longer, to extend the time she had left, or get it over with so she was no longer anticipating the painful end. Quick or not, the thought of her precious consciousness fleeing this world felt like a deal gone bad.

As the sparks grew hotter, leaping into the air above their prone bodies, Zuri got angry. She raged against the bindings then fell back against the stone in frustration.

Think, Zuri, think.

A million what-ifs ran through her brain. What if she'd never dated Blake. What if she'd killed him and taken control of his group. What if she'd rejected the path laid out before her and gone to another Hall. She would have been shamed by her peers, but at least she'd be alive.

No, I refuse to go out without fighting.

The ritual was rising to a crescendo with the air inside the circle whipping around, stinging her eyes as sparks leapt high.

She ran through every spell, every resource, everyone she'd ever known, trying to think of a way out of this mess. And then it hit her. She didn't know if she'd have enough time, or if it would even work, but she had to try.

"Orion, listen to me carefully. I need you to know something."

When he didn't respond, she said, "I need you to answer. You have to hear me."

"I hear you."

"Good. I need you to know that the Siren Sisters have been using alchemy recipes stolen from D'Agastine Industries and that your great uncle Leonidas Dreadmarsh tried to have his brother Magnus killed in the early '90s."

"Why are you telling me this?"

At first when nothing happened, Zuri feared that the curse couldn't penetrate the ritual circle, but then her body was wracked with pain. A bulb of dark energy lifted out of her belly button and then shot out of the room.

"If it works, I'll let you know, but until then, stay ready."

"Ready for what?" asked Iona, then realization dawned on her face. "Oh."

As the ritual culminated to its conclusion, Zuri feared that her last-second attempt to escape was in vain. Professor Cornwallis was either not in the Obelisk, or unable to find the hidden ritual chamber.

At least I didn't give up. At least I fought to the end.

She wondered what her parents would think. The only thing they'd probably know was that she won the Second Year Games, then unexpectedly died in the Obelisk. They'd probably quietly blame Blake, but never take action for fear of a reprisal.

The whole thing would be a mystery. The entirety of the winning team, minus Blake Lockwood, would either be dead or missing. And with the other vials of elixir, he would be poised to rule their class. Zuri wasn't sure which she hated worst, dying to the creature Am'attillazzi, or knowing that Blake would come out on top. Again.

The ancient creature was no longer speaking, which announced that the end was near. Zuri girded herself. The end would be swift, but it would not be without pain.

Am'attillazzi produced a ritual dagger from beneath his robes. It was the same one they'd found in the pyramid. The same one that had taken Justine's flesh body before she'd fled into the puppet.

"Let it be quick, let it be quick, let it be quick..."

The thick air inside the circle fled, and electricity no longer jumped from point to point. The robed figure stepped between Orion and her, glancing between them as if deciding which one to kill first.

When Am'attillazzi looked out of the circle, Zuri was confused. Then she heard a scream of rage.

"What in the seven hells is going on here?" asked Professor Cornwallis.

Zuri craned her neck to see the professor standing inside the room, eldritch sorceries roiling around her like thunderclouds. She looked like a woman stumbling upon her cheating husband.

Am'attillazzi spoke, which was quickly translated by Justine.

"This ritual does not concern you. Please take your leave and these beings will trouble you no longer."

"Bloody hell, I will not take my leave. This little bitch stole from me and there's only going to be one person who's going to punish her."

"Am'attillazzi regrets this choice, but will not back down."

"Good," said Professor Cornwallis with a growl in her voice. "I haven't had a good fight in a while."

A crack of blinding light splashed across the room, searing their shadows onto the stone briefly. Professor Cornwallis stalked forward, surrounded by three glowing balls that looked like miniature suns.

The creature met her in the wide part of the room. He'd summoned no sorcery and muttered no spell, but he looked formidable in his rune-lined robes and with his long snout filled with jagged teeth.

The three orbs whipped forward like meteors directly at Am'attillazzi's head. The creature swatted the first out of the way, and the second it dodged with a head feint, but the third slammed into his chest, boring into it like a drill, steam and sparks exploding from the corona. The creature growled menacingly, his voice rising to a crescendo as he grabbed the burning orb and ripped it from his flesh.

A smoking divot remained in the aftermath. Am'attillazzi squeezed the removed orb, shattering it into shards of light which created imprints on the nearby stone wall.

The creature stomped his enormous foot and slapped his hands together, rubbing them clockwise, while his fingers made hooks and curls.

When he finished his spell, the ground rumbled as a four-legged creature ripped itself from the sandstone. The hound-shaped construct leapt at the professor, latching onto her leg. She screamed and brought her fist down. It contained the one remaining orb that had circled back. The impact created a violent explosion, throwing sand and light in all directions.

Professor Cornwallis looked mad enough to spit with her thigh bleeding and her normally perfectly coifed hair plastered to her forehead. She took her remaining burning orb and with a muttered incantation, ripped it into smaller pieces that quickly grew into five separate balls of burning sun.

The creature was in the middle of his own spell. When he concluded, an armor of chipped stone flipped into existence, section by section, until he was completely covered except for his head. He shook his hand and a staff of obsidian appeared. Am'attillazzi was sprinting towards the professor when she unleashed the new set of orbs.

The explosion deafened Zuri, covering her in stone dust. Any exposed skin felt like it had received a bad sunburn. Before she knew it the battle had left the ritual chamber and entered the main level.

Iona was speaking, but Zuri couldn't hear. Nor did it matter. Their fate was tied to the winner. Or at least her friends' fate was. She was dead either way. The professor wouldn't forgive the theft, but at least Orion and Iona would escape.

When there was only silence, Zuri knew the end was near. She craned her neck, hoping to catch a glimpse of who had emerged victorious.

Her heart fell when she saw the long snout of Am'attillazzi as he dragged the body of Professor Cornwallis into the room. She was still alive. Barely. And looking like she'd been tossed into a washing machine full of sand and rocks. The creature didn't look much better with his sandstone armor barely hanging off his body and one eye looking like it'd taken a heavy gouge.

Am'attillazzi tossed Professor Cornwallis next to the circle. He looked tired. The left side of his body looked like it'd been dipped in molten lava with the scaly part of his flesh turned to heated glass. Zuri hoped he wouldn't be able to go through with the ritual until she saw his clawed hand had been untouched by the damage.

The creature knelt before the professor, who looked like she was trying to muster a defense, but her body had been shattered by the fight. She was bleeding from so many locations, she'd die if he left her on the stone.

Am'attillazzi repeated the incantation that he'd spoken before, his voice lacking the power that he'd displayed earlier. It was shorter this time. Rushed even as if he feared to delay too long.

The end was quick.

Zuri startled when the creature slammed the ritual dagger into Professor Cornwallis' chest. The savagery shocked Zuri, who was no stranger to brutality. He reached his hand into her chest and yanked out her heart. With a quick squeeze, the organ disintegrated in his clawed fist, releasing arcane energies which fled into his body.

With a soul-worn weariness, Am'attillazzi rose to his feet and took a long look at the scene of destruction, the ritual circle, and finally, Iona chained to the pillar. Zuri wondered which one would be next to feel the tip of his blade.

When he spoke, she could hear how much the battle with Professor Cornwallis had taken out of him. During his little speech, he gestured at each one of them, but motioned to Iona more than once.

"Am'attillazzi regrets to inform you that he will not be able to take you with him to his homeland. He thinks you would have enjoyed the journey, but this fight has taxed him and he must return quickly to receive healing."

The creature slowly tramped to the archway on the far wall. Using the hand that had crushed the professor's heart, he gestured to three points, which lit up the portal with swirling energies. The arcane energies that had been released before came rushing out and into the stone, intensifying the display until it was a full-fledged portal. He turned one last time and spoke, which was quickly translated by Justine.

"Am'attillazzi warns you this place is not what it seems and that you should not delve too deeply into its secrets or suffer the consequences."

In a flash of eldritch light, the creature named Am'attillazzi disappeared through the swirling portal, which winked out the moment he was gone, leaving Zuri numb with relief.

FORTY

In the aftermath of the battle, Iona wondered if they'd ever be freed from their bonds or if they'd be stuck forever, or at least until Blake found them because Justine didn't move for nearly ten minutes after the creature had left.

"I think she might be broken," said Iona after calling Justine's name for the dozenth time.

"Why are you calling the creature's puppet Justine?" asked Orion.

"No point in keeping it a secret now," said Iona, giving him the run-down of all that had happened, including how she'd come to be and the fight with Fenris last year.

A few minutes after the explanation finished, a small cry startled them as Justine came back to life.

"Oh, thank Merlin," said Iona. "Can you get us out?"

To everyone's relief, Justine held the keys which gave them quick freedom. Iona was stretching out her shoulders and rubbing her wrists in no time while the other two sat up doing the same.

"What are we going to do about her?"

No name had to be given. It was hard to ignore the body of Professor Cornwallis with a smoking hole in her chest and blood pooling around her. For once, Iona didn't feel the urge to taste the blood.

"It would be best if we're not associated with her death," said Zuri.

"Why did she come?" asked Orion, staring down at the professor's mangled body.

"Can we get out of here first? We can explain everything, but I don't want to hang around and wait for Blake to come back," said Iona.

"I hate to say this, but shouldn't we check the portal? I think there's a good chance it was Am'attillazzi keeping us from leaving the level. Probably left over from Fenris. But now that he's gone..."

Iona gestured to Orion.

"You good with that? Get to the next level, and then find somewhere private to discuss?"

The big man nodded, so the four of them returned to the pyramid with Justine in the lead. The little puppet led them through the traps and obstacles, turning them off with a few phrases and magical gestures.

In the depths of the pyramid, the four of them worked through the runic puzzle until it was complete. To everyone's profound relief the portal woke at the end.

"Together?"

The four of them traveled to the next level, which would give them access to return. The landing area was a large square room with three doors leading out and only a few hieroglyphs to suggest their purpose, but they were too tired for new challenges so they used the portal to return to the lowest level. The old mummy-mirror room was a safe place away from the others where they could discuss what had happened and what was to come.

They started off explaining everything they could to Orion. Iona alternated with Zuri with occasional interjections from Justine, who seemed to have returned to her former self. She explained that at some point, Am'attillazzi had taken control of her and she was merely an observer in her own wooden body.

Iona sensed there was more to Justine's tale than she was letting on, but there was no point on pressing her after their long absence from the Obelisk.

"The one thing I've never been able to understand," said Iona, "was why you were mixed up with our group for the Second Year Games."

Orion grunted, presenting a striking figure, hunched over like a gargoyle on an overturned armoire and staring into the distance as if there was a vast plain before them. Iona had the impression that he was a man out of time, less a student and more of a forgotten warrior. She felt a strange kinship and, for the first time, a romantic interest.

"I was on the third level during your fight with the warlock."

"That explains it," said Iona softly. "Whatever Fenris, or the creature did, must have blocked the portal for all of us. Then when it came to picking time for the Second Year Games, that link must have gotten us stuck together."

Zuri had been barely listening as she leaned against the wall where the old mirror had been before, the faded outline like a scab removed.

"I worry none of this matters, that we've delayed the inevitable with Blake and his elixirs. With that foresight at his disposal, we're in more danger than we've ever been."

She looked right at Orion, who didn't shy from the intensity of her gaze. If Orion was a warrior, then Zuri was the priest, slender and gauntly beautiful, knowledge burning on her brow like a fiery crown.

Iona knew that left her as the monster, for she couldn't be the jester, as that was Justine's role. But her thoughts were interrupted by Zuri's continuation.

"We can't continue in the Obelisk as a trio. Not that we're lacking resources, but Blake has a larger group and now he has the elixirs. I know you prefer to be a lone wolf, but we could use you in ours, Orion. If we're being bluntly honest, I don't think you can survive alone. Blake knows you too well now. He's not afraid of you anymore. Whatever myths you've wrapped around your shoulders all these years, keeping us away, that veil has been pierced."

The quick glance Orion shot Iona's way had her heart fluttering in her chest, but not for the reasons that first came to mind. When they'd first met, she'd thought him the monster and herself the fledgling hero, but now that she'd seen inside his head, seen the events that had made him and the unexpected lesser station of his family, she knew those roles were reversed. She was the monster and he was the one who slayed them.

"I can't."

Without further explanation, Orion surged from the room, hands clenched into fists. Zuri started to speak, but Iona cut her off as she rushed out after him.

"Orion!"

The big man was near the fountain, shoulders hunched and chin dipped towards his chest.

"Please. Don't go. Join us. But not for the reasons that Zuri said, as logical as they are. I mean, she's right. We need each other in this awful game. Blake will kill us if we even let our guard down in the slightest.

"But that's not why I'm asking. I feel like after almost two years, I know you better than anyone else. Which isn't much, but it's something. I know you didn't want me to see inside your head. I'm sorry. I didn't mean to intrude like that, or do what I did. But I wanted to explain. It wasn't about the game. I didn't do that because we needed you out of the shadow seed. I did that because I saw how much you were hurting."

She gestured towards their surroundings even though he was facing the other way and couldn't see her.

"I wasn't born into this and unless I misunderstand that vision, I know that you weren't either, despite your Dreadmarsh name."

Iona buried her face in her hands, growling under her breath in frustration which turned to a brief yell. Orion half-turned until he could see her over his shoulder.

"If you haven't figured it out yet, I'm a monster. I thought I was running away from Fenris, but really I was running away from myself. I'm scared of what I might become. The only thing keeping me sane, keeping me whole, is the people around me. Zuri, Justine...and you. Yes, you, Orion Dreadmarsh, feared second year of Coterie. I want you, as a friend, as a teammate, maybe...I don't know, maybe there's more. It feels weird saying this. I don't have very much experience with other humans, if that's what I can call myself, but I'd like to get to know you better."

The entire time she was speaking, Iona was aware he was rocking back and forth, leaning on his front foot, then his back, as if he were mired in indecision.

For a brief moment, she thought he would turn and agree to rejoin the group, or at least tell her he was considering it, but then he tensed up as if he were a towel trying to squeeze out every last bit of their relationship.

Orion marched away as if he were going to walk through a brick wall, disappearing into the complex shadows that made up the interior of the Obelisk, leaving Iona feeling like a fool.

§

Zuri was disappointed when Iona returned to the mummy-mirror room alone, even if she hadn't given Iona much of a chance to convince him to return. Her friend looked on the verge of either crying or punching a hole through a wall.

"I don't know if he *can* join a group," said Zuri. "Whatever goes on in the Dreadmarsh family, I think it makes it hard for them to connect with others."

Iona leaned against the wall, pressing her palms against her eye sockets and shaking quietly.

The contradiction of vulnerability and rage, combined with her pale blonde hair and the splatters of blood across her jaw from the day's battles, made Iona into an angel of vengeance.

Zuri didn't fear her friend, but she worried for her. This second year of schooling had unlocked things in Iona she clearly hadn't expected.

"If you need time, Iona..."

"No," she said right away. "I can't delay any longer. Ilyana wants me to join her for a feast in two days."

"You should kill her," said the puppet Justine, sitting on a chunk of stone, kicking her legs like a child waiting for candy.

The runes on her wooden flesh had faded, but she was still wearing the strange robes. Zuri was surprised how lifelike she seemed despite her diminutive size. Something about her time in the Obelisk during the year, or the capture by the creature had changed her.

"I can't," replied Iona. "She's too powerful. I've seen that firsthand."

"There's always a way," said Zuri.

"It's not like you're out of the woods either. What are you going to do about Adrian Constantin and the Dark Nines? He's going to come after you hard."

Zuri thought back to the moment she thought she was going to die in his care. *I need to be more ruthless.* She'd come to the Obelisk thinking she could somehow avoid the fate of every Coterie mage, that she could acquire that power without it changing her, but she was disabused of that notion now. If you wanted to gain and hold onto power, you had to set aside those weak human desires.

"I'm not going to let them come after me, if that's what you're asking. But that's not the important question here. What are *you* going to do, Iona?"

She looked up, devastation in her eyes.

"I don't know how I can say no."

FORTY-ONE

Ilyana tired of the smelly puddles covered in an oily sheen. She tired of the press of people, too oblivious with their mortal thoughts, bumping into her without regard for station. She tired of the care she had to take when hunting, leaving no trace and disposing of the bodies in ways that could never be linked to her.

She wanted to visit the smaller cities of this great country, following in the footsteps of her father as he harvested the little folk. The ones that wouldn't be missed. It would lack the culture and niceties of the shops in Eastern Europe, but it would make up for that in raw, primal feeding.

But first she had a score to settle.

Once and for all, she would learn if Iona had killed their father. And if so, she would rip her limb from limb. And even if she hadn't, but refused to leave Coterie and become her true self, well, she would kill her for that too.

Ilyana had grown tired of the cat and mouse game with Iona. For all the promise that their father had spoken of, she was blind to the possibilities of what she could become. A waste. Better that power had been gifted to her upon birth, not this upstart yokel with far too much caution to be relevant.

To her surprise, Iona was waiting for her at the corner near the park, despite the early arrival. She'd intended to spy on her approach to give her an idea of her mental state, which would help later when the cook gave Iona her meal, laced with a potent truth elixir, which would finally reveal what happened to their father.

"Darling sister, you look smashing," said Ilyana, kissing each cheek.

"You as well, sister," said Iona with a smirk.

Ilyana held her at arm's length, examining her outfit. The black leather pants and cream shirt conformed to her slender body, matching the messy pale blonde hair.

"You look like a rock star, Iona."

"And you look like you're ready to buy the third ward," said Iona.

Ilyana put a hand to her chest. The woman she'd killed last week in the first ward had an extensive wardrobe that just screamed to be freed from that ugly mansion. It'd taken months to get invited for a dinner with just the two of them and it'd been so worth it.

"Are you as excited as I am?" asked Ilyana, hooking her arm and pulling her towards the Vânatoare.

"I won't lie to you, sister, I'm nervous," said Iona, mouth twitching.

"It's understandable. It's your first time. Much like sex, it's both better and worse than expected, but also like sex, it gets better with practice."

"That's good."

The guards outside the Vânatoare were as expected, but none of the faces were.

"Where's Tiago?" she demanded.

The tallest and biggest with a bushy beard and muscles that looked like they could bend an iron bar approached, exuding a strange nervousness.

"He was sent to another part of the city. The boss is expanding."

Ilyana frowned and put her fingernail under his chin.

"I don't remember you."

He swallowed.

"Adrian has been recruiting."

"Recruiting?"

"Expanding."

"Interesting," she said, peering into his soul.

Not only was he nervous, but he was weak. Despite the muscles and the look, he wasn't much more than an empty shell. Tiago was smaller and meaner. He liked to kill. Ilyana was certain this one had never even strangled a rat. The others weren't much better, but she guessed that was what happened when you wanted to expand your business. Another reason Ilyana enjoyed being alone. Dealing with Iona this year had been annoying enough.

"Come, sister, I'm famished."

"So am I."

The secret door opened to her touch, revealing the long white hallway. Past the door was the hostess station. The normal sounds of the Vânatoare—the squelching of ripped meat, the muffled moans and thumps of pleasure—none of them were present. A few chopping noises and the scent of fresh blood was the only thing that told her she was in the Vânatoare.

"Welcome back, Miss Storm. Your feasting room is waiting."

Ilyana ground her teeth. The woman was the same, but she was unusually nervous. A bead of sweat ran down her neck despite the cool temperature.

She grabbed the hostess' wrist, pulling her close enough that she could smell her breath, faint with onions.

"What's going on?"

"What do you mean?" stammered the hostess.

"First the new crew outside, and then, I don't know, something's not right."

The hostess blinked.

"My deepest apologies, Miss Storm. The fault is mine. You're one of our most treasured guests and we want to make sure tonight's meal lives up to your high expectations. We've been preparing for this night all week."

"Very well. I will allow it, but you should have taken some calming elixirs or something. I can smell your fear."

"Again, my deepest apologies. We do have some extras planned for the meal. I do hope that you'll accept them as recompense for my error."

"We'll see," said Ilyana, shooting Iona a wink.

Her half-sister looked less anxious than she had outside. Good. The anticipation and hunger must have quelled her trembling.

The hostess led them to a special room at the end of the hallway. Three sets of chains were drilled into the wall with a porcelain trough running beneath. The table was longer than their previous meal, with cutlery and settings from Louis the XVI, which Ilyana had personally picked out.

"What do you think?"

Iona studied the chains, reaching out and tugging one as if to test its hardiness.

"Do they struggle much?"

"It depends on if you want them drugged or not. There are some that say their fear taints the flesh, makes it less appetizing, but I find it elevates the experience, making it fine cuisine."

"The screams must be difficult," said Iona with a knitted brow.

The earlier nervousness had returned, and for good reason. Ilyana remembered her first time. A back alleyway in Budapest under the watchful eye of her father. Fourteen and only a waif of a girl. A disadvantage for some, but she used her pink flesh as a lure, taking the man to a spot where the cobblestones were chipped from chopping firewood.

He'd struggled mightily, punching and kicking, leaving marks about her face and arms. The fight had only made the meal more delicious. She broke his neck when he tried to gouge out her eyes and then tore the flesh on his chest. Blood, skin, viscera—she gorged until Fenris dragged her away, warning of a bellyache.

He made her stay indoors until her wounds healed, fearing that someone might think he beat her. He was more of a dandy back then with expensive fitted clothes and a top hat. Somewhere between then and a few decades ago, he'd lost his appetite for civilization and returned to the lifelong study of his own hunger. It was one of the reasons she'd entertained Iona's story about Fenris disappearing unexpectedly, because he'd done the same to her, surfacing a decade later with a handwritten letter that had appeared as if by magic. After that, they'd traded messages for years, but she never saw him again.

Ilyana roused from her memories.

"They bind their mouths. I, myself, prefer their screams, but it upsets the other customers."

"I'm glad then," said Iona, circling the room until she stood behind the chair. "Do we sit?"

"Please, sister. I've been looking forward to this for a long time. And don't worry about the chains, that comes later. We have time for some amuse-bouches and other little delights. I think you'll find that these bites will enhance your hunger rather than dull it."

"That's good," said Iona, sneaking a glance back to the chains.

"Don't worry. You'll find your appetite."

"It's not that. I was wondering what kind of people they find. Are these bad people? Or do they find them on the streets without regard to their life history?"

"Does it matter?"

"It does to me," said Iona.

"I honestly don't know," said Ilyana. "Nor do I care. I come for the meal. Sinner or saint, they all taste the same. How the Vânatoare acquires them is not my problem. It's why we pay such exorbitant sums. But since it clearly worries you, I can summon the hostess to inquire if you'd like."

"I would."

Ilyana tried to hide her displeasure at this distraction as she hit the button on the table. The hostess appeared moments later.

"Is there a problem?"

"My darling sister would like to know the moral quality of the meal tonight. Are they gangbangers or janitors? Are they priests or elementary school teachers? Do they stiff the tip or are they generous?"

The hostess placed her hands behind her back.

"While we select the meal from the worst of society, we make sure that the flavors will not be tainted by bad elements like drugs, or other corruptions of the flesh."

"See?" asked Ilyana, arching an eyebrow.

"Thank you," said Iona with a tepid smile.

Before the hostess left, she said, "The first bites will be arriving shortly."

Ilyana's heart sped up in anticipation. She hadn't decided when she'd kill Iona if she detected that she had anything to do with Fenris' death. Maybe she would let her sate her hunger before ending her life, but that way was fraught with peril given the strength that Iona would gain. Not that she was worried about the fledgling mage. The girl, despite her potential, had no idea how to access it. It wasn't just a matter of indulging her hunger, she had to slough off those troublesome ideas of what civilization was to really find her strength.

"Congratulations on winning the contest. I suppose an apology is in order for my disparaging the time you spent pursuing it. I hear the prize was rather considerable."

An odd thought passed like clouds across the sun in Iona's eyes.

"I'm just glad it's over. It was exhausting."

"Is there any news to the disappearance of the other winner? The redhead? The papers are wild with speculation about what happened. I normally don't concern myself with affairs of the university, but I must say, this has been quite titillating."

Iona stared her straight in the eyes.

"They won't find her if that's what you mean."

Ilyana sat up.

"My word, Iona. I didn't think you had it in you."

"My time in Coterie has taught me a lot about the nature of power."

"Have you come to a conclusion?" asked Ilyana.

"It resides where people think it does."

"Interesting conclusion. I'm not sure I agree, but I can understand your point of view, given your newness."

Iona steepled her fingers.

"Then where do you think it resides?"

"Power is a force. You have it or you don't. The lion doesn't care what the antelope thinks about where power resides. The lion just eats."

"A fair point," said Iona. "But isn't that a simplified version? Don't we live in a complex society filled with overlapping power structures each vying for their piece of the pie? You might be powerful enough to take down a lion, but could you become mayor? Or could you make the masses love you? There's power in things like that too, not just physical power."

"Don't let their petty games confuse you, sister. A lion doesn't get confused by the nervous prattling of the antelopes. I learned long ago from our father that these games are meaningless. Better to play our own games than the ones rigged to lose."

Their conversation was interrupted by the hostess, who swooped in, depositing two shallow bowls of thick red liquid. She cleared her throat.

"The chilled soup has hints of rosemary and blackberry. Enjoy."

Iona stared suspiciously at the liquid.

"Problem?"

"How do they know if it will taste like that?"

Ilyana smirked.

"They purport to feed them specific meals before their harvesting. I'll admit, I can barely taste what they've described, but it makes a nice fiction."

The soup was a lovely beginning to the feast. Not too heavy. Not too sweet. Iona looked raptured by the effects, her eyes glittering with the power it gave. But more importantly, the blood soup was laced with the truth elixir. When Iona belched behind a cupped hand, she knew it had taken effect.

"How do you feel, sister?"

"Elated."

"The soup will help later when they bring the main course. You lack the finesse required not to make a mess otherwise."

As Iona went back for more soup, Ilyana let a grin rise to her generous lips.

"Did you enjoy killing the redhead?" she asked sweetly.

Iona stared into the soup with the spoon hovering over its dark red surface. A single bead condensed along the curve of the utensil and eventually released into the bowl, shattering the pristine surface.

"I didn't kill her," said Iona with a knitted brow. "It was Blake Lockwood. He killed her because he thought she would betray him."

"Oh, that's quite interesting."

Iona appeared confused about her salacious tongue, but she went back for another spoonful, relishing the liquid as it passed her lips.

Ilyana was satisfied that the elixir was working, but she wanted to work up to the big question in case there was resistance.

"What do you think of me, sister?"

The hesitation was brief, but suspicious before Iona let the words flow.

"You're beautiful and frightening. Like a dark angel. I want to be like you, but I don't know if I can."

Ilyana reached across the table and caressed her half-sister's hand.

"It takes time. I will teach you."

Iona tried to remove her hand, but Ilyana latched on hard, fingernails digging into flesh.

"Why are you doing that?" exclaimed Iona, struggling to pull away.

"Did you kill Fenris? Did you kill our father?"

Fear permeated Iona's eyes like lightning strikes. She yanked again, but Ilyana's grip was steel. She didn't want to kill Iona yet, but she would if she must. A feast could be enjoyed solo if necessary.

Ilyana sensed the affirmative answer forming on her lips and readied to leap across the table. She would have to be careful not to take Iona's blood, or suffer the elixir, which could complicate things later.

"I did not. I've told you before. He left me at the farmhouse without warning or word. I'm as mystified by his absence as you are."

The words took longer to process than Ilyana would have liked. It wasn't the answer she'd expected, or the one she wanted. There was something that had bothered her about her half-sister and not just the obfuscations about Fenris.

Iona yanked her wrist away, holding it to her chest. The accusation in her gaze gave Ilyana pause for the first time since she'd met her half-sister. The look was like a hook in her brain, wiggling deeper and causing pain.

Doubt had never been an issue, but she sensed she was missing something important. *Had the elixir worn off? Did the chef mess up the formula?* Ilyana had sent along the serum with explicit instructions.

"I know you're searching for answers, Ilyana, but I do not have them. I'm sorry. I wish I knew what happened to Father. I truly do."

The urge to rip out Iona's throat came on like a freight train. Despite knowing that the truth elixir was coursing through her veins, Ilyana was sure there was falseness afoot. She'd been certain that today would be the day she would expose Iona.

The awkward pause was interrupted by the arrival of the waiter with a plate of heart sashimi to be dipped in blood pudding. A favorite, but Ilyana was barely paying attention. She traded small talk with her sister while trying to figure out what she was missing.

The main course was upon them before she realized it when the hostess led three naked figures into the room on a length of chain. Two men and one woman. Iona averted her eyes from the nakedness, which amused Ilyana.

"Have you had sex?"

Iona swallowed.

"Once. Last year. It was rather messy."

"Most great things are."

Her eyes flashed to their meal, which was being chained to the wall.

"Would you like to go first?"

"I'd rather watch how it's done first."

Ilyana rose and approached the three, running her fingernail across their chests.

"Do you have a preference? I figured we could each have one for ourselves and then take the third together."

"Will we be able to eat that much?"

"The room is booked for the night. It will take us hours, but I assure you that your life will feel completely different afterwards."

"I plan on it."

Ilyana wrapped her hand around the balls of the first male. He was a healthy specimen and grunted at her touch.

"Perfect. Subdued but not oblivious. I like it when they squirm."

She pulled a thin blade from the hem of her jacket, holding it to the light before pressing it against his forearm, making a long cut between the muscles.

"If you cut the other side, the blood flows too quickly."

Ilyana licked the crimson blade, letting her tongue skirt the sharp edge while relishing the fresh blood. She gave a shiver while Iona watched her strangely.

"Care to join me for a drink?"

"I like watching you, sister. Please. Educate me."

Ilyana tapped the flat of the blade on the male's neck while blood dripped from his arm.

"This is the gusher. Never cut it unless you plan on a quick and messy meal."

"Good advice," said Iona.

"For a feast like tonight, we'll start with fresh blood. Maybe cut off some bits. Let him bleed, then when he's close to death, I like to slice open their chest and eat the heart. Biting into that organ while it's still pumping is something to be experienced."

"Delightful."

Ilyana gestured toward the other two.

"Please, don't be shy."

While Iona collected a blade from the surgical tray, Ilyana pressed her lips against the man's arm, sucking at it greedily, letting it fill her with divine purpose. The beat of his heart thumped in her ears, growing louder as she pulled. This was life. This was everything.

She drained a few pints before she forced herself to step away, delirious and a little unsteady. It was like her head was a great big balloon.

"Drink, sister. Your meal is waiting."

The little tugs of doubt that had been making her uneasy the entire night pulled harder. She felt loopier than normal, which was unlike herself. Ilyana preferred absolute control during her feedings.

When she looked into Iona's eyes, she didn't see fear or hunger, she saw anger. Intensity. A hawk watching a rabbit struggle through the grass.

Then it hit her. The unsteadiness of her feet, the way her head felt like it was growing larger by the second, the ache in her gut. The blood had been poisoned. She hadn't detected it at first, because it was subtle. A hint of waste. Not enough to notice from a small sip, but the volume she'd ingested made it abundantly clear.

What she couldn't understand was how. The Vânatoare's reputation was impeccable. How had Iona corrupted it? What did it matter. She needed to kill her. Now. Before the poison took over.

Ilyana surged forward to slam Iona against the wall, but tripped over her own feet, crashing to the ground. Her half-sister stood away, watching silently, repulsion on her lips.

"What have you done to me?"

"I poisoned you. *Sister.*"

The word came out as recrimination. Hatred. The lie exposed.

"How?" she asked as she lurched back to her feet, swaying drunkenly after Iona, but her half-sister pushed her away as easily as a child.

"Everything today has been a lie."

"But the Vânatoare..."

"Should never exist."

Ilyana's legs abandoned her, leaving her on her knees, wobbly as a drunken child. Her arms quivered and shook with palsy.

"First we took care of Tiago and the other guards," said Iona, leaning into her face until it was all she could see. "They were easier than expected, but then again, they didn't know we were coming. The fight was brief."

"But the guards, the hostess," slurred Ilyana.

"The guards are actors. Once the strength of the Dark Nine was eliminated, we took control of Adrian's entertainment business. It only took a little blackmail to convince everyone that it was in their best interest to help out.

"As for the hostess. We explained how easily we could ruin her life and she quickly agreed to help." Iona stood back and put her hand on the arm of the bleeding, naked man. "These fine folks were the ones that worked in the kitchen. Killing in the name of feeding monsters like you. We decided they would make fine bait as it was unlikely you'd ever bothered to meet them."

"The poison..."

Iona was back in the middle of her vision. A pale, white face like an angry moon.

"You provided that answer, *sister*. Thieves' Milk. You told me about it in the plant dome at the beginning of the year. Or I should say you accused me of using it to kill Fenris. It wasn't easy to acquire, but we managed to get enough for our purposes."

A slap to the jaw startled Ilyana out of the comatose state she was drifting in.

"Don't leave me just yet, sister. I have one more thing to tell you. One that you've suspected this entire time. Yes, I killed Fenris. I killed our murderous father. He would have done the same to me if I hadn't."

"You..."

The word turned to mush in her mouth. Ilyana tilted forward, but Iona held her up easily.

"I know now that I'm a monster, sister. I was born from one. Seven hells, I was nearly kidnapped by another a few days ago. One that you would find familiar even if you'd never met it. But I'm not a monster like you. You prey on the weak. You prey on those that can do nothing to stop you. We found men, women, and children in the Vânatoare's pens. These were poor people who were in the wrong place at the wrong time. Which makes you the worst kind of monster, sister. It makes you weak. I know that I'm a killer, but I'll never be a coward like you."

The fog descended, blotting out the word, but Ilyana raged against it, fighting until she'd climbed back into the feasting room in the Vânatoare. Iona was holding a thin blade. A familiar blade.

"If the world was just, I would put you through the pain and agony that you inflicted on these poor folks, but I'm not stupid. I don't want you alive any longer than necessary. You're that dangerous."

Iona swiped the blade across her neck. A bright flash of pain was followed by warmth spilling across her chest.

"The gusher. Goodbye, *sister.* I won't miss you. I don't think anyone will."

Ilyana could no longer hold up the strings of her body. She collapsed onto the tile floor, staring at the feet of the men and women that were meant to be her feast. Blood gurgled from her lips as she tried to tell Iona that she'd lied to her. That the family was larger and more prevalent than she'd let on before and that someone would find out and enact revenge on her behalf.

But the words never came.

A dry, bottomless pit that went on forever rose up and swallowed Ilyana. The last vision that imprinted on her dead eyes was Iona standing over her.

FORTY-TWO

The Ancient Wyrm was a starred sushi restaurant on the forty-seventh floor of a high-rise in the first ward. Rumors had always swirled around the venue about the chef and owner that he was actually a dragon in disguise that had given up his horde to serve raw fish to rich clientele. Zuri thought it bullshit, and probably a little racist as the chef was just an old Japanese man, but it gave the place an air of mythology.

Iona was seated at a private booth in the corner, staring out the window at the city during a heavy rainstorm while running her finger along the top of her beer glass.

"You okay?"

The darkness in her friend's eyes was like the storm outside: full of fury but not affecting her presently. After the restaurant, Iona disappeared for a few days before messaging her about wanting to talk.

"So far I've killed my father and my half-sister. I'm beginning to wonder what that makes me."

"A survivor. They would have done the same to you."

The waiter brought a glass of beer and an appetizer of a single slice of fugu covered in caviar and resting on a lotus petal. Iona continued staring out the window after they finished.

"Regrets?"

"No, but I feel like I lost a connection to my past. Or at least my history. How many of Fenris' kin are still out there? If there's a restaurant like Vânatoare, then there are more monsters like Ilyana."

"The guest list was protected by powerful enchantments."

"What does it matter, we burned it all down."

Zuri grabbed her beer and held it up.

"I know the last few weeks have been intense, but we survived it, as impossible as it seemed at times, and unless something crazy happens these last few weeks of school, we're moving on to our third year."

Glasses clinked together and Zuri let the smooth, bubbly liquid caress her tongue on the way down her throat. She'd never been a fan of beer, but this was something else entirely. It was like drinking a summer day.

"Anything from Cornwallis' death?" asked Iona with a raised eyebrow.

"The body was discovered as we expected. No traces were linked to us, though rumors already circulate, probably due to the Siren Sisters. Professor Sinclair told the Hall that she must have uncovered a dangerous mystery within the Obelisk and that we should all take it as a reminder that it's truly a dangerous place, even for professors."

"Shame the diary isn't useable anymore. Would be like that spiteful bitch to have it turn into a pyre upon her death."

"It's okay," said Zuri. "I've come to realize that using someone else's blackmail is fraught with hidden danger. I didn't know how she acquired the information, nor how much of it had been used already. It was a buried mine field. It's better that it burned."

"Using someone *else's* blackmail?"

Zuri let a grin rise to her lips.

"I used to think I could rise above the fray. Avoid the petty backstabbing that goes on in our world, but these last two years have disabused me of that notion. Everyone has too much at stake not to be playing for keeps. If I don't learn to play their games, I'm just going to get run over."

"And now we have Blake and the elixirs to worry about," said Iona.

"Another reason to tap any resource we can. He's going to be able to anticipate us, giving him the advantage. But not if we remake ourselves."

"Easier said than done."

"I'm not the same person I was even at the beginning of the year," said Zuri.

"None of us are. Not even Blake."

"I thought I could avoid the fate that comes for us all in the Obelisk. I thought I could show them that you didn't have to become a monster to succeed. Now I know different. But that doesn't mean that we have to lose ourselves. We can choose the monster we become."

"Sometimes it's chosen for us."

"I don't believe that's true," said Zuri, grabbing Iona's hand across the table.

"I hope you're right," she said, staring back with the intensity of a supernova.

Thunder rumbled against the window, reminding them of the storm outside.

"It's not going to get any easier. Without Scarlett tempering his ways, Blake is going to be worse. Much, much worse. And now he's armed with knowledge and foresight. We need Orion on our team more than ever. Do you think you could persuade him? Or do I need to get involved?"

"No. He'll come on his own power, or he won't come at all."

"Is that because of what you saw in his vision?"

"Maybe," said Iona frowning. "But I think it has more to do with the fact that he and I are much alike. We were born monsters, not made to be like one. The Dreadmarshes, the Storms, both families of monsters, but not all of us wanted to be one."

"You'll talk to him?"

"No. I'm going to give him time. And space. I think he's spent his entire life having people come to him with expectations based on who he is, and what his family name means. If he's going to join us, he'll do it on his schedule."

"Iona..."

"I know, I know. After your speech about taking control, I'm asking you to back off. Trust me. I know Orion better than you do. Trying to convince him would only turn him away permanently. The fact that he showed up to help that day should be proof enough that he's considering it."

Zuri sighed and leaned back in the booth.

"I hope you're right."

"Me too," said Iona wistfully as she watched the storm batter the windows with wind and rain.

Zuri was going to say more, but she saw her friend deep in thought. About Orion? About Ilyana? She couldn't tell, but the advice about giving time and space for decisions seemed relevant.

She held up her beer.

"To survival."

"No," said Iona. "It has to be more than that."

"Then what?"

Iona looked into her beer.

"I don't know. Something more. Otherwise, we're just killing each other for a slightly fancier dinner, a few more yards of space in a home, a ticket to an event with more famous people in the seats."

There was a time that Zuri thought that was enough. Everyone was striving for the best, so why shouldn't she? But she saw what Iona did. If you're stabbing each other in the back for a nicer cut of sushi, what did that make you? Worse than a monster, that was for sure.

"To finding ourselves," she said, offering the glass to clink.

Iona tilted her head, a smile following.

"To finding ourselves."

FORTY-THREE

"Congratulations on your baby," said the mother pushing a stroller with twins inside.

Iona didn't realize the woman was talking to her until she saw the broad smile and twinkle in her eyes.

Once she realized what was happening, she muttered, "You too?"

She quickly marched away, putting distance between her and the woman before she leaned her head back so she could see Justine through the hazy mesh.

"We're going to have to put a privacy shield on this baby backpack, or I'm not taking you out anymore," said Iona.

"I can do it," said Justine.

Ever since they'd upgraded her voice box, Iona was no longer creeped out by their diminutive friend. She sounded like the Justine of old, but without the endless self-doubt.

The streets of the third ward were packed with tourists for the beginning of summer. She dodged around the packs of kids headed to the second ward for the illusionary battles while Justine muttered incantations in the baby carrier. A few people gave strange looks but no one said a word.

Their second year at Coterie had ended two weeks ago. They managed to pass, only because most of their class had been stuck on the fourth level. Iona had a suspicion that was due to Blake, because he was equally screwed if the rest of their class moved too far into the Obelisk.

The Minoan Gallery had no sign out front. The entrance was an open archway with a glimmer shield keeping out prying eyes and insects. It wasn't technically open, but they had an appointment.

"Hello?" she asked.

The walls were covered in paintings. Iona immediately liked them more than the ones in the Obelisk. The art displayed in Coterie's home tended towards the idolization of its Patron, or the exaltation of the elite. She was sick of seeing statues of its famous alumni in preening poses.

While these paintings had some things in common, like the display of power and magic, the underlining themes were different. More warning, or introspection, rather than celebration.

Iona found herself drawn to a painting that showed a shirtless man with an impressive physique casting complex magics while his shadow showed the outline of a demon.

"Do you like it? It's called *The Maze*."

She turned to find a man approaching in open robes. His mane of dark hair framed his attractive face. She could almost imagine him lounging on a divan sipping wine and having grapes fed to him.

"Oh, I'm sorry." Iona smiled at the man. "Yes, it's intriguing."

"Are you a fan of art?" he asked.

"I'm new to it. Are you the owner? I'm Iona. We spoke on the phone, I think?"

She held out her hand but he only had eyes for the baby carrier.

"It's lovely to meet you, Iona. You can call me Dee. Can I assume this is the artist I see?"

Iona startled, peering over her shoulder.

"You can see her?"

Dee frowned precipitously.

"Let's not play these mortal games. Please. No one else is in my gallery. Let us talk, artist to artist."

Iona unzipped the carrier, releasing Justine to climb down. She was wearing an outfit that looked like black pajamas with her hair in a high ponytail.

"It's an honor to meet you, Dee," said Justine with her tiny, wooden hand held out.

Dee shook it while bending into a deep flourishing bow. He gave no indication of the strangeness of interacting with a two-foot living puppet, but then again, Iona wasn't quite sure he was human.

"The honor is all mine. Did you bring the painting?"

Iona held out the protective carryall that had been slung over her shoulder. He set it on a nearby table and unzipped the carrier, then folded back the cloth to reveal the painting, which elicited a gasp.

"It's exquisite. A masterpiece."

Iona hadn't known what to make of it when Justine had first revealed it and asked for help in finding a buyer. The shapes and angles were all wrong and the colors brighter than she would have used, but the image was unmistakable. At least for her. It was the scene of the ritual with Am'attillazzi. Iona could pick out her figure chained to the wall while Orion and Zuri were strapped to the center of the ritual circle. Strange lines connected various figures in the painting, for reasons Iona was less clear on, but they formed a secondary structure beneath the explicit use of magic.

Dee held his fingertips to his lips as if he were afraid of what he might say. His interest was unmistakable. Light seemed to burst from his brow as he made noises of pleasure in the back of his throat.

"Tell me, Justine. Do you enjoy the works of Mistropholies? I find your use of color invoking his techniques without resorting to pastiche."

Justine placed her arms behind her back, which gave credence to the illusion that she was a normal little girl, despite the serious mien on her brow.

"I find his works lacking depth, but enjoyable all the same."

"Yes, yes," said Dee, placing his hand against his chest. "I agree wholeheartedly. Can I show you his latest? I acquired it a few months ago."

The two of them wandered into the gallery. Iona felt like a third wheel and despite the interestingness of the paintings on the wall, she chose to step outside to give the artist and the gallery owner a chance to speak in private. The fact that Dee made no special mention of Justine's puppetness let Iona know that she was in good hands.

"I'm going to walk around," Iona called out. "Message me when you want me to pick her up."

She wasn't two steps outside before she ran into the towering figure of Orion Dreadmarsh. The big man seemed an inch or two taller than she'd seen him last. He glowered at her with the intensity of a loaded gun.

"Hey?"

He cast his gaze around them, the reason for his unease clear as passersby gave them a wide berth and concerned looks.

"How did you know I was here?"

"Can you…?"

He nodded towards the distance. Heavy weights hung on his shoulders.

"Sure, what do you need?"

Orion turned and strode towards the sidewalk, and to her surprise, raised his hand to wave down a taxi. The first three sped past, making her realize why he walked everywhere, so she made him move back to the building side. The first taxi she signaled made its way over.

She climbed in the opposite side, feeling the vehicle sink when Orion forced his way through the opening. The taxi driver was alarmed, his eyes wide with fright. Orion mumbled an address and the vehicle lurched into traffic.

"Is everything okay?" she asked.

Orion chewed his words, swallowing before daring to let them out, which left Iona sighing heavily.

"You're going to have to eventually explain something."

When his gaze cast to the driver's rearview mirror, Iona understood his hesitation.

"Fine. I'll wait."

Her mind was filled with the possibilities of what he might have to say, or want to show her. Maybe it would be Blake tied up in an abandoned house? Wouldn't that be nice. All their worries about the next year eliminated. But she knew that wouldn't be the case. Wishful thinking and all that.

The taxi let them out at Atlas Gardens. The taxi driver sped away as soon as they exited, not bothering to collect his fees.

Orion marched towards the knot of gang members loitering near the apartment sign. They greeted him with hellos and waves, which he returned tepidly, steering her around the building and into an entrance he bypassed with a key card.

His shoulders scraped the narrow stairs, leading up to the third floor, but he didn't go in when he stopped at a doorway.

"What is it? What do you want to show me?"

"She can be difficult..."

Orion went through the door, leaving her wondering why he'd brought her. The interior reminded her of the old house in the vision, including the shelf of colorful figurines in a long hallway, which sent shivers down her spine.

The living room shared many small items from Orion's memory, but she only had eyes for the central figure: a massive hulking creature sitting in a steel rocking chair knitting a black sweater. The woman covered in blankets made Orion look small as her head scraped the ceiling. She had to be nearly eight feet tall the way her back arched in the sitting position. Iona couldn't even begin to guess how much she weighed.

"Hi, I'm Iona."

Gnarled hands retreated into the blankets as the knitting was released into the lap, and then the hood was pulled back. The old woman was monstrous, with two nubs on her forehead, one of which was bleeding around the edge.

"Hello, Iona, I'm Adeline Dreadmarsh. My grandson, Orion, tells me much about you."

"He does?" she asked, checking back to him.

His chin dipped towards his chest as he averted his eyes.

"My grandson is shy. It's difficult when you look like him and have his last name."

"He's a good person."

Adeline used a handkerchief to wipe the bloody nub, then the cloth disappeared back into the folds.

"He is. Sometimes to a fault. It makes him vulnerable. He didn't want to join Coterie, but I insisted. He needs to toughen up. The world is not a kind place."

"It's not," said Iona.

"He admires your resolve, my Orion," said Adeline. "You're a survivor. I like that."

"I haven't had much of a choice."

"Most survivors are like that."

Adeline coughed which sounded like drums rumbling in the deep. The old woman's amber eyes glowed from beneath her heavy brow. Iona could see that in past times, a woman like Adeline would have been hunted down and killed as a monster.

"You're not afraid of me," said Adeline.

"Should I be?"

"It depends."

"I would say the same of myself," said Iona.

Adeline chuckled, which sounded like a great boar truffling in the bushes.

"Does it hurt?" asked Iona.

"Does what?"

"The growth. I saw"—she was going to explain the vision from the Games, but the enchantment kicked in and strangled her voice until she pivoted—"a picture of you when you were younger and Orion's father was alive. You were much smaller. Does it hurt to grow so large?"

"Some days, but there are potions and poultices. Unlike the main branch of the Dreadmarsh family, we've not been gifted with infernal good looks. Our gifts are more obvious."

"I'm lucky to have Orion as a friend," she said, staring him straight in the eyes. "A better gift than anything the others could offer."

He didn't look away, which she took as a win.

"Oh, you wouldn't say that if you knew what Leo or Jackie or Magnus could provide, but they would never associate with you. Nor us for that matter. We're an inconvenient rotten branch of the family tree as far as they're concerned. One they would have liked to have pruned a long time ago."

"I take it you didn't invite me here because you wanted to tell me about the Dreadmarsh family scuttlebutt."

"Perhaps I did. I could wax all day about the awful things that part of the family has done over the centuries but I doubt you care that much. You've more important things to worry about, like surviving your final three years at Coterie."

"It does weigh on my mind."

"Orion's too, not that you would know that by looking at him. Which is why I wanted you here, so I could tell you that he accepts your offer of joining. He would tell you himself, but he fears that he's too dangerous to be around others."

"I would fear more for his safety than mine," said Iona, thinking of her hunger.

Orion's head snapped towards her. She'd surprised him. It brought a smile to her lips, one that she deepened with amusement.

Adeline broke out in laughter, slapping the metal arm of the rocking hair. The shaking of her enormous body rattled the windows and plates in the kitchen.

"While I appreciate you speaking on his behalf, I think it's best if we leave that decision to him. We don't want a reluctant partner."

"A wise, but foolish sentiment. But I will allow it."

She turned towards him.

"Do you want to join us, Orion?"

The question seemed to cause him pain. He shrunk inward, but then his enormous head bobbed up and down twice.

"Good. We're glad to have you."

"I am"—he closed his eyes momentarily—"glad."

"Excellent," said Adeline. "Now there's just one more thing, and then I'll let you go. I know you have an appointment at the art gallery to return to."

"You're the one who knew where we were. Is that part of your gifts?"

The enormous woman reached into the folds of her robes, producing something small that fit in her basketball-sized hand.

"Not my gifts."

When she opened her hand, a familiar vial was revealed. The Elixir of Foresight. Half of it remained. She held it towards Iona.

"Mee-maw," said Orion, turning on the old woman. "You can't. I gave it to you so you could figure out an answer to your pain."

"And now I'm giving it to Iona, which will benefit you as well since you're part of the same team. But I figure she's a bright young woman who won't squander her advantages on an old woman who has lived far longer than necessary. Better it help a young man who is in a difficult situation. He told me what happened after the contest. That poor girl should have seen that coming. You all should have."

Iona collected the vial and slipped it into a pocket.

"We knew he would strike, but didn't think he'd do it so soon. Or to Scarlett."

"I drank half the elixir so I'd know how best to help Orion."

"What did you see?"

Adeline gathered herself and Iona sensed beneath the blankets she was a formidable warrior, but the expectations of society and her last name had kept her hidden.

"*Beware the shadows of occlusion*
When time stands still
And fate hangs in the balance
This cursed light brings death
For those daring to look upon its face
Bringing an end to the stolen tower."

"What does that mean?" asked Iona.

"I don't know but I saw your face in the vision too, which is why I asked Orion to bring you here. I'm sorry, I wish I could tell you more, but prophecies are like that. They often only make sense after it's happened."

"Better than nothing. Thank you."

"I hope so. I didn't do this for your benefit, but his. Keep that in mind. I might be an obscure branch of the Dreadmarsh family, but I'm still a Dreadmarsh."

"Warning received."

"And I didn't just see your face, but some of the struggles you will face in the Obelisk. I didn't understand most of them, but know they will be fraught with peril. Now, if you could step into the hallway, I have a few words for my grandson about these visions before he escorts you back to the gallery."

"It was nice meeting you, Adeline."

"You as well. Try not to die next year."

Smirking, Iona returned to the hallway, head spinning with how the day had unfolded. The addition of Orion Dreadmarsh and half an Elixir had increased their chances of survival. Iona was under no illusion that things would be easy, but it gave her hope. She couldn't wait to tell Zuri and Justine about the day's events.

As she shifted down the hallway, she saw a darkened side room and peeked inside. It looked like a guest room by the old faded yellow comforter and the family picture frames on the dresser. Iona casually leaned in, examining the people in the pictures. She saw lots of Orion and Adeline, and a few with a woman she assumed was his mother, though none of the father, for obvious reasons.

There were others with people she didn't recognize. Other branches of the Dreadmarsh family, she assumed. As she moved across the dresser, she saw Adeline in smaller and smaller forms. In one, she almost looked normal sized, but the photo was in black and white from what could have been the Old West as she was wearing a fancy dress.

When she heard the low murmur of conversation from the other room end, Iona returned to the hallway as Orion appeared.

"Hey, I know it wasn't your idea to join our group, but I'm really glad and not just for the safety in numbers."

His forehead knitted as he silently chewed his words. Iona started to move towards the door, but he motioned for her not to go.

"I didn't want you to die alone." He smirked. "Again."

§ § §

This ends the second book of the Cotere of Mages series. Stayed tuned for the third book:

VISCIOUS

Special Thanks

A long series like this doesn't happen without readers and an excellent support team. I can't express how much I appreciate all the help I've recieved over the years in getting this massive world of books out to the public.

First and foremost, my wife and first reader, Rachel Carpenter deserves a lot of credit over the years keeping me on the right path with this series. At times, some of my ideas have strayed too far from what makes a good Hundred Halls novel and she's nudged me back to where I'm supposed to be. I must also thank my team who help make each novel as best as it can be: Sasha Almazan & Gene Mollica from GS Covers, Tamara Blain from A Closer Look Editing, the beta reader team (Tina Rak, Lana Turner, Phyllis Simpson, and Melanie Coupland), as well as my writing group that we affectionately call the Murder Cabin (Andrea Stewart, Anthea Lawson/Sharp, Annie Bellet, Megan O'Keefe, Marina J. Lostetter, Jamie Thornton, and Tina Gower). Additionally, the Vanguard plays defense for little errors that sneak through the cracks, and for this book, I have Tony Lavely, Jane Peatling, Paige Grimmer, Roe Adams, Jeremiah Vaille, Inger L. Ticker, Debbie Davis, Phyllis Simpson, and Brian Busby to thank.

ABOUT THE AUTHOR

Thomas K. Carpenter resides in Colorado with his wife Rachel. When he's not busy writing his next book, he's hiking, skiing, and getting beat by his wife at cards. He keeps a regular blog at www.thomaskcarpenter.com and you can follow him on Bluesky @thomaskcarpenter.bsky.social. If you want to learn when his next novel will be hitting the shelves and get free stories and occasional other goodies, please sign up for his mailing list by going to: https://thomaskcarpenter.com/sendy/subscription?f=1Lnd7j2n0ZXtOzPUaaV7892afuK-38926t4ZDTPrWw3bnlViLZdE7R5fE35C8922xbGounE. Your email address will never be shared and you can unsubscribe at any time.

www.ingramcontent.com/pod-product-compliance
Lightning Source LLC
Chambersburg PA
CBHW030423310726
48979CB00009B/1582/J

* 9 7 8 1 9 5 8 4 9 8 2 9 3 *